Our Little Secret

By

Kevin A. Carey

This book is a work of fiction. Places, events, and situations in this story are purely fictional. Any resemblance to actual persons, living or dead, is coincidental.

ISBN: 1-4033-8041-4 (softcover)
ISBN: 1-4033-8040-6 (electronic)

This book is printed on acid free paper.

1st Books - rev. 11/27/02

..... to those individuals who have been robbed
of innocence and the capacity to love
by the abuse and violence
of others.

And the world will be better for this:

That one man, scorned and covered with scars,

Still strove, with his last ounce of courage,

To reach...the unreachable star...

Don Quixote De La Mancha

ACKNOWLEDGEMENTS

I am deeply grateful for the generous help and support I received while writing this novel. Drew Denning, without whom this book would not have been possible. He had the courage to help me dredge up many lost memories and to pull the words from my head and onto the page. Robert Cutting, for his masterful and insightful editing skills. Every writer should be lucky enough to have a Bob Cutting in his life. Serge Zavyalov, for his incredible cover designs. Serge is a very talented young man with a bright future ahead of him, no matter where life chooses to take him. Juan Fernandez, for his vast photographic and computer graphics knowledge. Glenn Coleman, for taking the time to proof read. Glenn is living proof that something great can come from something tragic. Harry Gonzalez, someone I can honestly call a true friend for all seasons. He has always been there through thick and thin and has pushed me every step of the way to see this project through to completion.

Table of Contents

CHAPTER ONE

Heat waves shimmered along Pennsylvania Avenue as the pavement baked under a mid-July sun. The air was oppressive, even by Washington, D.C. standards. Inside the Oval Office— climate-controlled at sixty-eight degrees— I could feel rivulets of sweat trickling down my brow. My long blonde hair, neatly braided and tied back for the occasion, was soaked.

The sting of the sweat in my eyes broke my trance-like state, bringing me back to the activity in the room. My attempt to remain cool and composed for the afternoon's ceremony had failed. I was proud that all the years of diligent effort had brought me here, but was nearly overwhelmed by the aura of this special place, filled with the most powerful people in the country. Today's special ceremony was for me— Geoffrey Brooks— and my nervousness was evident to everyone. I marveled at the President's desk, picturing in my mind that now famous photograph of little John John, President Kennedy's son, playing under it while his father worked.

1

I scanned the room looking at familiar faces and some less so, trying not to let my eyes betray the anxiety I was feeling. To the left stood Lieutenant General Lincoln D. Fauer, the esteemed Director of the National Security Agency. With him was Ann Caracristi, the Deputy Director of the NSA. Next to her were the President's National Security Advisor, Richard Allen, and Chief Justice of the United States Supreme Court, Warren Berger. Chief Justice Berger, a tall, austere man, dressed in his black robes was holding a bible in his right hand. Lastly, standing between Chief Justice Berger and myself was William Schuster. He was the man who had made all of this possible, and, more importantly, he was my grandfather.

A single bong sounded. The Sergeant-at-Arms, who was standing at the entrance to the Oval Office, turned, saluted everyone and closed the double doors behind him. The side door quietly slid open. Everyone stood at attention as President Ronald Reagan entered the room. He gave us all a warm smile and slowly made his way around the room greeting each one of us personally. I was the last person he came to. Seeing my obvious nervousness, he took the white handkerchief from his jacket breast pocket and silently offered it to me to wipe my noticeably wet brow. "Congratulations, Geoffrey," he said as I discreetly passed the handkerchief back to him. "This is a day you will remember for the rest of your life. I cannot tell you how proud we all are of you. You have just completed quite an arduous journey and now the world is at your feet. Take it into your most capable hands and mold it the best way you know how. You now have the tools and the power to make this world a better place for generations to come, and I look forward to sharing at least part of this journey with you and providing you with some of the wisdom I have collected through the years. Best of luck, Geoffrey, and May God bless you and be with you."

"Thank you, Mr. President," I said, smiling as I shook his proffered hand. I could feel my anxiety and tension fading.

Although I had met the President on several occasions, I remained in awe of Ronald Reagan. His

3

ability to make each person in his presence feel special was well recognized, already earning him the title, "the Great Communicator."

President Reagan gave a nod to Chief Justice Berger who stepped forward, asking me to do the same. Chief Justice Berger asked me to raise my right hand and place my left hand on the Bible he was carrying. "Repeat after me," he said. "I, Geoffrey S. Brooks, in recognition of the critical importance of the sensitive cryptologic mission and activities of the National Security Agency to the defense and national security of the United States, do solemnly swear, understand and accept the need for extraordinary security measures and high standards of personal security in the Agency. I acknowledge my obligation to comply with the Agency standards of conduct and the Agency policy relating to safeguarding of information regarding Agency organization activities and functions deemed by the Agency to require protection in the national interest. I agree to report only to the Director of Security or his representative and not to succumb to any attempt to blackmail me or subject myself to coercion or duress because of my sexual preference or behavior related to that preference. I will not violate the laws of any jurisdiction in which I find myself as they relate to conduct in public. I further agree not to condone, support or participate in any activity not consistent with the Agency's policy on anonymity or which may bring disrepute or notoriety to the Agency, so help me God."

I rightly perceived this to be an attack on my homosexuality, but I took the oath without comment, knowing full well that I was entering into a sacred world where homosexuality was not tolerated and absolutely forbidden. By even acknowledging that I was gay, the United States government was making a concession beyond any normal realm of possibility. With the oath administered, President Reagan stepped forward and announced, "Language Specialist Geoffrey S. Brooks, it is with great pleasure and pride that I present you with this gold shield. You are now a Special Operations Agent and Profiler for the most elite organization in the world. You will be serving

God and your country, reporting only to the people in this room."

As he handed me the wallet with the gold shield in it, the others in the room applauded and came forward to shake my hand. As if on cue the Sergeant-at-Arms opened the doors and a tall man in a neatly pressed tuxedo entered the room with a tray of champagne-filled flutes. We each took a glass and waited for the server to leave the room and the doors to be closed.

My grandfather, looking as dashing and debonair in his well-deserved retirement as he did in the prime of his career when he worked under such luminaries as Presidents Eisenhower and Kennedy, was given the honor of making the toast. "Geoffrey," he said, as everyone raised their glasses, "today, after countless hours of study and dedication you have fulfilled your lifelong dream. You are now a member with full privileges in the most elite organization in the world. Good luck and God bless you." President Reagan was right: This was a day I would never forget.

Almost as soon as it had started, the ceremony was over. President Reagan came over to me, put his arm around my shoulder, and with a broad smile told me to take the rest of the afternoon off. Before anyone else in the room decided that the President was joking, I hastily thanked everyone and bolted out of the room, not giving anyone a chance to object. As I made my way down the hall, I could hear them all loudly laughing. Without looking back, I left the White House and made a dash for my new metallic-blue BMW which Grandfather gave me the weekend before. "Your graduation present," he had beamed!

As I drove through the North Gate of the White House grounds, I began to wonder if I was ready to undertake the job I had just been commissioned to do. The job of a profiler was an easy one in theory. It was simply to meet people, get to know them and gain their confidence. Each assignment would consist of convincing the subjects to which I would be assigned to trust me unconditionally. Ultimately, my job would be to cajole their innermost secrets out of them, secrets they would not have told even their closest confidants, secrets imperative to the national security of the United States of America. To gain the trust of my subjects I would have to live their lives, become their best friend, their closest confidant. I would learn their hobbies, their personality traits, their loves, their dislikes, what gave them joy and what caused them sorrow. I would study their habits, their patterns and their characteristics. I would memorize their daily regimens. By the end of each assignment, if all went as planned I would know what made them tick, what turned them on and off and which buttons to push to cause whatever desired effect the Agency sought. If I were to fully accomplish the job I had been so painstakingly and diligently trained to do, I would know more about these individuals than they would ever know about themselves.

Now, while honing my language skills, I also took psychology courses that sometimes lasted ten hours a day. I went through defense training where I learned not only how to defend myself, but also how to be the aggressor when situations called for it. Finally, I spent an hour a day at the FBI firing range. This was my favorite part of the training. In nine short months, I worked my way up to "Sharp Shooter" and was issued my very own semiautomatic Glock Model 20 10mm pistol, a weapon I respected like my best friend.

My first assignment was my actual on-the-job training as a profiler. I was given rather unusual orders to befriend a Rhonda Hertz, the manager of a local restaurant in Tirol, Maryland, a suburb of Baltimore. I assumed that since this was considered a training assignment, it must be a very low priority and not at all dangerous. The only thing I was told was that the manager was under investigation for heading up an international drug-selling ring.

The assignment had been projected to take about eighteen months. However, in less than a year Rhonda Hertz had given me all the information the Agency needed to convict her, together with her subordinates and some acquaintances. The case turned out to be one of the largest international drug busts ever made and created international headlines. As for me, I faded into thin air, no one ever aware that I was the one who made the bust happen!

Although I was not scheduled to receive my shield for another year, my induction into the Agency was accelerated by a full ten months. There was still an element of disbelief, but the shield was tangible proof that the President had just made me a Special Operations Agent.

I pulled into my parking space in front of my apartment building in Georgetown. As I got out of the car, I suddenly realized that I could not recall anything I had seen since I had left the White House. I could not remember any of the details of the ride home. Evidently I was that deep in thought. It was amazing that I managed to make it all the way home without wrecking my new car.

I walked into my first floor apartment, tossed my keys on the coffee table, went to the kitchen, popped open a can of beer, went over to the hall closet and pulled out a heavy box filled with all of my photo albums. I placed the box on the coffee table and made myself comfortable on the couch. A warm feeling came over me as I leafed through the first book, seeing the pictures of people who meant so much to me. One of the pictures that especially caught my eye was a family shot taken the day before we moved from the house in which I had spent the first eight years of life. The picture made me laugh. Ben, my younger brother by eighteen months, and I looked pathetic. I recalled thinking how cruel Mom and Dad were, uprooting us and moving to what seemed to be another country. Life as we knew it was being taken away from us. How would Ben and I ever get over it and adjust? Would we make friends? We both doubted it at the time. Mom and Dad, on the other hand, appeared to be very happy. Mom was holding Natalie, my baby sister. She wasn't yet two years old in that picture. I remember Mom sitting Ben and I down and talking to us right after this picture was taken. She knew how unhappy we were about the move, even though it was only a few towns away. She explained to us that we were moving to a better neighborhood, an upper-middle class neighborhood where the schools were the best in the area. She was so optimistic!

The next picture to catch my attention was one of Jay and me by the pool at the Country Club. I vividly remember meeting Jay during recess on the first day of third grade. I had only been in the neighborhood two days and was really depressed — maybe a little scared. Jay came up to me and introduced himself. We became fast friends. His given name was Jason Scott, but I was the one person who could call him "Jay". Even his mother called him Jason.

Jay and I went everywhere and did everything together, so there were a lot of pictures of the two of us. He had become my best friend: later I would realize he was my first love. Ever since I could remember that I knew I was "gay", though I didn't fully comprehend all the consequences of what this meant. Jay knew how I felt about him and while he cared for me he made it clear that he was not "queer", even encouraging me to "act" straight. Because of Jay's attitude and all the jokes I'd heard, I tried to hide my feelings. If this wasn't enough, my dad's outspoken condemnation of gay people, whom he detested, scared the hell out of me. Dad thought homosexuals were sick and deviant. I recall him saying, "If I were President, I would have them all gathered up, put on a deserted island in the middle of the ocean, nuke it, and rid the world of the problem!" Once, when a co-worker of his confided to him that his son was gay, Dad said that if he ever found out that one of his kids were gay he would throw him out and never let him come back. So, I knew from a very young age that I was in big trouble and, if I didn't keep my feelings to myself, my father would throw me out — and would nuke me if he had his way.

I paused for a moment, took a sip of my beer and thought about how unfair and cruel life could be. No matter how many years had passed and how comfortable I was now about my sexuality, I still had an irrational fear of my father and avoided him as much as possible. He had given me little encouragement throughout my childhood but in the end, I guess, I was the one who alienated him.

The reality was that my father and I never saw eye-to-eye about anything, especially about the role of Grandfather in my life. Given the secretiveness of my work with the agency, he could never understand my life choices either. When I finally did get the courage to tell him I was gay, my father didn't send me away, but he would never accept my homosexuality. For good reason, my grandfather had been the nurturing parent my father could not be.

By choosing a career with the government I was aware that I would have to remain closeted, especially after the oath I had taken about an hour earlier. I kept telling myself that I had worked hard for this opportunity, that my work must take precedence over my personal life. One thing was certain — the Agency did not tolerate homosexuality. It was their position that gays were promiscuous, unstable security risks whose behavior made them vulnerable to compromise. If not for Grandfather's influence and power, no matter how qualified I were this job would not have been mine. I knew full well that my personal life would be closely monitored to ensure I didn't cross any imaginary lines in the sand. However, I still needed to be true to myself and refused to compromise or abandon my personal relationships. I was protected by the people closest to me who knew that I was gay but observed an unspoken rule of never talking about it.

CHAPTER TWO

I gazed back down at the pages of my photo album, my eyes focusing on a picture of Jay's mom and dad standing by their backyard grill where steaks cooked during one of their annual Independence Day barbecues. Shelly, Jay's mom was the type of mom all the neighborhood kids wished they had. She was hip with her bouffant hairdo, miniskirts and white go-go boots. The other moms always talked behind her back about what a bad impression she was giving the kids, not to mention their seething jealousy from the straying eyes of their husbands. Without a doubt Shelly was a stunning woman. No one dared confront her because they knew how influential her husband Peter was and to not be included in the annual Independence Day barbecue would be unimaginable. For many of the kids she was our second mom. If anyone was in trouble at home we knew Shelly would listen to our problems, make practical suggestions on how to correct or make them better, and best of all, she would not take any of our complaints back to our parents. She let us play and make as much noise as we wanted. She didn't even mind that we played our music full blast, as kids were prone to do. She even served us milk and cookies after school knowing full well that dinnertime was just a few hours away.

Then there was Jay's dad, Peter, whom all the guys called "Coach" because he was the head of the little league. Most of the guys, including me, admired him and looked up to him for guidance and leadership. Just as Shelly was our second mom, Coach was our second dad. He was a very handsome man with muscular arms and legs. He always had a deep, dark tan. It was no secret that both he and Shelly went to a tanning salon at least once a week. Of course, this "unnatural behavior" as many of the moms called it fueled the neighborhood gossip mill. In this particular picture, he was wearing his tortoise-shell Aviator sunglasses, which made him really hot looking. Now, as I stared intently at that picture of him, the feeling I felt was not one of admiration, but one of betrayal, hatred and disgust. I could not bear to look at his face. I quickly turned the page, hoping against hope that his image would disappear from my mind, knowing that it would always be lurking somewhere in my psyche for the rest of my life.

On the next page was my sixth grade class group photo. I could feel the tears beginning to well up in my eyes. I spotted Jay in the middle row, the best looking guy in the class. He was shorter than the rest of us, something he absolutely hated. To compensate for his size Shelly let him wear two-inch platform shoes. Whether he knew it or not, he was the envy of all us whose moms would have no part of such things as platform shoes.

I continued to look over all the other faces of my classmates, though most were now a distant memory. However, standing only three classmates away from me was Kenny Masterson. How innocent he looked, with his curly brown hair and darting hazel eyes and that angelic expression on his face. There we stood with eager anticipation, everyone so excited that the following year we would all begin Junior High School, on our way to becoming young adults. All of us were embarking on new adventures, none of us aware of the fate that would alter the course of our young lives.

On Friday, June 13, 1969, a few short months after that class photograph was taken, the dominos began to fall. When the day began, there was a certain specialness about it. It was like a thousand spring days rolled into one, when all you feel is the warmth of the sunshine on your face and the gentle breeze blowing through your hair. I was bubbling over with excitement and anticipation. Mom and Dad were letting me go down to the seashore with Jay and his folks for an entire weekend by myself, without their supervision. We were going to Cape May, New Jersey, to visit Jay's grandparents and celebrate his grandfather's 55th birthday. I can still remember going to the Ben Franklin 5 & 10 Cent Store with my allowance money. It felt so good picking out a present all by myself. I could not wait to see the look on Jay's grandfather's face when he opened it up.

As the memories continued to pour back into my mind, I could not help but remember that first moment of separation from my mother. Up until the last second,

I was convinced that she was going to change her mind. There she stood in our driveway wearing one of her frumpy "old lady" housedresses, which she insisted on always wearing. She was not a small woman by any means, so these dresses made her look even bigger than she was. She had flaming red hair and a face full of red freckles. She was a sight, but that was my mom. I managed to ignore her for the most part as she went through her usual long list of do's and don'ts and rules of etiquette. As I fidgeted with the tassels on the handlebars of my bicycle, I suddenly realized that she had stopped speaking and she had her arms held open for a goodbye hug and kiss. I quickly got the deed over with, ran back to my bike and sped off before she had one last chance to stop me.

When I arrived at Jay's house, I parked and chain locked my bike as usual to the iron fence post in the backyard. Once it was securely locked, I ran up the steps and knocked on the backdoor. After what seemed like an eternity, Coach wrapped only in a towel answered the door and ushered me into the kitchen. He took my backpack, sat me down at the table, poured

19

me a glass of milk and gave me some Oreo cookies. "Yummy, this is going to be a great weekend!" I proclaimed. I was embarrassed and excited at the same time seeing Coach nearly naked. I was beginning to feel that scary tingling sensation stirring inside me. He appeared also to be embarrassed because he stumbled through his words, uncomfortably apologizing for Mrs. Scott's and Jason's absence and quickly explaining that they had gone to do some last minute shopping for the trip.

No matter how hard I tried not to I could not stop staring. As insane a thought as it was, I wanted to touch Coach's body. My mind was out of control. If Coach had even an inkling of what was going through my mind, I would be in a lot of trouble. Finally I asked, "May I go into the living room and watch TV while I wait for Jay to come home?"

"Of course you may," he said, winking at me.

I ran into the living room and turned on the television. I mindlessly turned the dial and eventually found an old episode of "The Little Rascals."

A few minutes later, Coach came into the living room presumably on his way upstairs to get dressed. However, instead of continuing up the stairs he crossed the room, came over to the couch where I was sitting and sat down right next to me. When he did, the towel he was wearing fell from around his waist. My jaw dropped and I tried to turn away so he would not see my reaction. I knew the expression on my face would reveal that I was highly intrigued and aroused. If he had any idea what I was feeling, I had no doubt he would lose his temper, as I had seen him do from time to time. He was only human after all. He would most likely tell my parents who would send me away forever. I felt my heart racing a million miles an hour. As if he were reading my mind, Coach turned to me and assured me that everything was going to be okay. I tried to open my mouth and say something, but nothing would come out. Coach was now laughing almost uncontrollably at my obvious embarrassment. Then, without warning, he grabbed my hand and began slowly rubbing it across his chest. I was shaking so badly, but Jesus, it felt like nothing I had ever touched

21

before, it was great. There was so much hair. He guided my fingers all over his chest. I squeezed my eyes shot not knowing what to do next. When I again opened my eyes, I realized that he was no longer guiding my hand. I was doing it all by myself. Much to my surprise he was not in the least bit angry. In fact, he seemed to be enjoying it because he just kept smiling and making these oooh and aaah kind of noises. I was being lulled into this crazy comfort zone, and I could do nothing about it, nor did I want to. It was like I was in some kind of a trance. Coach suddenly reached over and with one quick swipe pulled my shirt off over my head. I screamed and tried to run, but he was too strong. He kept telling me to relax, that it was okay as he ran his hands all over my chest and back. It was so magical. I was flying. Coach obviously knew what he was doing, and it could not be wrong. He was, after all, the man whom I had grown to admire and idolize. I trusted him with my very life. I respected him more than I respected my own father. I could not even fathom that he would or could do anything to hurt me.

He was so kind and gentle. Boy, I thought, Jay was so lucky to have a dad like Coach.

What Coach suggested next really excited me. He told me that he and Jason often took showers together and wouldn't it be fun if we could do the same. My heart almost stopped beating. I felt like I couldn't breathe. I was feeling things that my ten-year-old brain couldn't really comprehend as I shook my head "yes."

This worried look appeared on my face, and I questioned out loud when Jay and Mrs. Scott would be back. Coach again laughed like there was some joke that I was not getting and told me I worried too much, and they would not be returning for quite a while and that they had lots of errands to run. He then reached over and grabbed my pants. I shook my head "no" and tried to stop him but he was too strong for me. As my pants and underpants came down together, I was exposed in all of my nakedness, complete with a pre-adolescent erection. I began to cry because I knew that my life was about to come to an abrupt halt.

"Oh please Coach," I said, "please don't tell my parents. They will send me away forever."

"Relax," he said, "I am not going to tell anybody."

"Promise?" I asked, trying to stop crying.

"Promise. Come on, where's that big, beautiful smile of yours? And that sparkle in your eyes? Ya know, Geoffrey, you are a real charmer. You are going to be quite a lady killer when you grow up."

I tried hard to smile, but it wasn't working as I followed him upstairs to the shower in the master bedroom. I figured the Scotts were getting ready to paint because the room was completely covered in heavy plastic. Everything was covered, even the floor. Though Shelly was a neat freak, this seemed a bit extreme. There were at least two layers of the stuff! In fact in some parts of the room the plastic was taped halfway up the walls. What was that all about? Jay hadn't told me that his parents were planning any major painting or redecorating, but hell, my parents don't tell me everything either.

When we got into the shower, Coach took the bar of soap from the soap dish. He lathered up his hands and reached for my penis and began to soap it up. It was a weird yet wonderful sensation to have someone else play with my penis. He handed me the soap and told me to wash his penis. It was huge! I was in awe, still shaking like a leaf. I could tell he really liked it. He kept running his hands through my hair and telling me how beautiful I was. I thought for a brief instant that I was hurting him because he started breathing heavily and told me to stop because he wasn't ready yet. I had no idea what he was talking about, but I decided that now was not a good time to ask.

I was so relieved when he took the bar of soap from my hand. He then took a hold of my shoulders and turned me around and started to massage my back. It felt so good. He slowly moved down to my butt. He was massaging that as well. It was an incredible feeling.

Even now as I look back at the events of that day, I can hear Mom's voice in my head warning me, as she often did, "Pay attention, Geoffrey, you never pay attention. One day it's going to get you in trouble!" Yes, it's true. I was not paying attention. How could I? In my wildest dreams I could never have imagined what Coach was going to do. I know I was only ten years old but was I that dumb and naive to think that it was okay to take my clothes off in front of my best friend's father? Did I think so much of this man to allow him to take advantage of me the way he did? How could I have allowed what started out as an innocent moment of exploration get so out of hand? Could I have stopped what happened if I had only said "no"? I thought so at the time, but now I realize that I had absolutely no control over the situation.

I felt his hard penis rubbing up and down my butt. And then it happened. I suddenly felt this jolt and then excruciating pain, the likes of which I would never have imagined. I was in such shock that I had no idea what was happening. Coach was no longer laughing. "You fucking bitch!" he yelled as he shoved his penis deeper and deeper into my butt.

I began screaming at the top of my lungs. "Please don't! Oh God, it hurts, it hurts!" Through my tears I pleaded with him to stop. "I don't want to play anymore. I just want to go home. Please stop and let me go home." All of my efforts were useless. He just kept right on ploughing away and yelling all kinds of obscenities, many of which I did not understand. He was unrelenting. He began to breathe faster and heavier, gripping my shoulders so tightly that his fingernails were piercing my skin and drawing blood. Finally he thrust his penis into me one last time harder than ever, and he held it there. As he moaned with some kind of sick pleasure, I felt wave after wave of this hot liquid shooting into my body. When he finally took his penis out of me, I looked down and freaked. There was blood running down my legs. It was all over the place. I was screaming not only from the excruciating pain but also from the horror of seeing my own blood. I began to get lightheaded. The last thing I remember yelling as my legs went out from under me was, "Jay, where the fuck are you? Help Me! I'm going to die."

When I woke up, I found myself stretched out on the Scotts' bed with my wrists and ankles tied to the bedposts on top of all of the sheets of plastic. The pain seemed to be getting worse by the second. It hurt so badly that I just wanted to crawl into a corner and die. I had no clue what I had done to deserve such a fate. Through a hazy fog I looked down and saw blood, *my blood*, all over the place. Then I slowly looked up and there was Coach, standing over me smiling and laughing. "Now that wasn't so bad, was it?" he sneered.

My body shook out of control. I was overcome with fear and panic. Coach was pointing a sword at me. It was the same sword that was usually displayed in a handmade glass case, mounted prominently on the bedroom wall amongst his various coaching and work awards. His father had given the sword to him for his 21st birthday. It was a souvenir from World War II. Coach would periodically parade all of us kids up to his and Shelly's bedroom and we would all sit on the floor around him as he retold his father's stories about the war. Coach was so proud of his father. The sword had these magnificent sapphire blue gems encrusted into a long, beautifully engraved silver handle. If we were lucky, he would take the sword from its place of honor and let each of us touch it. The sword had a mesmerizing and hypnotic effect on all of us. However, at this moment its luster and beauty meant nothing to me. I was sure that he was going to kill me with it.

Coach continued on his tirade, "Shut the fuck up. You are such a big baby and an ungrateful son-of-a-bitch, and, if you don't stop crying right now, I am going to have to hurt you, and I really don't want to do that." His voice lowered almost to a whisper, "This is to be our little secret. This is just one of the ways a father shows his love for his son, and I consider you to be one of my own children. I am warning you here and now that if you have any crazy ideas about telling a single soul I will kill you, and don't think I don't mean it! You had better hope that I kill you, because no one will believe you. You will be called a liar, and you'll be severely punished. I will tell the whole world that you are a faggot." To make his point and to show me that he meant every word he was saying, he took the handle of the sword with its many jagged edges and rammed it up into my already aching butt. The force he did this with was incredible. I tried to scream but I couldn't breathe. The pain was so overwhelming that I again blacked out.

I don't know how long I swayed in and out of consciousness, however, when I finally was a bit more coherent, Coach said in his normal nonthreatening voice, "If you're a good little boy, I won't hurt you anymore. Let me assure you, my friend, that the first time is always the worst. It gets much easier each and every time. The next time it will not hurt nearly as much."

Oh God, I can't go through that again. I started to cry and asked, "When is Jay coming home?"

"Not for a longtime," Coach answered matter-of-factly.

"Did you hurt him too?"

"I didn't hurt anybody, not even you. No, it's much better than that. You see, Geoffrey, I've been planning this little private party of ours for quite some time."

"But where are Jay and Mrs. Scott?"

"Now give me a chance to explain. Before you got here last night, I told them that your mother called and cancelled because you had a family emergency."

"But what about you? Weren't you supposed to go too?" I asked.

"My boy, you underestimate me. Don't worry. I've taken care of everything. You see, I made it look like I was unexpectedly called out of town on business. I even had my secretary make travel arrangements. No one will ever know that I didn't keep them. Brilliant...don't you think?" he asked with this twisted look of pleasure on his face.

"You fucking asshole!" I yelled, not thinking about the consequences.

"You don't talk to your father like that!" He yelled back and again shoved the handle of the sword up my butt.

I could not hold in my emotions any longer. Before I again blacked out, I shouted against the pain, "You are one sick mother fucker!" Then I looked up to the sky and muttered, "God, please let me die, it hurts so much."

Of course death never did come that day. God apparently had other plans. Unfortunately for me the weekend and the roller coaster ride were just beginning.

I regained consciousness, thinking for a brief instant that perhaps all of this was only a very bad nightmare. For a split second I actually began to feel better. I looked up and saw sunlight peeking through the curtains. Oh God, no, I thought, there are no frilly curtains on my windows, as a matter of fact there were no curtains at all on my windows. This really was happening and not a nightmare. As all of my senses returned, I felt my butt throbbing as pain seared through it. I had to go to the bathroom but I dared not move for fear that my insides would come out. I looked down and the blood was gone. I was lying on a clean sheet of plastic. I tried to get up but I could not. My wrists and ankles were still tied to the bedposts. I turned my head and there he was, standing over me and still smiling that grotesque smile of his. Every vivid detail of the night before came flooding back. What a monster this man is, I thought.

He said, after a long period of just dead air, "If you can behave and be a really good boy, I will untie you."

I really had to go to the bathroom. Despite the fact that I knew I would die, I just could not hold it any longer. I put on my best happy face and said, "I promise to be good and not cry anymore."

"Good Boy. I knew I could count on you."

"Coach, may I go to the bathroom?"

"Of course you can," he said as he untied my arms and legs.

Once untied, I raced into the bathroom and slammed the door behind me. Coach was laughing like a hyena. "What the fuck do you think is so funny you sick bastard?" I whispered to myself hoping he couldn't hear me.

Going to the bathroom hurt so much. I held my breath as I relieved myself. Thank God my insides didn't fall out. I was not going to die after all. As my eyes drifted around the bathroom, they stopped cold on the shower stall door. There was still blood all over it, my blood I was sure. I began shaking again. My resolve to survive must have kicked in at that moment.

33

I knew instantly that if I was going to get out of this alive, I had better behave myself and do exactly as I was told, and I had better keep my emotions in check. I pulled myself together and stopped shaking. I took my time washing my hands, and then, as calmly as I could I opened the bathroom door and went back into the bedroom. I walked over to the side of the bed where Coach was now sitting and sat right next to him.

He smiled and said, "I am so proud of you, Geoffrey, you have taken your first big steps to becoming a man. However, my young one, you still have many more lessons to learn." He then pulled me toward him, holding on to me and stroking my hair. He was holding me so tight that I could barely breathe. I could not believe what was happening. Coach was crying. How could this horrible beast of a man be so mean and nasty one minute and so warm and loving the next? I was so confused. He stared at me with these glassy eyes and said, "I am so sorry for making a complete fool of myself. Lie down on your back, Geoffrey, I want to treat you to something very special and wonderful, something you are really going to enjoy."

I was so tired of the pain that anything pleasurable would be good. I lay down, praying that Coach meant what he was saying. He leaned over me and began to lick my chest and nipples. I am very ticklish. Through the foggy pain I was in I squirmed and laughed, almost forgetting about the pain. He gently held down my arms and legs. His tongue traveled down to my little penis, which was again erect from all of the excitement. Any fear about getting in trouble for having a stiff penis had completely vanished. I just could not believe what I was feeling. It was so incredible. He rolled me over onto my stomach and began licking my butt. He told me that he knew I was hurting, but not to worry that he would make it all better. He was turning out to be such a sensitive person. I felt his tongue slowly massaging my butt. Then, he slowly slid it in. The feeling was so awesome. Coach's tongue was acting like Bactine. I mean it stung for a brief moment as the tip of his tongue hit the open sores which had formed on the inside of my butt.

Then, as if by magic, the stinging sensation was immediately replaced by this wonderful warming sensation. It was so marvelous. He was trying to heal my wounds. Thank God the pain was over and Coach was back to his good old self, I happily thought. The feeling was so great that I just did not want it to stop. He, of course, did eventually stop. I rolled over onto my back and stared up into Coach's eyes. They were beautiful. We were both smiling at each other.

"Don't ever lose that smile my friend. It is your best asset," he said.

I was so happy at that moment that I just wanted to shout with joy. If only the weekend had ended right there, perhaps all would have been forgiven and forgotten.

I suddenly had the urge to return the pleasure that I was feeling. I crawled up next to Coach and started to play with his chest. He was so hairy and it felt so amazing. I was nervous and even a little bit reluctant, even though, subconsciously, I knew there was no reason at all to be either. I'm sure Coach understood and knew that each new experience brought with it its owns fears to conquer.

"Don't be so shy and bashful," he said with a playful look on his face.

His tenderness helped me relax and all of my cares, fears and worries vanished. I imitated what Coach had just done to me. I began licking his nipples. It was so funny because they were nice and soft when I started, but they suddenly became hard and erect, just like his penis. I never knew that such a phenomenon was possible. Just to make sure, though, I asked if I was hurting him.

He laughed and replied, "No Geoffrey, quite the contrary. It really excites me, see," he said, as he turned my head toward his lengthening penis. I still could not believe the size of it. It was so long and so thick. Could that thing have really been inside of me? Unfortunately, there was no question about it as the pain, which had dulled only a little reminded me.

Coach gently steered my head down his torso until I hesitated over his gigantic penis. I think I was more awestruck than afraid. With a little bit more coaxing, I opened my lips and mouth and began to timidly lick Coach's penis. All of a sudden he yanked me by the back of my head and pulled me right up into his face. He looked me square in the eyes, his eyes now terrifying. In that brief second I knew I had seen the fires of hell. The book "Dr. Jekyll and Mr. Hyde" popped into my head. Coach was a real life Jekyll and Hyde. He began to speak, his words boring into me with the scariest stare I had ever beheld. He slowly and deliberately growled, "You fucking bitch, everything I have done for you, everything I have taught you and this is how you show your gratitude, with this poor excuse for a blow job?"

Before I had time to react, my head jerked again as Coach pulled it back toward his penis. He forced it into my mouth and shoved it down my throat. I couldn't breathe. He was choking me.

He finally took his penis out of my mouth while yelling at me the whole time. "You fucking faggot, stop biting down so hard." And then he hauled off and slapped me across my face. My mind was in such a frenzied state. I was gasping for air and my face was stinging so badly I thought my teeth were going to fall out. Just when I thought it couldn't get any worse, he shoved it back down my throat, and suddenly I felt spurt after spurt of hot gooey liquid pouring into my stomach. I was gagging and choking. As I faded yet again into unconsciousness I thought, I'm going to die. Thank you God.

Now, sitting on my living room couch, amazing myself at how often I had cheated death that weekend. I realize that the inner strength and determination I somehow mustered up was the beginning of my mental as well as my physical preparedness for my position with the National Security Agency.

I clutched my throat still recalling the pain of that day. I got up and went into the bathroom and gargled with salt water to soothe my throat, as if the incident had just happened, something I have done each time I recall the episode.

CHAPTER THREE

Unfortunately it didn't take long for me to be drawn back to that wretched weekend. I was so engrossed in the memories that it felt like I was back in Shelly and Coach's bed reliving the nightmare. In my perplexed mind I heard crying from somewhere behind me. I knew it wasn't Coach. I rolled over and saw Kenny Masterson, a friend and schoolmate, lying next to me crying and sobbing. He was tied to the bedposts just as I had been. I was so confused. What the hell was he doing here? Although my mind was swimming in confusion, and I could not properly focus, I got up and made a futile attempt to untie the rope holding Kenny's left wrist. "Kenny, what the fuck are you doing here? Run for your life before Coach hurts you too!" I yelled hoarsely.

Confusion gave way to pain as I turned around and saw Coach standing there holding the sword. Grinning, he said, "It's no use, Geoffrey, Kenny's not in a hurry to go anywhere."

I looked down at Kenny and saw blood — this time it was his blood — all over the plastic. Oh Jesus, I thought, had Kenny just gone through the same suffering I had? Why was this man doing this to us? Had Kenny also put up with the pain of that sword? I knew the answer to all of those questions, but couldn't comprehend why any of this was happening.

Coach continued, "Say hello to our guest. Aren't you happy to see your friend?"

"Kenny, I am so, so sorry." I said as I started to cry.

"Now," Coach said, "it's time to see what we have learned. You didn't use your mouth as well as you should have on me. Let's see how you do with our guest. Be nice and show him how pleasurable it is."

"No," I pleaded. "Why are you doing this to us?"

"Don't you get it yet? I'm not hurting you, I'm helping you. I'm helping you become men. Now do as I tell you or I will have to discipline you again, and I don't think you want me to do that."

"Kenny, I promise I won't hurt you," I said to him.

Coach was now acting like a Drill Sergeant, yelling out all kinds of orders and commands. I did as I was told trying to be gentle. In an instant, however, everything began to unravel. Coach pushed me out of the way and shoved his penis down Kenny's unsuspecting throat. The sounds coming from Kenny were bloodcurdling. He was choking and gurgling and gasping for breath. He suddenly threw up all over himself and Coach.

Coach jumped up with this annoyed look on his face. I watched in complete shock as Kenny stopped moving. I was sure that he was dead. I did not think it was possible, but Coach appeared to be angrier than I had ever seen him. He turned to Kenny's limp body and started yelling, "You sorry ass little pig, you will never do that to me again."

Then he turned to me. I was doing everything I could to keep my emotions in check, but I could not do it. I just sat there and openly and shamelessly wept. Coach continued on his tirade as he cleaned up the mess Kenny had made. "You fucking little faggot, what's your fucking problem? What are you crying about? I didn't do anything to you, now shut up!"

Kenny began to make these gruesome noises. Despite how chilling they sounded I was relieved that he was still alive.

Coach, still livid, looked into Kenny's blank eyes and said, in a low grumble, "It's time for you to be punished, and you're going to take it like a man."

I watched in horror as Coach made a fist and started rubbing Kenny's butt with it. When I saw what was about to happen something deep inside of me snapped. I had to stop him. "No you asshole. Stop it!" Then I went ballistic. Everything started moving in ultra slow motion. I lunged at Coach but it was too little too late and I hurdled off the bed. I screamed as Coach's fist plunged deeply up into Kenny's little butt. I watched from the floor in complete shock. I was paralyzed and could not move. Kenny let out a bloodcurdling scream. Then, Coach made this really strange face that turned to a look of satisfaction. In an instant Kenny stopped screaming, a look of sheer terror and panic running across his face; suddenly his eyes rolled back up into his head. I tried to scream, but nothing came out.

Coach grabbed me by the scruff of my neck and slapped me hard across my face. His hand was covered with Kenny's guts. The smell was so awful. Is this what death smells like? I wondered.

"Geoffrey, my friend, it's your turn. Kenny got his punishment, he will never talk back to me ever again and neither will you!"

"Oh no, please don't," I begged. He threw me down onto the bed like a rag doll. I felt no connection at all to my extremities. Without hesitation he rammed his fist up my aching butt. The pain was so excruciating, but I just could not fight anymore. I just lay there and sobbed, waiting to die. In an instant, I understood Kenny's expressions of pain and then terror when Coach was torturing him. There was no mistake in what I was feeling. Coach's fist opened into a hand deep inside of me. It was like no other pain imaginable.

The only way I can describe what Kenny and I experienced that day, although it sounds so macabre, is to call it hand puppets. Coach was the puppeteer and we were his puppets, being manipulated as he saw fit. My short life flashed before my eyes. There was no question that I had lost the will to live. I just wanted to be dead. If I were dead, I would not have to endure Coach's brutality or hear his voice ever again. My insides were throbbing and pulsating with such pain and I was so weak. The one thing I do remember clearly was that, even though all of these things were going on inside of me, I absolutely refused to give Coach the satisfaction of seeing me suffer.

With all of the strength I could muster, I put a smile on my face. Kenny was still lying on the bed next to me still alive somehow. We stared into each other's eyes, acknowledging without words the torment we were both suffering. "I want to go home." He finally managed to murmur.

"I know you do Kenny, so do I, but hang in there and hopefully this will be over soon," I whispered.

45

It was so amazing the way Coach's emotions changed in a split second. He put a hand on my shoulder and in a worried voice said, "Geoffrey we have a big problem here, Kenny is very unhappy with us. It appears that he does not want to be a part of our little playgroup. He is going to tell on us and we cannot let him, now can we? If he reports us to the police, they will send us both away for a very long time, probably forever."

As he continued to speak of the terror of being sent away, he took the sword from its case and placed it in my hands. It was so heavy. I didn't think that I had the strength to hold on to it, but I did. There was no way that I was going to let anybody take me away. I was so scared that I lifted the sword high over my head like a golf club and froze. As I stood there motionless, Coach whispered into my ear, "Don't let him hurt you and make you have to go away forever." My mind was blank and my emotions took over. Without any forethought or hesitation, I swung the sword down at Kenny. Blood went flying everywhere. Coach continued whispering into my ear, "Do it Geoffrey, do it, and don't stop until it is finished. Kenny has been a very bad little boy, and he needs to be punished."

I again lifted the sword and began hacking at Kenny's body. Pieces seemed to be flying in all different directions. I don't know how many times I hit him. When Coach finally stopped me, I felt like Jell-O. I looked down at Kenny, but what was left of him was little more than a pool of blood and torn flesh. Kenny was barely recognizable.

Coach turned me away from Kenny's body. He smiled at me and said, "Geoffrey, you did a great job. Kenny can never hurt you or me ever again. Isn't it great? You and I are one now. This little act of love joins us forever. Always remember, you can never tell anyone about this, because you are the one who killed Kenny." He paused for a few moments as that thought sank into my already saturated mind. He continued, "If you tell anyone, you will be telling on yourself. This will always be our little secret. Now, let's get this mess cleaned up."

I was so numb I couldn't even feel my own pain. I just sat across from the bed on a chair, which was also covered in that wretched plastic and watched Coach wrap Kenny's lifeless body up in the many sheets of plastic. As Coach carried Kenny away, bundled up in his plastic coffin, I continued to sit and stare into space. My mind, which had been on overload for so long, was now totally void of anything.

When he had finally finished cleaning everything up, he came over to me and without a word picked me up and carried me toward the bathroom. He could have done anything to me and I wouldn't have been able to react. I was completely spent. As he carried me across the room toward the bathroom, a very strange thing happened. I suddenly realized that I was looking down from above, and I wasn't feeling any pain. I felt like I was floating. I felt like I had finally been freed. I looked up and thanked God for releasing me from all of the pain. I even began to laugh watching Coach carry my lifeless body. Wow, this is great, I thought. I'm dead at last. Death was such an incredible feeling, a feeling of freedom from all that bound me. Floating above, I watched as Coach placed me into the shower and turned the water on. He was cleaning me up. He scrubbed every nook and cranny, every crevice of my body. He washed my hair, not once but twice. Outwardly, except for a couple of bruises, there was no indication of the brutality I had just experienced.

He must have known that I was dead because he did not perform any more perverse acts on me. He turned off the water and began drying me off. I felt him roughly drying off my body with a towel. Worse yet, all of the pain had returned. I looked around. I was no longer hovering from above. Fuck, I thought, I hadn't died at all.

I was the one who finally broke the silence. Even though I already knew the obvious answer to the question, I had to ask it. "Is Kenny really, really dead?"

Coach smiled and said, "Yes, Kenny really is dead and you are safe now. You have absolutely nothing to worry about ever again."

"You have absolutely nothing to worry about either," I said.

"What do you mean by that, Geoffrey?" he asked.

"Coach, I promise not to tell a single soul ever. This will always be our little secret."

"That's my boy! Here's your backpack. Now get dressed. We're going for a little ride."

With all the trauma my body had been through I could barely walk, but I bit my lip and pretended to be fine. I could never again let him know what I was feeling, neither physically nor mentally. I was going to have to really work hard at not showing the physical pain, however, hiding the mental anguish would not be so hard, because I had died a long slow death that night. If not physically, then mentally.

Coach opened the passenger side of the car door and sat me in the seat. He took some rope from his workbench and began tying me into the seat. "You don't need to tie me up. I promise I won't run away," I said.

"I know you won't Geoffrey. But we don't want to take any chances now do we?"

"No sir," I calmly answered.

When we finally pulled away from the house, I looked around. I figured that it had to be really late at night because the roads were empty; in fact they were downright deserted. All of the stores were closed and the parking lots were completely empty. The clock in Coach's car was broken so I was clueless as to what time it was. We drove in silence for several minutes before Coach finally started talking. "We are taking Kenny to a place where nobody will find him. That way nobody will know that he is dead. They will just think that he ran away from home."

Jesus, he sounded so sure of himself, almost as if he had been through this sort of thing before. My mind went into overdrive yet again. Oh Christ, had he killed before? Would he kill again? Would I be next? Those simple little questions solidified in my mind the indisputable necessity to remain calm and stay silent, if for no other reason than for sheer survival.

Coach eventually got off the highway. We were going down a weather-beaten road through what I recognized right away as the swampland behind the Philadelphia International Airport. He drove past the lake where Mom and Dad took us kids ice-skating every winter. I tried to hold on to those memories of happier times, if only for a fleeting moment. Coach turned off his headlights and drove by the light of the full moon. We twisted and turned in the dark for what seemed like miles. After a while, we came to a stop at the edge of another big lake. The smell was really putrid. Coach looked over at me and flashed me a big smile. "It's almost over. You never have to be afraid of anything ever again." Then he leaned over and gave me a big hug.

I shrank back in my seat ever so slightly aware that any sudden movement might set him off again. He continued to hold on to my aching body and said, "Geoffrey, don't worry. I promise not to hurt you like Kenny almost did to you. You are like a son to me. I could never hurt you."

He finally let go of me, telling me to sit quietly while he took care of things. He got out of the car and opened the trunk. He lifted Kenny's plastic-shrouded body and laid it by the water's edge. Going back to the trunk, he took out some rope and threw it next to Kenny's body. Then Coach darted into the tall reeds by the lake, quickly emerging with an armful of cinderblocks. I watched as he placed the blocks on top and then used the rope to tie the cinderblocks to the bundle of plastic. I was in awe and amazement at what happened next. Coach picked up Kenny's plastic coffin with the cinder blocks on top and heaved the entire package far out over the water. It hit with a loud splash, but there was no one else around for miles to hear it.

Coach stood on the bank of the lake for several minutes staring out at the now calm water. What was he thinking? Was he feeling at least a little bit of guilt? I hoped so, but I truly doubted it.

He returned to the car, dusting himself off and taking off a pair of gloves. They were brown cloth, loose-fitting gardening gloves. Coach loved to grow things, and he was really good at it. How strange is that, considering his disregard for Kenny's life, I thought.

Coach finally got back into the car wearing a funny grin on his face, a look of accomplishment and satisfaction. He turned to me and said, "See Geoffrey? It's all over. I've taken care of everything, just as I

53

promised I would." He turned the radio on and the time suddenly lit up. It was 3:45 a.m.! He then said, acting as if nothing bad had just happened, "You look really tired. Why don't you try to get some sleep? It's been a long day."

My brain could not handle one more thing. Coach was singing along with the radio — the song was "Oh Happy Day" — as I drifted into a fitful sleep.

CHAPTER FOUR

I was jolted back to the here and now by the incessant ringing of the telephone. I stared at it until it stopped. I was not in the mood at the moment to talk to anybody. If it were important, they would call back. Although the air conditioner was making the place feel like the Arctic, I was sitting in a pool of sweat.

Thank God for the bizarre workings of the human mind. The moment Coach began singing "Oh Happy Day" my mind opened a door, shoved everything that happened that Saturday inside, and quickly closed it. The memory of murdering one of my friends left my conscious mind, only to be unlocked a few years later when the time would be right for my psyche to handle and process the information.

I quickly turned the page of the photo album to try and wipe those memories away again. I now stared down at a picture of Jay and me. I was wearing the tee shirt from Cape May, New Jersey that Jay's mother bought me on that weekend. God, how I had trusted her and believed in her. What a fool I had been, I thought, as my mind was drawn back to that hellish weekend.

When I woke up, I was lying on clean linen sheets, not on plastic ones. In fact, as I began focusing on the room, I saw that all of the plastic had been removed. I rolled over and realized that I was no longer tied down. I looked at the clock on the nightstand by the bed. It was after 4:00pm. The afternoon sun was shining brightly through the windows. I looked up and there was Coach sitting on the edge of the bed next me, asking me how I felt. I lied and told him that I was okay. He was not going to know that I was still in a lot of pain from the previous evening's torture. My throat was killing me, and my voice was rather raspy. Coach handed me a glass of water with some salt in it. He made me drink the bad tasting stuff, telling me that it would make my throat feel better. I tried to remember back to the night before to figure out what I had done to make my throat feel so horrible, but nothing came to me.

My eyes slowly moved up the wall to see the sword, which had so brutally assaulted me only hours earlier. It was now safely stored away in its glass enclosed display case. I could not stop staring at it and asking myself why this was happening and what I had done wrong that had made God so mad at me.

Coach saw me staring at the sword. He smiled down at me and said, "There won't be any need for that 'silly old thing' anymore."

Boy, I thought, was he ever right about that. I would be damned if I was going to go through that shit again. I gave him a big smile, but knew that I could never trust him again. My best plan of attack would probably be to just play his fucking game and then just maybe I could go home.

Coach's head jerked around. He heard something that alarmed him. I heard it too. It didn't take long to figure out what it was. It was the sound of the garage door opening. Coach and I both ran into Jay's room and watched the shiny black Caprice slowly pull into the garage. Then the garage door slammed shut with a thud as it hit the cement floor. Without warning, Coach turned back into a wild monster. He started yelling at me again. The only difference was that this time I could detect fear in his voice. Now he sounded more like a child about to get caught. He was screaming at me to sit back down on the bed and to keep my fucking mouth shut if I knew what was good for me. He glanced up at the sword and I got the message loud and clear.

I heard voices as the door from the garage to the laundry room opened. Shelly was telling Jay to take off his shoes. She was such a stickler for taking shoes off before coming into the house.

From the bottom of the living room stairs I heard Shelly call out, "Peter, what are you doing home so soon? I didn't expect you until at least tomorrow." She hurried upstairs.

Before Coach had a chance to answer, Shelly saw me sitting on the edge of the bed. Her face suddenly began to contort, and she turned white as a ghost. She reached the doorway in a flash and stared at Coach and me in utter disbelief. "My God. Peter, what is going on here? Please, please don't tell me— "

Shelly's face was now turning several shades of red. I had never seen her this upset before. In a whispered, angry voice she continued questioning Coach, "You didn't, did you?" I watched as she slowly moved passed him, never taking her eyes off him. She came over to where I was sitting on the edge of the bed and sat next to me. It was as if the wind had been knocked out of her. The look of disgust and anger on her face began scaring the hell out of me. With clenched teeth she said to Coach, "You did. Didn't you? Oh sweet Jesus, no!"

Coach just stood there, completely speechless, completely inanimate. She turned back to me and now her demeanor changed instantly from anger to compassion. Boy, I mused, as she put her arms around me, she changes emotions just as quickly as Coach does.

"There, there, Geoffrey, it's going to be all right," Shelly said reassuringly.

Coach was still standing at the doorway immobilized like some stone statue. She looked straight at him and barked, "Get downstairs in the

59

recreation room and stay there until I am finished here."

Jay was standing in the doorway with a dazed look on his face. Shelly ordered him to go back to his room, shut his door, and not to talk to his father. I had never seen her this angry, yet so in control. Jay immediately did as he was told, leaving us alone.

After a brief moment, she turned back to me with tears in her eyes. For several moments there was a calm stillness as neither of us spoke. In the safety of Shelly's arms I was now able to openly cry. She just held me and rocked me back and forth, stroking my long hair. Eventually I stopped crying, but I could not stop shaking. I said to Shelly, "Please tell me it's over. Please tell me Coach won't ever hurt me again."

"Yes, honey, it's over. Are you okay?" she asked.

"Yeah. I guess so. He didn't hurt me that much," I lied. Of course I could never tell her the truth. I needed to go to the bathroom, but I made Shelly promise to wait for me. She continued to assure me that I was indeed safe now. As I got up, Shelly let out a horrible shriek. She scared the shit out of me! Coach and Jay both came running into the bedroom. Shelly chased them both back to their respective rooms. I turned to see why Shelly was screaming and looked down where I had been sitting. There was a big pool of blood on the white bedspread. The sight of it made me throw up. "Oh Jesus," I yelled, "I'm bleeding to death."

Without hesitation Shelly picked me up and whisked me down the hallway to the bathroom. "Oh Goddamn it, Peter!" she kept repeating furiously as she carried me down the hallway. "What have you done? Geoffrey, I am so sorry. You must understand Mr. Scott is not in his right mind. He didn't mean it."

Once we reached the bathroom, she sat me down on the floor and began to run the bath water. The only thing I could do was sit on the floor and shake uncontrollably. My mouth tasted terrible from the vomit so I got up and went to the sink to rinse my mouth. The pain was really bad. I kept muttering incoherent stuff like, "I'm going to die," and "Will I ever get to see my mom and dad and brother and sister again?"

Shelly finally calmed down enough to hold a conversation with me. "Now, Geoffrey, no matter what Mr. Scott said to you, no matter how much he threatened to hurt you if you told on him, I want you to tell me everything. Remember, you are safe now, he can't hurt you anymore."

I wasn't about to take any chances. "There is nothing to tell. I just want to go home. Can I go home now?"

"In due time Geoffrey."

"Why not now?" I wanted to know.

"We have to get you fixed up first."

"Okay. But then can I go home?"

"Relax. Mr. Scott isn't going to hurt you anymore," she said sounding a bit irritated.

"I promise I won't tell my mom and dad," I blurted out.

"Oh no, your mother and father don't need to know about this. No, no, no, don't worry about that, Geoffrey dear. I just want to help you and make you feel better. If you tell me what Mr. Scott did to you, I will know how to take care of you and make you feel better. Please Geoffrey, tell me everything."

Feeling better already just knowing that Mom and Dad would not be told about this, I began my story, trying to be as vague as possible. As I spoke, she had this perplexed look on her face, but she listened nonetheless and did not say a word. I told her, "I came over last night to go down to the Shore to see Pop-pop and celebrate his big birthday. When I got here, Coach answered the door and told me that you guys would be right back that you had some more shopping to do before the big weekend. Coach must have just gotten out of the shower, because the only thing he had on was a white towel around his waist."

"Oh Jesus," Shelly cried, "I knew it! Oh Geoffrey, I'm so very sorry. Do you understand what Mr. Scott did to you?"

"Yes, I think so," I replied turning my head away from her.

The bathtub finished filling up. Shelly asked me to take off my clothes so she could wash them. She said the warm water would make my backside feel a lot better. The pain was so bad that I was more than willing even if it meant getting undressed in front of a girl. At least this time, when I took off my clothes, my penis didn't get erect like it did when Coach undressed me.

Shelly helped me into the tub and I slowly sat down. She was so right. The water felt great. "Relax for a few minutes. I'm going to put your clothes in the washing machine."

A sudden tinge of panic came over me. "Please don't leave me alone," I pleaded.

"Oh honey, it's okay. How would it be if Jason sits with you? Would that be okay? I'll make sure Mr. Scott stays downstairs with me."

"Okay," I said.

Shelly went to the doorway and called down the hall for Jay to come into the bathroom. Jay was there in a flash. "Jason, honey, I want you to stay here with Geoffrey while I take care of a few things." Then she said, almost with a smile on her face, "The bad man inside of daddy hurt Geoffrey a little bit, but it's nothing we can't fix."

At first I couldn't even look at Jay. I was so embarrassed; I just stared down into the water, which now had a light reddish tinge to it. I put my hands over my privates because just the sight of Jay in his underwear was making me tingle inside and my penis was getting erect again. Please God; don't let him see my stiff penis. I thought.

Jay closed the lid on the toilet seat and sat with his hands folded in front of him. Although I was not crying out loud, Jay saw the tears rolling down my cheeks and said, "Don't cry, Geoffrey, my daddy didn't mean it. It's just that sometimes he gets, you know, a little weird. He becomes a different person. He can't help it."

"Jay," I asked, "has your dad ever hurt you, like he's hurt me? You know what I mean, don't you?"

"Yeah, I know what you mean, and yes he has hurt me in that way too. But, when he gets that way, it's not my daddy, it's this bad man. Besides, Mommy always knows how to make it all better."

I finally got the nerve to look at Jay. He was also crying. "Why did he do this to me?" I asked.

"I don't know, but I'm sorry Geoffrey. I'm so sorry. Please don't look at me, I am so ashamed. Daddy would be so mad if he saw me crying."

"Jay," I said, "we both had better be good and maybe he won't hurt either of us anymore."

I wish you were right," he sadly said. "Geoffrey, I have to tell you a secret, but you have to promise that you will never tell anyone."

I spit in my hand. He did the same. We held up our hands, palm to palm and both promised never to tell a single soul what he was about to confide in me. We then promised to never speak of it, ever again.

Jay continued, "I have this secret place where I go whenever Daddy becomes the 'bad man.' I will take you there later. It's a place I go to make all the hurt go away. Now it will be our secret place."

I, of course, was fascinated and broke into a genuine smile for the first time that afternoon. Shelly returned with a plate full of cookies for us. I was really hungry because the last time I had eaten was last night when Coach gave me milk and cookies.

"Mom, is it okay if Geoffrey and I stay home from school tomorrow? We're not doing anything anyway, and there's only two more weeks to go?" Jay asked.

I started laughing and blurted out, "Don't you know that tomorrow is Sunday, stupid?"

They both looked at me like I was the stupid one. Shelly gave me the same perplexed look she had given me when I was explaining to her what had happened. She said, sweeping the whole thing under the carpet, "No, honey, this is Sunday evening, you must be confused. Why, with what has happened it is perfectly understandable. Let's not talk about it anymore."

After a few moments of again going over everything in my head, I confidently pointed out that I knew I had gotten there yesterday afternoon almost right after school.

Jay and Shelly again looked at me like I had two heads. "No, honey," Shelly said, "it's Sunday evening. You must be mistaken."

I was still very much confused, but maybe Shelly was right, maybe I had lost all track of time. Shelly said with a smile, "I tell you what. I will call your mother and tell her that we had car trouble and we will be back tomorrow. And yes, you two can have a free day off from school."

Shelly emptied the tub and refilled it, and I soaked a little while longer. Jay went to his room and came back with some of his space men and joined me in the tub. We must have played for what seemed like hours. I must admit that with Jay sitting naked next to me in the tub it was difficult to concentrate on playing with the space men, but I somehow managed to play and hide my stiff penis from him.

Shelly finally came up and gave us towels and told us to get dressed and come down for dinner. My clothes were all freshly washed and laid out on Jay's bed. Jay and I got dressed and fooled around as we listened to The Archie's singing, "Sugar. Hey Sugar, Sugar, You are My Candy Girl . . . "

It wasn't long before Shelly called us for dinner. I suddenly panicked. "I can't go down there," I whimpered.

"What's the matter?" Jay asked.

"I'm afraid to see your dad. He might hurt me again."

"It's okay. Daddy probably isn't even there. Mommy always makes him go down to the recreation room to do exercises and that makes him feel better. That makes the bad man in him go away." Just to make sure, he called his mother who came running in from the kitchen. She looked up the stairs and saw the tears streaming down my face.

"What's wrong, honey?" She asked.

Geoffrey's afraid of Daddy," Jay answered.

Shelly came up the staircase to where I was standing and put her arms around me and reassured me, "Now, I told you not to worry anymore. I promise Mr. Scott will never hurt you again. Besides, he is down in the recreation room. You won't even see him. And please, Geoffrey, always remember that it was not Mr. Scott who hurt you, he would never do that. No, it was the bad man inside of him and he's gone now."

I tentatively made my way downstairs with both Shelly and Jay. Sure enough, Coach was nowhere to be seen. The three of us had a really fun dinner, more like a picnic. We had hot dogs, hamburgers, potato salad, and baked beans. Shelly really had a way of making me feel better. She was great!

After we had dessert, we went into the living room and watched The Wonderful World of Disney. "Wow! It really is Sunday!" I marveled out loud.

During the show, Shelly went downstairs to the recreation room to be with Coach. When the movie ended she reappeared and told us that it was time for bed. I started to panic again. I thought I was going to have to sleep alone on the couch in the living room like I usually did when I stayed overnight. My fears quickly subsided when Jay whispered to me, "Come on, we can play camping and make a tent in my room. I have a couple of flashlights."

With that we raced up to his bedroom. As we topped the steps I glanced into the Scotts' bedroom. I quickly closed my eyes trying to block out the memories of the previous Friday night.

Shelly yelled up to us, "Boys, you have one hour."

Once we were safely behind Jay's bedroom door my fears dissipated. Jay stripped down to his underwear. I just stood there and stared. "Come on, what are you waiting for? Get undressed and let's play."

"Okay," I said quickly stripping down to my underwear too, praying that he would not notice my stiffening penis. Without a glance, Jay handed me one of the flashlights and turned off all the lights in the bedroom.

We managed to build this really cool tent with the bed sheets. I was really tired. Jay saw me yawning and said, "We had better get ready for bed now. Mom will be up soon to tuck us in." We disassembled our tent, turned out our flashlights and got under the covers. The feeling of being in the same bed in only my underwear with my best friend was euphoric. I looked over and started to talk to Jay, but he was already fast asleep. Before I drifted off to sleep, I slowly manipulated my arm so that it lay across Jay's chest. I knew he was sound asleep because he didn't move a muscle. In no time, I too was fast asleep.

*****

"No, stop, please, Oh God it hurts so much! Jay, help me. Help me! He's going to kill me!" I felt several pairs of hands pulling at me as I opened my eyes. Shelly and Jay were shaking me trying to get me to wake up. I was drenched in sweat. I was shaking so badly that even Shelly had a hard time calming me down. "You just had a bad dream," she said. "I told you, the bad man is gone, and I promise you, Geoffrey, he will never, never ever come back to hurt you again."

Shelly leaned over to Jay and whispered something into his ear which I could not make out, and then she got up and quietly left the room.

"What time is it, Jay?" I whispered.

"It's four o'clock in the fucking morning. Jesus, Geoff, you scared the shit out of us. What's wrong with you?"

"I'm sorry, it's just that I keep seeing your dad and that fucking sword." I realized the minute I opened my mouth I was in trouble.

"Oh fuck no. Please don't tell me he threatened you with granddaddy's sword?" Jay cried out.

I began to sob again. I just could not hold it in, as hard as I tried. Jay needed to know. He needed to know what kind of a monster his father really was. "I have a secret to tell you," I confided in Jay, "but you have to promise that you will never tell a single soul." We again swapped spit and I continued. "He not only threatened me with that sword, he, you know, used it on me!" As difficult as it was to recount what had happened to me, I took a deep breath and said, "Your dad is a monster. He hurt me so bad with that sword that I thought I was going to die. He shoved the handle of it up inside my butt and told me that if I ever told anyone what he did to me he would kill me. Oh God Jay, I don't want to die! Please don't let him hurt me, don't let him kill me!"

Jay moved next to me and lovingly put his arm around my shoulder, just like Shelly had done. He said, "I can't believe he did that to you. I promise I won't tell anybody. I have a secret too. Something I have never even told my mother. Daddy has hurt me many times with that mother-fucking sword. I can't even look at it anymore without feeling pain." Jay cried as

73

he told me how his father had hurt him many times before, and how when his father was really angry, he would go to the display case and pull that "ugly prick of a sword" out and shove it into him. He paused for a second then said, "I hate my father. He scares me to death. Although he says he does these things because he loves me, I know he really hates me too."

We heard Shelly coming up the stairs. We quickly wiped our eyes dry on the bed sheets and started talking and laughing like everything was okay. She came into the room with a tray in her arms. First she gave me two aspirin and some water to wash them down. Then she offered us more chocolate chip cookies and milk. "Cookies and milk," she said happily, "are the best medicine for my little boys."

After we finished, she put the tray on the nightstand, lay down between us and told us to get some sleep. She turned to me and said, "Don't worry. Mr. Scott doesn't even remember what happened, and when he can't recall anything I know he's back to his normal self again." Then she added with a smile, "Isn't it wonderful?"

To this day, her words boggle my mind. She was so nonchalant about it. The scary thing was that she honestly believed every word she was saying. There was no question in my mind that he was lying to her. How many times before this had he hurt Jay? How many times before this did she have to take care of Jay because of what this monster had done to him? How could she have been in such denial? There was so much I did not understand then and still don't understand now, many years later.

As I woke up from a very restless sleep, all of my fears returned. I realized that I was in bed all alone. Jay and Shelly were nowhere in sight. I sank deeply under the covers knowing that Coach's door was right across the hall. Oh Jesus, please God; don't tell me that he got rid of them again. I began to shake, but quickly stopped. I could not and would not let him see that I was weak and vulnerable. I hastily crawled under the bed hoping that he would think I went home or something. I tried not to breathe or utter a sound as I heard footsteps come up the stairs. The bedroom door swung open. There was so much clutter under Jay's bed that I could not see who was standing there, but I knew when no words were spoken, it had to be Coach. The bedroom door slammed shut leaving me alone in the darkness. I knew exactly what he was doing. He was covering his room with those plastic sheets. He was going to get the sword out and this time he was definitely going to kill me.

The bedroom door again swung open. This time I heard Shelly frantically say to Jay, "Where did he go? Are you sure he is not here? He couldn't have gone home. If he tells his mother what happened to him they will take your daddy away for sure and you'll never get to see him or Geoffrey ever again! We've got to stop him."

Just the thought of never seeing Jay again was so horrible that I yelled out that I was right here and proceeded to crawl out from under the bed. They both looked at me with this dumbfounded expression on their faces. Shelly asked, "Did you hear everything I said?"

"Yes," I replied, "that's why I came out from hiding. Please don't let them take Jay or me away. I'm not a queer. Please make them understand that."

"Honey, what are you mumbling about?" Shelly asked. "Nobody is going to hurt you or take you away. I told you everything is going to be all right." I watched as she paused and took a deep breath searching for the right words. "Now, what is this nonsense about being queer? What a terrible word that is. My God, the things you boys think up now a days. I swear that you both are growing up way too fast."

I was so relieved to hear Shelly tell me that nobody was going to be taken away. I knew she didn't want Coach to be taken away either.

Shelly continued to look at me with this concerned look on her face. "Now Geoffrey, honey, you have got to promise me that you will not tell your mother and father about this. Do I have your word?"

Without hesitation I replied, "Yes, Mrs. Scott, I mean Shelly, you have my word."

"Good boy, Geoffrey. Now get dressed. It's already one o'clock in the afternoon. Jay and I bought you a new tee-shirt while we were on the Boardwalk Saturday night."

"Thank you," I said as Shelly turned and left the room.

As I got dressed, Jay told me that his mom wanted him to tell me all about Pop pop's birthday party and the Boardwalk and stuff like that. That way I would have something to tell my parents when I got home. He continued to yak and I listened intently. We went downstairs and Shelly made us a peanut butter and jelly sandwich. After we ate, she let us go outside to play.

Jay unlocked the shed and got his bike out while I unlocked mine from the iron fence post. "Come on, slowpoke, I've got something to show you! You won't fucking believe it!" He said.

We sped down the street and made our way to the entrance of the park where we played little league. Today, however, we had no intentions of playing ball. I knew, even without asking, exactly what Jay had in mind. Behind the ball fields was a wooded area with lots of quarries and caves and a stream that ran through it all. Even though these woods were forbidden territory, and our parents had always threatened us with the severest of punishments if we were ever caught going back into these woods, many of us took our chances and snuck back there to build the coolest forts and to play ultimate hide-and-seek.

We made the final turn into the park at breakneck speed. As we made the turn, we saw two cops blocking the entrance and several others in the ball field and the woods beyond.

"Slow down, boys!" one of them called out, hands up motioning us to stop.

We slammed on our brakes, doing everything we could not to wipe out and crash. After we were both safely stopped, the cop came up to us and asked, "Where are you guys going in such a hurry?"

"We just wanted to ride around the field and play," Jay immediately responded.

"Not today boys," He stated rather sternly, "there's a police investigation going on here."

"What for," I asked.

Kevin A. Carey

"That's not important, but I would advise you boys not to play down here unless you're with your parents. It just isn't safe here," he looked down at his watch and inquired, "By the way, shouldn't you two be in school? Do I need to call your parents and the school?"

"Oh no sir!" Jay responded, speaking rather fast, "You see sir, we just came home from my Pop-pop's down in Cape May. It was his birthday and we walked the boards and everything. See my friend's new shirt? Isn't it great? Anyway we couldn't come home until today. My dad's car, well it broke down when we tried to leave yesterday. We just got home and now we're out playing. Oh yeah, and my mom called the school and all and told them all about it. Is that okay, sir?"

With all that fast talking babble the cop had just heard, he just shook his head and said, "Okay, okay, but you kids should not be down here playing without adult supervision. It's a very dangerous place, now go on home."

We thanked the officer, turned around and walked our bikes up the very steep hill which we had just came barreling down a few short minutes earlier. Now that we were taking our time, we both noticed something that neither of us had seen on our way into the park. There were policemen all over the neighborhood. They were going door to door, talking to anybody who would answer. "What's going on?" Jay asked.

"I'm as clueless as you are," I answered.

"Something big must have happened!" Jay exclaimed.

"Yeah, I wonder what."

We finally arrived back at Jay's house, still worn out from that stupid hill and parked our bikes in the driveway. As we were walking up the driveway, Shelly came out of the front door escorting two policemen. I couldn't help but notice the peculiar expression on her face.

"What's going on?" I asked again.

"I told you, how the fuck should I know?" Jay whispered back to me as we approached the front door.

"Jason, honey, Geoff, honey, there seems to be a little problem. Come in and let's talk about it." Shelly ushered us into the living room and sat us down on the couch. "Wait here boys. I have to call your mother

Geoffrey and let her know that you both are home and safe."

"Your mother is acting really weird," I said after she left the room.

"Yeah, she seems upset about something. I wonder what it could be?"

A funny thought occurred to me. "Do you think the cops found somebody dead in the park? Like maybe they were chopped into little bits and pieces."

Jay interjected, "Yeah, and they found an arm in old Mr. Beyer's backyard and a leg in Miss Tibit's tree." We both howled with laughter just at the thought of those two old geezers coming out to their yards and finding body parts strewn all over the place. We continued to add to our little scenario. By the time Shelly came back into the living room, we were laughing ourselves silly. Shelly's mood was the complete opposite. She seemed to be very disturbed about something. When Jay and I quieted down, she turned to me and asked, "Geoffrey, honey, is there anything you're not telling me? You can tell Shelly anything. You know that, don't you dear?"

Although I was panic struck that Coach had told her more than I did, I looked her straight in the face and simply said, "No."

"Are you sure?" She kept prodding me. "What about Saturday? Tell me what happened. It's okay, honey, you can tell me. I promise I won't tell a single soul."

"I told you everything I can remember," I said, getting frustrated.

Shelly was also getting agitated. "Okay Geoffrey, when you're ready to talk about it remember I'm here for you."

Jay finally chimed in, "So what's going on? Why were the police here? Why are they everywhere? Why are you questioning Geoff like he's a criminal or something? He didn't do anything wrong. It's Daddy who hurt him."

"Jason, you take that back right now!" Shelly shot back. "You know your father isn't like that. You know he can't help it when he gets that way. Now, I've heard enough out of you, Mister!"

Jay and I sat there in complete silence. Neither of us could believe what was coming out of her mouth. Suddenly Shelly turned real serious, took a deep breath and said, "Boys, Kenny Masterson went out to play on Saturday morning and he never returned home. The police are searching the park and asking if anyone has seen him. I know he is one of your best friends. Would you boys perhaps know where Kenny would have gone to hide?" Then, as an afterthought, Shelly turned her head away from us and said to no one in particular, "Things must really be terrible at home for a little boy to run away like that. I can't imagine what would have possessed him to do such a thing?"

Jay and I just stared at each other in mutual confusion. We had all been playing together at Kenny's house just last week. "If he was planning on running away," I asked Jay, "wouldn't he have told us? I mean his mom seems nice and Kenny has never said anything bad about her or his father."

"Yeah," Jay replied, "us guys, we always tell each other everything."

"Geoffrey, darling," Mrs. Scott interjected, "are you absolutely positive you did not see Kenny on Saturday?"

"No!" I shouted, now totally sick and tired of having to explain myself yet again. My frustration finally got the best of me and I angrily shouted, "I told you what happened! Why won't you fucking believe me?"

Without skipping a beat Shelly hauled off and slapped my mouth and yelled, "I don't know what your mother lets you get away with at home, but cursing is not allowed in this house! If I ever hear such language come out of your mouth again I will call your mother and tell her what you said and tell her to wash your mouth out with soap."

I sulked back into the couch trying to hold back the tears.

"I'm sorry Geoffrey," Shelly said, calming down. "I am only looking out for your best interest. I don't want either of you boys growing up using foul language. Only uneducated low-life's use profanity. You boys are much better than that. You are gentlemen and cussing is very unbecoming of gentlemen." After her speech, she leaned over and gave both of us a hug.

"Now," she continued, "is there anything either of you can tell me that will help the police find Kenny? His parents are worried sick."

We looked at each other and shrugged our shoulders reading each other's thoughts. I answered first, turning and shooting a look at Jay so that Shelly could not see it. "No, I can't think of any place, can you Jay?"

"No, I can't either," Jay answered, fully understanding what I was trying to silently convey to him.

"Okay, but if either of you think of anything please tell me. Geoff, it's almost time for you to go home. Go upstairs and pack your backpack. First I have to make a phone call. I will meet you boys upstairs in a few minutes."

With that, Jay and I both ran up the stairs to his bedroom. Once we were safely behind closed doors Jay turned to me and asked, "Where do you think Kenny is?"

"I don't know," I said. "I mean, he could be anywhere, but I just don't get it. Why would he run away? I've never seen anything wrong between him and his mother and father, have you?"

"No, but maybe his dad is a bad man too. You know, like my dad. Do you think he might have a secret place, like I do?"

"Yeah," I said, "I bet he's hiding out somewhere. Maybe we should sneak out and try to find him. I know a couple of places where the cops would never look."

"So do I," Jay said.

Before we had a chance to formulate a plan, a knock came at the bedroom door. We quickly changed the subject and spoke louder so that Shelly could hear us. Jay said, "Sam Levy called. Being that it's the first weekend the pool is open for the summer, he is trying to get up a water basketball team to start practicing early to beat that bully team of Rod and Eric. And you are the best swimmer. Well, besides me."

Shelly opened the door and walked into the room. She smiled and said, "I didn't mean to eavesdrop boys.

But of course, Geoffrey, the summer is here again. You will be joining us as usual. Right?"

I eagerly replied, "Yes, I really want to, if Mom lets me."

"Don't worry. I'll talk to your mother. I'm sure it won't be a problem."

I finished packing my backpack and the three of us made our way downstairs.

"Jason, put Geoffrey's bike in the trunk of the car. I think it best that we drive him home." She stated in a cautious tone. "I don't want him out there by himself. It's much too dangerous out there right now."

Once my bike was in the trunk, we headed to my house. Shelly talked incessantly about the weekend and all the things they did while they were down the Shore. I guess it was for my benefit. It was a lot of information to digest all at once, but I listened intently so that I could tell Mom and Dad all about my weekend.

When we got to my house, I jumped out of the car and ran to my mother who was coming out of the front door and gave her a big hug. Mom gave me a look of surprise, but she was grinning like the proud mother she was, enjoying the attention. "Wow" she said, "I should let you go away more often." My body shuddered at the mere thought of ever being separated from her again.

Shelly went around to the back of the car and unlocked the trunk so that Jay could get my bike. Mom saw the tee shirt I was wearing and commented, "Look at the new tee shirt. Did you buy that all by yourself?"

Before I had a chance to answer, Shelly cut in: "Hi Jeannie. Do you like it? Peter bought each of the boys one, just as a memento." Then she took a camera out of her handbag and asked Mom to take a picture of the three of us, promising to give me a copy. I loved taking photographs, so this was a thrill for me. Mom and Dad had given me a camera for my eighth birthday and I took pictures whenever I got the chance. Mom was always more than happy to buy film for me and to send my pictures away to be developed. Her philosophy on the matter was that there were a lot more worse things with which I could be occupying my time and energy. With my allowance money I would buy photo albums and spend hours and hours arranging the pictures in the albums to eventually show my family and friends. On this particular trip, however, she would not let me take the camera. She informed me that it was too expensive to get ruined by the sand and grit of the beach. As it turned out, that decision was a blessing in disguise.

Shelly then turned to us and asked, "You guys had a great time, didn't you?"

"Yeah!" Jay and I both said nodding our heads in unison.

Shelly continued, "The boys play so well together. They always have such a good time and Geoffrey is such a wonderful young man, a real gentleman"

"It sounds like you all had a great time," Mom said.

Everyone froze for a second as two police cars, with sirens wailing, came down the street heading in the direction of the park. Shelly sighed a nervous sigh of relief, "Well, maybe they have finally found little Kenny. I hope he's okay. He was probably just trying to run away from home. These kids nowadays, they can be too much to handle sometimes."

Mom laughed, albeit nervously, at the prospect of Kenny just pulling a childhood prank on everyone and said, "I hope you're right Shelly. If it were one of my kids, I'd be going out of my mind with worry right now."

Shelly replied, "Oh so would I. At least I know when Jason runs away from home he always comes back." Then she winked at my mom and whispered loud enough for all of us to hear, "I know he'll be back by dinnertime. He would never miss a meal!"

Again Mom tried to laugh. This time you could tell it was not really genuine because none of her children had ever tried to run away from home. The concept was truly foreign to her. "Whatever the case may be," Mom said, "I don't want you boys anywhere near that park. It is just not safe." She then turned toward me and said, "I don't mean to sound like a mean mother, but I need you to understand me and hear me loud and clear. The only time I will allow you to go to the park, Geoffrey, is with your father or Mr. Scott. Promise me that you will never ever go down to that terrible place without supervision."

"Yes ma'am," I responded half-heartedly, dreading the thought of going anywhere with Coach.

"So Shell, how is Peter? I'm surprised he didn't come with you."

"Oh, he was so upset about the car breaking down, and the kids missing a day of school, that he got one of his migraine headaches. I left him at home to relax and get some rest."

"Oh dear. Tell him I'm sorry and I hope he feels better. Please thank him for me. You two are wonderful. Thank you for everything." Mom then turned to me and said, "Geoffrey, what do you say to Mrs. Scott and Jason?"

"Thank you for a great weekend. I really had a lot of fun," I answered less than enthusiastically hoping that no one would notice my edgy tone and how I was really feeling.

Shelly turned and said, "Jeannie, I'll let you know if I hear anything about Kenny. I'm sure he's okay."

"Thanks for everything. I'll also call you with any news."

Shelly and Jay got into the car and drove away. I was alone with Mom. I was always taught to be honest, however, the weekend changed that forever. Not only was I going to have to lie about everything, I was going to have to do it convincingly. Of course, in this case, I could tell her anything. How would she know whether or not I was lying? If anything ever came up in conversation, Jay, Shelly and Coach would back me up no matter what it was.

CHAPTER FIVE

As I sat back on the couch, still thinking back to that afternoon, I thought, yeah, I am going to be really good at this job. I learned how to lie well at a young age. It would become an art form.

*****

It was not going to be the lies that caused me problems. It was the nightmares that began almost immediately. I can still remember that first night I was awakened by Mom and Dad. "No, please, don't, not again! Oh God, why can't you make him stop!" I awoke with a start. Mom was shaking me. She was shaking me so hard that I could feel her fingernails piercing into my shoulder. Dad was holding my arms down. My first waking thought was that they had found out, and they were preparing to have me taken away. I began to fight even harder, but it was no use. It took a couple of minutes before I realized that they were not trying to hurt me at all. They were trying to wake me. "It's okay Geoffrey. You just had a bad dream," mom said.

Here, take these son," Dad said as he handed me a glass of water and two aspirins.

"What were you dreaming about that was so terrible?" Mom asked.

"I don't remember," I lied.

I'm sure you are worried about Kenny. They'll find him. Don't worry. Now get some sleep. Tomorrow's a school day."

Sleep? Yeah right. That's easy for you to say, I thought. I was going to have to be extra vigilant in my efforts to act as if nothing was wrong, but how was I going to control the nightmares? They were something I had no power over, and I couldn't stay awake the rest of my life.

Only after Mom and Dad felt reasonably certain that I was okay did they go back to bed. I laid awake for quite awhile fearing sleep, fearing the bad man, fearing that I would reveal my secret in my nightmares.

Kevin A. Carey

When Mom woke me up to get ready for school the next morning, I was so tired. I was usually chipper in the morning. I loved going to school. I loved being with my friends. Hell, I even loved my teachers. This morning, however, I felt different. I felt dirty, and all the showers in the world were not going to change that. I did not want to go to school. I was still in a lot of pain and I could not face my friends. I knew they would figure out that something was wrong with me even if my parents could not.

I took my time and moped around until Mom finally came up to see what was taking so long. "Honey, what's wrong? Are you feeling all right? Does this thing with Kenny still have you upset?"

"Mom, do I have to go to school today?" I asked avoiding her question, "I don't feel good, my stomach hurts," I lied.

"Now Geoffrey, you missed yesterday, don't you think that was enough?" She asked.

I pleaded with her, "But Mom!"

"Don't 'but mom' me. We are all worried about Kenny and we're praying for him. There is nothing you can do about it by staying home and worrying. Don't you think it would be better if you went to school so that you could be with your friends? I'm sure they could use your support, and I bet they will raise your spirits too."

"Oh okay, but if I still feel sick tomorrow I'm not going to school!" I shouted angrily.

"My goodness, Geoffrey, what has gotten into you?" Mom asked, taken aback by my outburst.

"Nothing, I just feel sick."

"Everything will be alright. I promise," Mom said with compassion. "They are going to find Kenny safe and sound, you'll see. Now finish getting dressed and come downstairs for breakfast."

I begrudgingly finished dressing and made my way down to the kitchen. Although I was running late I slowly drank my orange juice and nibbled on my toast. Mom practically had to push me out of the door. I meandered down the street and around the corner to where Jay usually met me on our way to school. As usual, he was impatiently waiting for me. "Hey," he barked, "what the fuck took you so long, slowpoke?"

"Oh you know, I just can't get into it today. My, you know, butt, still hurts like a motherfucker and this thing with Kenny. Where the hell could he be?" I snarled.

"Don't take it out on me!" Jay snapped back. "You are such a sorry wimp! The pain will go away, just don't think about it. Just do like I do when it hurts."

"So what do you do when it hurts so bad, Mister Know-it-all?" I asked, still sounding angry.

"For your information, faggot, I make the pain go away by thinking up ways to hurt and even kill the bad man the way he hurts me. It's as simple as that. Try it."

I barely heard the last part of what Jay had just said. My mind was still reeling from him calling me a faggot. "Who the fuck do you think you are calling a faggot, faggot?"

"Hey, take it easy, I was only playing with you," Jay reeled back, obviously at a loss for what to say or do next.

I finally backed off, but we still ended up walking the last two blocks to school in complete silence.

The kids in class were very quiet. Kenny's disappearance had everybody on edge. There were policemen posted all around the school. Jill Baxter, the girl who sat directly in front of me by the luck of the alphabet, seemed to be the authority on what was going on. Her father was the Chief of Police of our town. She spoke to us as if we were her loyal subjects, "Kenny's mom told the police that he was going up to Jason's to play, but there obviously was no answer, because the Scotts, and Geoffrey here had gone down to the Shore for the weekend and didn't come home until yesterday."

Amy Winston, who I always thought was a bratty girl anyway, turned to me, "We thought you were sick, jerk!"

"Anyway," Jill continued, shooting a nasty look at Amy as if to say that while she was speaking everyone had better be listening to her and only her. "Somebody in the neighborhood said they were pretty sure they saw Kenny going into the park. What an idiot. Doesn't he know how dangerous it is down there? My dad is always telling me they are always catching those drug

99

pushers and dealers down there. I bet they're going to find him dead, or maybe they won't even find him at all. Don't people read the papers? Do you guys know how many kids have disappeared and never come home because they go to places they're not supposed to? I'm talking about kids right in our own backyard. I don't know the exact number of missing kids from our area alone, but it's a lot."

Was Jill ever going to shut up, the little Miss Know-it-all? Just because her father was the Chief-of-Police, she always seemed to think she knew more than everybody else about what was going on. I mean, yeah, it was nice that she knew the scoop, but all that other stuff about Kenny. What bullshit! I am sure he had a damn good reason for doing what he did. Maybe he was coming over to Jay's to tell him about his problems with his family. He obviously never made it or I'm sure I would have heard him at the door.

Mr. Ewing, our homeroom teacher, advised us that a representative from the FBI was here and that he would be talking to each of us individually. If we had any questions we wanted to ask, now was the time to do it.

As the day progressed, one-by-one, we were called to the principal's office. My turn finally came. The FBI agent asked how I was doing and if I had any questions. After I convinced him that I was okay and had no questions, he asked me a bunch of questions like, did I know where any of Kenny's hideouts were, and if I knew of any reason why he might want to run away from home. I answered "no" to all of his questions and then went back to my classroom, wondering how Jay had answered all of those stupid questions. I met up with him after school as usual. He looked unhappy, even angry. I hoped he wasn't upset over this morning's little riff. That would be ridiculous. We always banter back and forth like that and by the end of the day, it's usually all been forgotten no matter how much we might have hurt each other.

"We've got to talk," Jay said seriously.

"Okay," I agreed, "let's talk. What's up?"

"You told my mother everything. Right?"

"Yeah, that's right. You were there."

"You weren't honest about the sword, so why should I believe you about anything else?" Jay said accusatorially.

"You're fucking crazy! Are you telling me that you think I was lying?" I shouted.

"Well, are you? The FBI man told me that Kenny came to visit me Saturday morning. Neighbors even saw him around my house. You can't tell me you didn't hear somebody knocking at my front door. You know how loud that fucking door is when someone is knocking. It's impossible to sleep through that! Not even the dead can sleep through that noise."

"Why won't you believe me?" I angrily whispered. I was getting really frustrated and ready to run so that I did not have to listen to him anymore.

"I'm sorry Geoff. I do believe you," Jay finally said apologetically. "It's just that I know you and Kenny weren't the best of friends. If you know anything that could help the police find Kenny, please, please tell me. I promise I won't tell the police where the information came from."

"Really, Jay, unless I was asleep when he came. I mean, I suppose something could have happened, but I doubt it. Besides, Jay, you know I would tell you if I knew anything. You're my best friend and best friends tell each other everything. Don't they?" I said.

"You're right. I'm sorry. It's just that I'm so scared for Kenny," Jay replied.

"Why don't you ask your dad?" I said, as a light bulb went off inside of my head. "Maybe he remembers Kenny coming to visit. He couldn't have slept through it too!"

"Oh no, like I told you before, when he becomes the 'bad man' he's a different person, he is not my dad, and after it's over he doesn't remember anything. Anyway, I could never ask him, he would just yell at me and probably beat me with the belt," Jay said resignedly.

"Oh God, Jay, I didn't know it was that bad. I'm so sorry. That really sucks. Would you be mad if I told you I hated him too?" I said.

"No." Jay was starting to cry now. "You have every right to be mad and to hate him. He's such an asshole. He probably upset Kenny even more. If Kenny is found hurt or something, I will never be able to forgive that bastard. He probably made Kenny even sadder than he already was!"

"Jay, don't cry, it's going to be okay. It has to be!" I said.

"You're right," Jay tearfully acknowledged. "Do you mind if I just go home today? I'm really tired and I have a lot of homework to finish."

"Yeah, I'm tired too. I almost fell asleep in history class today," I said.

Jay finally laughed and confided, "I fall asleep in that class all the time. It has nothing to do with being tired. Mr. Haversham is so dull. He bores me to tears."

I began laughing as well, easing the tension if only for a little bit, something we had not been able to do for a couple of days.

*****

Time seemed to pass at a snail's pace. My nightmares refused to go away. They were always of the same kind. Coach would be standing over me laughing that sinister laugh of his and grasping the sword preparing to insert it into my butt. A bright light somewhere in the background shined down and reflected off of the blue gems on the handle, increasing my fear even more. Thankfully, the nightmare would end before Coach would actually commit the act. The really ghostly thing about the nightmare was there was always someone else there screaming and it wasn't Coach. I could never figure out who it was. When I woke up I was always drenched in sweat and Mom or Dad would be at my side. Because the nightmares began occurring when Kenny disappeared, my parents, although concerned, attributed them to the trauma of having a close friend vanish off of the face of the earth. Mom always asked what the nightmares were about. I always responded by telling her that no matter how hard I tried, I just could not remember.

As days passed Kenny's whereabouts remained a mystery. School was not fun or festive like it should have been, considering there was less than a week to go. The mood was quite somber. Each morning after the beginning of the daily announcements and the "Pledge of Allegiance" the Principal had a two-minute moment of silence so that the whole school could pray that Kenny would be found safe and sound. But, as time marched slowly on, it became apparent to most of us that Kenny wasn't coming back. We would never get to play with him again. Okay, so maybe Jay was right, maybe Kenny and I were not the best of friends. At times we had our differences. But that did not mean that I would never want to see him again or have anything terrible happen to him. No way. Kenny was a really cool guy. He was just a little too stubborn and even arrogant sometimes, and he always thought that we should do things his way. I, on the other hand, was the only one in our group who had the guts to tell him off when he needed it.

Jay and I walked to and from school together every day but we didn't spend the afternoons together like before. When I got home I would try to read, but the only thing I managed to do was stare off into space. One day when I got home from school, Mom was on the phone with Shelly. When she hung up, she told me that she and Mrs. Scott thought it was odd that Jason and I were not spending our afternoons together and they were somewhat concerned. Although I was missing my best friend's companionship something awful, I flashed Mom one of my big smiles and said, "Oh Mom, it's okay. You know Jay has stuff to do and I have stuff to do. Besides, we're going to the pool on Saturday. I told you, Shelly even promised to pack us a picnic lunch and everything."

I know she didn't completely buy the lame excuse I had just given her, but Mom being Mom said, "Okay Sweetheart, I guess this deal with Kenny still has the two of you out of sorts. It will get better. Don't lose hope. Kenny's okay, I can feel it."

"Whatever you say, Mom. But I know that something bad has happened to him. I can feel it too," I said.

"Oh, don't be so pessimistic. We have to be positive and think the best. We can't give up hope," Mom said, a less than enthusiastic smile on her face.

Saturday had finally arrived. I was so happy not to have to go to school. I was looking forward to spending the day at the pool with Jay. The country club that Jay's family belonged to had the neatest pool in town. Even though Coach was going to be there, he usually spent all of his time with his friends playing bridge. We were always all the way down at the other end of the pool area having our own private picnic and having our own fun.

I got up, ate some breakfast, and took my book outside to read. I loved to read. While my brother, Ben, watched cartoons, I would go outside. If it were nice out, I would set up a lounge chair and read all day if Mom would let me. My brother always called me a sissy. Many times we would have a fight, and Mom would have to break it up, but I always got to go and read.

About 10:30 I heard the phone ring. After a few minutes, Mom came out and told me to get ready because Mr. Scott would pick me up on his way back from the grocery store. I hoped she meant Mr. and Mrs. Scott and not just Mr. Scott; there was no way in hell that I was getting in the car alone with that monster.

My worst fears were however, realized when Coach's car pulled up into the driveway. I looked out from my bedroom window and to my horror he was alone. I began to shake all over as Mom called from downstairs. I immediately ran into the bathroom to hide. Mom kept calling, she sounded annoyed now, but I just didn't know what to do.

"Okay Geoff, get a grip," I mumbled to myself, "the only way you are going to get to see your best friend today is to go with Coach. But what if he has other ideas. I can't, I just fucking can't!" I looked out the window and there was Coach standing down there smiling and waiting for me. He looked normal, but shit, that didn't mean anything, I thought. He changes so fast, it's not funny. He glanced up at the window and shouted, "Hey, Geoffrey, Jason and Mrs. Scott are waiting for us at the house. Are you almost ready? Mrs. Scott and I have a bridge tournament today and it starts in less than an hour. We're late, we're just barely going to make it as it is."

Okay, I reasoned, so if he's telling the truth, we'll be alone for maybe five minutes at the very most. I mustered up everything I could, stopped shaking and called out the window, "Sorry Coach. I'm coming."

I jumped back when I opened the bathroom door. Mom was standing there with her hands on her hips giving me this angry look. "What has gotten into you young man? Why are you being so rude? If you don't get a move on Coach will leave without you."

As I made my way down the stairs, I muttered under my breath, "Christ, why is everyone on my case. I hate my life!" Apparently I didn't speak low enough because Mom heard me. She smacked the back of my head and stated, "Your father will deal with you later. Now get going."

When I opened the front door of the house, I had this sudden urge to run as fast as I could in the other direction as far away as possible. Instead, I forced a smile on my face and made an effort to show both Mom and Coach that there was nothing wrong. Mom walked out with me and started apologizing for my tardiness. "Sorry Peter, Geoffrey's been a bit out of sorts since Kenny Masterson's disappearance."

"It's okay. We can still make it to the club in time for the first rubber," Coach said with a smile on his face that I knew was fake. "Jump in," Coach said as he held the passenger side door of the car open for me. "Thanks Jeannie. Will we be seeing you and Doug and the kids for our annual Fourth of July picnic?"

"Oh yes, we will definitely be there. We wouldn't miss it for the world. Have fun Geoff!" Mom shouted, sounding a little less angry, as I climbed into the car.

Coach got into his side of the car, reached over me and pressed the lock down on my door. I suddenly froze. I put my head down as if I were looking for something in my backpack so that neither Mom nor Coach could see the look of panic and fear on my face. I was scared out of my wits. Coach smiled and waved to Mom and said to me under his breath, "Look happy and wave bye-bye to your mommy."

I followed his orders to the letter feeling like a trapped animal

"Buckle your seatbelt," he said.

"No!" I barked, realizing as I said it that that was the absolute stupidest thing I could have done.

111

"Look you little bitch, put that seatbelt on now, or I'll do it for you, and trust me you don't want that to happen," he said with his teeth gritted together.

"Yes sir," I replied, complying with his demands.

"So," Coach began, "You're doing really well at keeping our little secret I hear. I'm sorry but you and Jason both have a lot to learn about life. If you didn't have me to teach you, you both would be going into this world completely unprepared. I just can't let that happen."

The man was completely grossing me out. I wanted to scream and yell at him and ask him why he thought it was okay to hurt me, but I knew that wouldn't be too wise, especially after my last little outburst.

He continued, "So you told Mrs. Scott that you don't remember much. Even though it sounds really lame, it was very smart. That cunt will believe anything. You just keep up the good work my boy or you know exactly what will happen to you."

"Yes sir," I again replied, now wondering if I had forgotten something. No, that's impossible, I said to myself, shaking the thought completely out of my head.

We rounded the corner and there, thankfully, were Shelly and Jay standing outside the house with all their bags. Shelly gave Coach a dirty look as we were pulling into the driveway. At first I thought maybe it was her silent way of saying to him, "if you hurt that boy again you will live to regret it." That was only wishful thinking because the minute he stepped out of the car Shelly started in on him, "What the hell took you so long to get back here? You know the bridge tournament starts in forty-five minutes and it takes over a half an hour to get to the Club. I just can't plop myself down and play. I need time to compose myself!"

Coach just shook his head as he opened the trunk and threw in the several bags Shelly had lined-up along the side of the driveway. By the amount of stuff lined up you'd have thought we were going away for several days, not just an afternoon at the pool. We all got quickly into the car. Coach put the car in reverse and off we went. He didn't say a word. Shelly had again turned him into a quiet little church mouse. Boy, what power she must have over him, I thought, as we sped off.

*****

The weekend flew by and it was time to go back to school. This should have been a fun time for me and my friends. It was the end of our elementary school years. Next year we would begin junior high school. This would be the last time we would be seeing all of our teachers. I really was going to miss them. There was a whole graduation ceremony planned but no one was really into it. Policemen were still posted throughout the school. They were still doing everything they could to find Kenny, although most of us had given up hope. I was trying as hard as I could to keep my chin up, but my mood was full of gloom and despair. The principal continued the two minutes of silence each day and she tried to lift our spirits with some inspirational mumbo jumbo, but no one was buying it. It was all so depressing.

Graduation day finally arrived. It was a day we had looked forward to for so long but without Kenny it just wasn't going to be the same. He had been selected to read a poem for the ceremony that our class had written together. I was asked to "pinch-hit" for him. I was honored to be asked, even though I was disappointed not to be picked from the get go. Now I would have given anything to have Kenny here reading it instead of me.

Before I did my reading, the principal introduced Linda and David Masterson, Kenny's parents. It was such a sad moment. They thanked the entire school for their support during this very difficult time. They told us not to give up hope that they were confident the police and the FBI were eventually going to find Kenny safe and sound. Before they walked off the stage they gave me a big hug and told me what a good friend I had been to Kenny. Mrs. Masterson looked into my eyes and said, "Please tell your friends to be careful and don't play in that drug infested park. You're such good kids; it would be terrible if something bad were to happen to any of you."

115

"I will," I promised.

"Thank you. Now go up there and make us proud. Make Kenny proud," Mr. Masterson said.

After the graduation ceremony was over several of the parents got a car pool together and took a bunch of us to Pizza Hut. I was surprised to see Mr. and Mrs. Masterson standing in the parking lot talking to several of the other kids' parents. Why did they want to be around us kids at a time like this? I watched intently as Mom, Dad, Shelly and Coach approached Mr. and Mrs. Masterson. First Shelly and then Mom gave Mrs. Masterson a big hug. The dads shook hands with each other. All three women were crying.

"Come on, slowpoke!" Jay yelled toward my direction, "Last one in only gets the crust!"

I'm glad he was only kidding, because I, as usual, was the last one in. Jay saved me a seat right next to his. The two seats next to mine had someone's sweaters on them. They obviously belonged to two adults. Coach being Coach, appointed himself the leader and told us all to sit down, that the pizza had already been ordered and the waitress would bring us soda once we were all seated. The mood was finally swinging in the other direction. Everyone seemed more relaxed and more jovial. Even I was starting to feel better.

The Mastersons came over and sat down next to me. I nodded hello and quickly excused myself to go to the restroom. I felt terrible for them. Why would anyone want to take somebody's child away from them? That was just plain sick. I got it together and was just getting ready to return to the party when I looked up and saw the missing persons poster with Kenny's picture on it. Somebody mentioned last week that there were posters made, but this was the first time I had seen one. Oh fuck. I thought. I wish there were something I could do to make Kenny come back home. I couldn't believe that his parents were so bad that he would want to run away.

I went back to my place at the table. Before I had a chance to sit down, Mr. and Mrs. Masterson both stood up and gave me another big hug. Mrs. Masterson said, "You did a great job today, Geoffrey. Kenny would have been so proud of you. He always spoke so highly of you."

I almost blurted out, "Jesus Christ, people. Stop talking about him like he's dead. He's not! He can't be!" Thankfully, before I had a chance to open my big mouth, a chorus of "For He's A Jolly Good Fellow" rang out. They were singing to me. I turned beet red with embarrassment. Everybody clapped and cheered and Jay made me stand up. "Speech, Speech." They were all yelling and clanking their hard red plastic cups with their silverware. It was an awful sound. I would rather have crawled into a hole. But since there were no holes available at the moment, I slowly stood up. As I did, I glanced about the room, my eyes locking on Coach's. It appeared that he was cheering and clapping the loudest.

"Thanks, everyone," I said. "You guys are the best. You really did it, not me, I just read it." Then, I don't quite know where from inside of me it came from, but I looked up into space and added, "Kenny, you bum, you'd better come home soon. You don't know all the fun we're having without you. Besides, we miss you, buddy."

When I looked down after a brief pause the whole dining room was staring at me in total silence, many of them with tears in their eyes, even people who were not part of our party. Then I heard a single clap. It came from Coach. Suddenly everyone stood up and clapped and shouted their approval.

*****

The first day of my summer vacation was finally here. It promised to be a good day. Even though the nightmares persisted, I accidentally came upon a way to wake myself up. My sister, Natalie, must have been playing in my room and she left one of her stuffed animals, a little bunny rabbit with bells on its ears. I didn't see it because it was tucked under my extra pillows. When I started tossing and turning I suddenly heard bells jingling. They woke me up before I had a chance to make any loud noises. At first I got mad at my sister for playing on my bed and leaving her stuff, but then I realized that I wasn't as scared when I woke up because the bunny rabbit's bells woke me up before the nightmare could intensify. I had to think fast. How was I going to keep the rabbit without everybody thinking I was a big sissy and without upsetting Natalie? I knew exactly what Ben was going to say. Well, I would just have to beat him up, like I always did.

I summoned Natalie to my room to make a top-secret trade with her. I traded Edgar, my six foot prized stuffed snake, for the bunny rabbit. She had always wanted Edgar, but I wouldn't let anyone touch him. He was a very special snake. My grandfather, the person I loved most in the whole world, had won him for me at the Saint Jude Church Carnival last summer.

After the trade was complete, I took the rabbit to my room and took off its frilly little dress. This would help me avoid a confrontation with my jerk of a brother. I had one of those beds with shelves on the headboard. I put Mr. Rabbit, my new name for him, into the nook where he'd be within easy reach at bedtime. No one could see that I was taking him off the shelf at night.

Later that afternoon, I sat outside in the backyard finishing a great Hardy Boys Mystery while Mom hung up the laundry. Natalie appeared at the back door and came outside dragging Edgar behind her. He was over twice her size. It was very painful, yet very comical to watch. I mean, I know I did the right thing but she was getting poor Edgar all dirty, dragging him around like that. Mom stopped what she was doing and approached Natalie. "Young lady, your brother is going to be very unhappy with you. You had better put Edgar away, now."

"No Mommy," Natalie said, "We made a trade, I gave Geoffrey Bun Bun and he gave me Edgar."

I peered at Mom out of the corner of my eye to see her expression. As expected, she was perplexed. "Geoff, did you trade Edgar for Bun Bun?"

"Yes, Mom," I said, not lifting my head from my book.

"But why?" she asked.

"Because," I said, "I know how much she likes Edgar, and now that I'm going to be starting Junior High, well, you know, I just couldn't let her have him for nothing, so, I traded him for Bun Bun."

"Mommy," Natalie chimed in, "I don't like Bun Bun anyway. She makes too much noise."

I could tell Mom was not exactly understanding or buying any of what was going on. She finally shrugged her shoulders and went back to hanging up the laundry. I went back to my book and poor Edgar continued to be dragged around in the dirt.

The phone rang. I jumped up out of my chair and ran to answer it. It was Jay. "Hi," I said, "what's up dude?"

Jay whispered into the phone, "Can we go bike riding or something? My daddy didn't go to work today and," he continued in even a more hushed voice, "he is really being a jerk. I think he's turning into the bad man again. Can you meet me at the corner deli in five minutes?"

"I'll be right there," I said. I ran outside, trying not to let Mom know that I was in somewhat of a hurry.

"That was Jay. We're going bike riding. I have to meet him at Carmen's Deli in five minutes."

"You boys," she said. "You are always in a hurry. You have all summer. Oh, since you're meeting Jason at the Deli I need you to pick up a couple of packs of cigarettes. I'll write you a note."

"Oh Mom, do I have to?"

"Yes, you have to."

"Okay, but please hurry."

"Take it easy," she said smiling. "I'm happy to see that you're back to your old self. I was beginning to worry about you." She went inside, wrote the note and got money and came back outside where I was waiting by my bike. "Here you go. I gave you some extra money. Get a treat for you and Jason."

When I arrived at the deli, Jay wasn't there yet. I hoped he was still coming because I was late too. God, Coach had just better leave him alone, I thought. I went into the Deli to get Mom her cigarettes and some candy for Jay and me. As usual Old Man Carver was running the counter like he always did. He studied the note I gave him and handed me three packs of Pall

123

Malls. I was quite sure the note said two packs not three. Before I said anything to Mr. Carver I checked to make sure I had enough money to pay for all three packs. Sure enough, I even had enough left over to buy two packs of jumbo bubble gum. Yes, this was going to be our lucky day. Jay and I had always talked about buying a pack of cigarettes, but we were always scared that Mr. Carver would tell on us. Once Jay stole a couple of cigarettes from his mom, but he put them in his pants pocket and they were all broken up before we got a chance to smoke them. Stealing cigarettes from my mother was next to impossible. She never left them sitting around. If she wasn't carrying them in her housedress, she put them up high where us kids couldn't reach them. Even though she smoked two packs a day, she would forever lecture us on the evils of smoking. She would say stuff like, "It's not at all becoming," or "If I had known that smoking causes cancer when I started smoking I wouldn't have started, so you shouldn't because now you know better."

As I walked out of the deli, Jay was pulling into the parking lot. I called out to him, "Hey buddy, who's the slowpoke today?"

As he came nearer to me, I could tell he was pretty upset about something. I had just the thing to cheer him up.

He started to say, "Daddy's . . . "

I cut him off in mid-sentence, "Wait! Look!"

I pulled the pack of Pall Mall's from my bag and slipped them into my pocket with a pack of matches. Jay stared at me in complete awe. "Wow! How did you get those?"

"Mom gave me a note to give to Old Man Carver. It said, "two packs of cigarettes." He must have misread it and gave me three packs. You know he's blind as a bat!"

"Wow!" he said again, "That's great. You don't think we'll get caught do you? You know our parents. They'll kill us if they find out."

"Oh stop your worrying you big chicken shit." I reached into my pocket and produced the two packs of jumbo bubble gum. "I've thought of everything. They will never know."

Jay was beaming. Whatever was going on with his father was now unimportant. He smiled at me and said, "You are the smartest person I know! So let's get going, slowpoke!"

I felt my face turn red from the compliment. I smiled and said, "But first we have to drop off Mom's cigarettes."

With that we both raced down the block. We stopped at my house just long enough to give Mom her cigarettes. Before we had a chance to make our big get away Mom warned us, as she always did, to be careful. "I don't have to tell you boys not to go anywhere near that park."

"Okay, Mom, no problem." I chuckled to myself and thought there were lots of other places to go that Mom didn't know about.

Jay and I decided to go to the Hidden Falls. They were a few towns over from where we lived. The Hidden Falls got their name because even though you could hear the crashing water from the road you had to hike a pretty good distance into the woods to actually see them. We probably weren't allowed to go there either, but we were never told we couldn't go there.

It took us about forty-five minutes to get to the path that would lead us to the Falls. We got off of our bikes, locked them to a bike rack and made our way along the small dirt footpath. I was feeling quite confident and good about pulling off this little coup. I knew there was little chance of us getting caught because it was pretty secluded, and nobody knew us around here. We slowly walked along several intertwining trails catching our breath along the way from the long, primarily uphill ride we had just completed. Jay stopped and turned to me. I could tell by the look on his face that his mood had turned somber again.

"I'm really scared," he said.

"What's the matter? Are you still worried about Kenny?" I questioned.

"No, no, it has nothing to do with him. It's my dad. For the past two weeks, he's been meaner to me than usual, and if he finds out what we're doing he'll—"

"Oh God," I stopped him in mid-sentence. "What has that monster been doing to you? Has he been doing, you know, bad things to you?"

"No, nothing like that. He hasn't become the 'bad man' or anything. But he beats me with his belt for no reason at all."

"What's his fucking problem?" I snorted disgustedly.

Jay's head sank to his chest. He began to cry and said, "I don't know."

I pretended not to notice his tears as we continued walking. Eventually we came upon several large boulders. We stood in complete silence for a minute. The only sound we could hear was the loud crashing of the waterfalls. I took the cigarettes from my pocket and opened them. I gave one to Jay and put one between my lips. Little pieces of tobacco fell into my mouth. It tasted pretty nasty but I figured that must be a part of the whole smoking experience. After a couple of tries I lit a match and Jay held his cigarette out for me to light it. It took almost the whole match before it lit. I almost burnt my fingers. I took my cigarette out of my mouth. "Well, come on, smoke it," I egged him on.

"No, you light up yours then we'll take a puff together."

"Oh Jay, don't you know anything. It's not cool to say 'take a puff,' you're supposed to say, 'take a drag'."

"Okay, Your Coolness, we'll take a drag together."

I nodded my approval and put my cigarette back in my mouth and lit another match. Trying to repeat the way Mom lit her cigarette, I took a deep breath as I put the lit match up to the cigarette and began to deeply inhale. I felt smoke filling my lungs. I immediately began coughing and gagging. "Oh Jesus Christ, I can't breathe!" I yelled. All of a sudden a wave of nausea hit me and I threw up my entire breakfast. Jay just stood there and laughed and laughed. He laughed so hard that he had to run behind a tree and pee.

Needless to say, that was the last time I would light up a cigarette for a very long time. Jay didn't even try his. He dropped it and stomped on it. We decided to have a formal burial of the cigarettes and matches, leaving no evidence of what we had just attempted to do. We grabbed a couple of flat rocks, dug a deep hole and put the rest of the pack in it with the matches so that no one would ever know we had them. At least the fiasco with the cigarettes took Jay's mind off of his father for a little while.

"I have a great idea," I said, "how about if I ask Mom if you can stay at our house tonight? You think it'll be okay with your mom?"

"Oh Geoffrey, that sounds like so much fun."

"Okay, when we get home I'll ask first and then you can call and ask your mom."

"Great, but if your mom says it's okay, can she call and ask for me? I'm afraid that if I ask my mother she'll say no. I really want to spend the night at your house."

The way he said it started making me get that tingly feeling again. I couldn't help it. I was in heaven. Mom had better say yes. I was counting on it! We made our way back to my house, this time at a much slower pace. We talked about our favorite television shows and laughed and even disagreed on a few things.

That was okay though because we were just having a lot of fun together.

As luck would have it, Mom thought our sleep over idea was swell until she got a closer look at me. "Are you feeling all right?" She asked as she reached to feel my forehead. "You're very flushed and pale. On second thought maybe this isn't such a good idea."

"No, no Mom. I'm fine. I'm just a little bit tired. We were racing over at the playground with the other kids," I lied.

"Alright, but you boys had just better be careful. That's all I've got to say," she commanded sternly.

"Mom, can you call Mrs. Scott and ask if it's okay for Jay to stay the night?" I asked impatiently.

"Okay, dear," She said as she made her way to the phone. "I haven't spoken to Shelly in a couple of days. I need to ask her what she wants us to bring to the Independence Day barbecue."

Jay and I hightailed it into the living room, and turned on the TV.

Mom was on the phone for a long time with Shelly. She finally returned to the living room. She had a big smile on her face. "Jason," she asked, "how would you like to stay both tonight and tomorrow night?"

I could not believe my luck. I couldn't help but smile from ear to ear. When I looked over at Jay, he was doing the same. I was sure it was for a whole different reason than I was smiling, but it didn't matter to me. I had Jay all to myself for two whole days and nights and that was all that mattered.

"You see," Mom continued, "your mother and father are doing some painting and I suggested to your mother that maybe it would be better to keep you away from the paint fumes. They can be dangerous to your lungs. I offered to have you stay with us until the work is finished."

"So, that was what all that plastic was for," I blurted out.

"What plastic are you talking about?" Jay inquired.

"When I was—" I stopped in mid-sentence realizing that my enthusiasm had gotten the best of me.

"Huh? When you were what?" Jay prodded on.

"Oh nothing," I said, "I must have been thinking about something else."

I tried to drop the subject, but Jay was being too persistent. "No, tell me, what plastic?"

I finally leaned into him and whispered into his ear, "Shut up, asshole, or you're going to get us in trouble!"

"Oh yeah, that plastic. You're right, they bought lots of it," Jay said, finally getting it.

Mom added, "I told your mother that when Mr. Brooks gets home from work tonight he would bring you over to pick up some clean clothes."

"Yeah, and I can pick up my matchbox cars, too," Jay gleefully shouted.

This was just too good to be true. I really was going to get to spend two whole nights with Jay.

Dad came home from work and we all sat down to dinner. Mom made spaghetti and meatballs, which was Jay's and my favorite meal. Boy, Mom is the greatest! I thought. After dinner Dad promised to take us all for ice cream after we stopped at Jay's to pick up his stuff. We all piled into Dad's new 1969 Ford station wagon. Jay and I got to sit all the way in the back of the car where the extra seat was situated. We couldn't have been happier.

When we arrived at Jay's house, we saw Coach and Shelly standing out front talking with Mr. and Mrs. Masterson. Jay and I were getting ready to jump out of the car when Mom, sensing that there might be some bad news, said, "You kids stay in the car! Your father and I will be right back." With that, they got out of the car and walked over to where the others were standing.

After a short while, they all made their way to the car. Dad motioned for us to get out. Thank God, I thought. If I had to listen to that nincompoop of a sister of mine cry for Mommy one more time, I would have had to beat her up like I did my brother when he got stupid.

I noticed that Mrs. Masterson was wiping tears from her eyes. She came over to our car and gave Jay and me a big hug. She said, "Hi, guys, how are you doing? Why don't you come over and visit sometime? I would love to see you, and I know Kenny would like it too."

I misunderstood what Mrs. Masterson was saying because I got all excited and yelled, "Kenny's home? Where is he? Is he okay?"

"I'm sorry," she said. "They still haven't found him. In fact, if they don't find him by tomorrow night they are going to call off the search and open the park again. Oh, I wish they would close that park for good. It's so dangerous down there."

Jay and I were at a loss for words. Wouldn't it be awkward to visit without Kenny there? Shelly broke the awkward silence and said, "The boys would love to stop by and say hello. Wouldn't you, boys?"

We both nodded yes, although I could tell that Jay was thinking the same thing I was. Shelly then said, "Jason, why don't you and Geoff run upstairs and pack your backpack. I've already laid out some clothes on your bed for you."

As we turned and headed for the house I heard Mrs. Masterson comment, "Isn't it wonderful how well those two boys get along. I miss my Kenny so much."

She began to cry again as Shelly put her arm around her. Mrs. Masterson continued, "Please God, bring my baby back home to me safely."

It was so sad. I wanted to stay and listen but Jay grabbed my arm and dragged me into the house. We hurriedly packed his stuff and came back outside with his now full backpack, matchbox cars and Star Trek action figures in tow. Shelly was telling everyone about plans for the upcoming Independence Day extravaganza. It promised to be the Scotts' best annual barbecue yet! Even Mr. and Mrs. Masterson said they were looking forward to it, and to being in the company of good friends during this very difficult time. I took everything from Jay and loaded it into the back of the station wagon while he made his ceremonial goodbyes. He went over to his mother and kissed her goodbye and then he told both his mom and dad that he loved them. Shelly told Jay to have a great time and reminded him that both of us should be ready bright and early on Saturday morning for the pool, because she didn't want to be late for her bridge game two weeks in a row.

"Your father will be by to pick you up after he drops me off at my hair dresser appointment, that way we won't be late again," she said, making it clear that she wasn't fooling around with either of us.

Okay, Shelly, I thought to myself, you've made your point. Now, can we please go before Dairy Queen gets too crowded? I didn't dare say it out loud. I wasn't that stupid.

*****

Jay and I had a great time playing together, although the time was zipping by much too quickly for my liking. Kenny was still not found so the word spread quickly through the neighborhood grapevine that the search had been called off and no further efforts would be made. The park would soon be reopened. Things were not looking good for Kenny and with the passing of time he receded further and further from our thoughts. I hated to admit it, but the last thing on my mind was Kenny. I had Jay all to myself and nothing was going to distract me.

The two days went by too quickly, and before you could blink, Saturday had arrived. It wasn't even eight o'clock in the morning and Mom woke us up. "Okay, you sleepy heads," she said, "Time to get up. Jason, your mom just called. She said that your father will be picking the both of you up right after he drops her off at the beauty parlor."

Knowing it didn't take much to get Coach ticked off these days, Jay and I quickly gathered everything together. We were waiting by the front door when he pulled into the driveway. Mom tried to get us to eat some breakfast, but we were both doing everything we could to keep Coach in a good mood. Jay opened the front door first and yelled, "Hi Dad, we're ready!" Then he turned to me and said, "Come on, slowpoke, hurry up!" I was right behind him. Neither of us was taking any chances. Mom ran out of the house behind us, yelling to Coach that we didn't eat any breakfast. Coach told her he would take care of it when we got home.

"Well," Mom said, exasperated, "the boys need to keep up their strength."

If the five-minute ride to Jay's house was any indication of Coach's mood, then we were in the clear. He asked us if we had a good time. We both answered at the same time trying to tell him everything we had done. We all ended up laughing, because none of it made any sense. When we arrived at the Scotts' house Jay jumped out of the car and opened the garage door. Coach pulled in and Jay closed the door behind him. The three of us proceeded into the kitchen and automatically took off our shoes. Jay and I started to run for the recreation room to play. "Not so fast," Coach snarled. "It's time you boys learned a lesson or two!"

A wave of panic came over me and I began to shake so hard my teeth were chattering. The last time I heard that tone of voice was the Friday night I was supposed to be going down the Shore. Coach took one leap forward, grabbed my forearm, squeezed it really tight and commanded, "Stop that twittering right now! I'm going to make a man out of you yet, you little faggot!"

Jay began to plead with Coach, "Dad, please stop! Geoffrey didn't do anything. Leave him alone!" Coach was now livid. "You don't tell me what to do, young man!" With that Coach took off his belt and gave Jay a big whack across his backside. I stood there in complete and total shock. Although I could tell that Jay was in a lot of pain, it amazed me that he showed no sign of it. He just nodded his head and said without any emotion, "Yes, sir."

"That's better. Now, you know what to do," Coach snapped.

Jay grabbed me by my wrist and whispered into my ear, "Come on, follow me, the 'bad man' is here. If we don't do what he say's, he will kill us both."

I whispered to Jay, "No, this is crazy, I have a better idea." With that I reached out for the front door. Before I had a chance to turn the knob I felt a stinging pain across my butt. Coach was whipping me with his belt. I reeled back from the pain. He yelled at me, "Don't even think about it, asshole. Now march up those steps right now! You obviously have a lot to learn."

I opened my mouth without thinking. "God damn you Coach, what is your fucking problem? Please Jay, don't let him do this again. Make the bad man, or whoever the fuck he is, go away."

Jay looked absolutely horrified. He continued to do as he was told and insisted that I do the same thing. Coach shoved us into the master bedroom. He took some sheets that were crumpled up in the back of his closet and laid them across the bed. Jay started to take off his clothes. I just stood there and stared.

Coach barked at me from behind, "What are you waiting for, get your clothes off!"

I turned to see that Coach had already taken off most of his clothes. Even in my state of mind I noticed again that he was so muscular and so hairy. Jay sadly looked at me and said in a robot-like voice, "Come on, slowpoke, the sooner you get undressed, the sooner it will be over."

I just couldn't do it. I could not take off my clothes. Coach grew impatient with me. All of a sudden he was grabbing at me and taking my clothes off, being careful not to rip them. Once he had them off he threw me on the bed face down and with one swift motion proceeded to force his penis up inside my butt. It felt like he was ripping my insides open. I began screaming uncontrollably as the pain seared throughout my entire body.

That fucking bastard lied to me! He said it wouldn't hurt the next time. I closed my eyes and tightly squeezed them shut, trying to make the pain go away. Then, without warning, it happened again. The pain had subsided as quickly as it had started. I opened my eyes in disbelief. I was no longer in my body. I was floating on the ceiling, watching Coach do his damage to my lifeless body. It was great. No matter how much pain he was causing, there was no pain up here. I swung myself around and there was Jay, floating next to me. He was smiling, something I hadn't seen him do in a long time. "Hi," he nonchalantly said.

"Hi," I nervously replied, "What's going on? I don't understand. How the hell did we get up here?"

Jay was ecstatic. He exclaimed, "I'm not really sure how it works, but it's great, isn't it?"

Yes, the feeling was wonderful. There was no pain at all up here. I felt nothing at all. I looked over at Jay and we both started to laugh.

Jay said, "This is only one of my secret places. I find my way up here when Dad, you know, gets like this."

"Only one of your secret places?" I asked.

"Yes, the other place is in the park. It's the place I wanted to show you when that cop stopped us last week. Now that the park is open again I'll take you there, if my asshole father lets us go before we have to go pick up Mom."

I was fascinated at the prospect of a secret place. Jay looked down then turned back to me and said, "It looks like he's finally finished with us. It's safe to go back now." As we floated down and returned to our bodies I heard Coach telling us that it was now time for us to learn about life. He was staring at us with a look of uncertainty. He started lecturing us; "You boys will be starting Junior High School in the fall. It is a lot different than elementary school. You will be meeting lots of girls and you both need to know how to treat them and what they want. Even you, fag boy," he said staring directly at me. "Today's lesson will be real easy. I just want you to touch each other all over."

We both hesitated. Finally Jay leaned towards me and whispered, "I promise to be gentle and not to hurt you. You treat me the same way."

"I promise," I said.

We began touching each other's arms and then each other's chests. "That's really good boys." He instructed us to touch each other's nipples. "Girls really like that," he said with some satisfaction. The feel of Jay's body was so incredible. It felt so good. His hands were rubbing all over my body. It was really making me crazy. My penis was stiff as a board and there was nothing I could do to hide it. I looked down at Jay and noted with satisfaction that his penis was also stiff. I could only hope that he was feeling about me the same way I was feeling about him.

Coach appeared to be really enjoying watching us. He smiled and said, "That's real nice boys. You both are doing great for your first lesson." He was stroking his penis. His breathing was growing heavier and

144

heavier. I could not help but notice that he had our underwear in front of him on the bed. All of a sudden Coach's body bucked forward. His head jerked back and he made a loud groaning noise. Stream after stream of thick white liquid came flying out of the head of his penis. The stuff landed first on my underpants then Coach moved a little bit and it continued to fall into Jay's underpants. I had never seen anything like that come flying out of my penis. I was in awe. I couldn't believe and didn't understand what was happening. My mind was a complete blur. When Coach recovered, he told us to get dressed and not to forget our underpants. I thought I had heard him incorrectly. I asked, "You want us to put on these underpants? But, they're all, you know, gooey."

"You heard me right, I told you to put them on!" He then picked up my underpants and threw them at me. "I don't want to have to repeat myself. Is that clear?"

"Yes, sir," I said. I was shaking again. Without another word, I slipped into them. The feeling of that warm wet gooey stuff was gross and disgusting.

145

After Jay and I finished getting dressed, he asked his dad if it would be all right if we went outside to play. He said it would be fine, but only for an hour, and we had better not be late. Jay had his watch on so we could keep track of time. Coach again made it clear that this was our little secret. He glanced over at the display case that held the sword. Both Jay and I knew the painful consequences if he decided to use it on us. We ran downstairs, grabbed our sneakers and ran outside. We sat on the back stoop and tied our shoes. We simultaneously got up and shot out of there like someone had yelled, "fire!" I followed Jay as we raced down the big hill and into the park. We ran past the ball fields and right into the woods. All of a sudden Jay came to a dead stop. My heart was pounding so hard that I could hear it beating. There was no longer a trail to follow. After we both caught our breath, I watched him move a pile of rocks and long logs, revealing an opening in the side of a large hill. It was so well hidden that the cops hadn't discovered it. It was an entrance to one of the many caves scattered throughout the area.

Without a word, Jay led the way into his secret hiding place.

"Wow, this has to be one of the biggest caves in the park!" I exclaimed.

"And it's all mine!" Jay said smiling proudly.

"Gosh, this is really great, but it's really dark in here," I said, a bit hesitant to go any further.

"Relax," Jay assured me, "I've got it covered." With that he moved some more rocks that covered a hole. He reached in and took out a pack of matches and a little lantern with a thick candle in it. He lit the candle and suddenly there was tons of light. The place was huge! I had never dared to explore these caves before. I was awe struck at what my eyes were seeing. Jay placed the candle on a flat rock and turned to me and said, "Welcome to my secret hideout. This is the place where I come to get the bad man off me."

I watched the candlelight reflect off of Jay's face. There were tears streaming down. As badly as I felt for him at that moment I could not cry. I was too drained. Coach was evil and I would never again think of him as anything else. Jay looked straight in my eyes and said, "Now, there is something we have to do. Take off your underpants."

My mind suddenly took off like a shot again. Oh man he does feel the way I do. I began to smile, but stopped cold when Jay saw the smile on my face and said, "Don't get any crazy ideas or I will never talk to you ever again."

I quickly turned away, embarrassed that I'd given myself away like that. Something entirely different was going on inside of Jay's head and I was about to find out what that something was. He gathered a bunch of sticks and newspaper together which he had apparently brought into the cave at an earlier time. "You're building a campfire? I don't get it. Isn't there enough light from the candle? What are you doing?" I asked.

"I am making a fire, so we can burn our underpants. I hate it when he cums in them. It's dirty and disgusting." Without another word, we both took off our pants and then our underwear. We still had not spoken a single word about what had happened earlier. Stupid me refused to let it go. Even though I was fully aware that Jay meant what he said when he threatened never to talk to me again I had to ask anyway. "Jay?" I asked. "Did you, you know, like it when I touched your body? I mean, your penis got hard too." I could not believe what I was saying.

Jay quickly put his pants back on and looked over at me and said, "Geoffrey, you're my best friend. Of course it felt good — hell anything would feel better than having to do it with my father, I mean the 'bad man'. Besides, we were only doing what we had to do."

"But did you like it?" I asked.

"Come on, cut it out right now! We're two guys. Guys aren't supposed to do it. You are queer, just like my dad said, aren't you?"

"No, I'm not, you big jerk!" To show him that I was not queer I continued, "You know how much I like that girl at the pool, Sharon. Why, we even kissed underwater last week. I bet you didn't even see it!"

"You kissed Sharon? The daughter of the president of my dad's firm, that Sharon? When?" Jay asked. He was now full of questions, but at least I made him stop

149

thinking I liked other boys. I knew now that I couldn't let him know how I really felt without losing his friendship.

"Jay," I finally said, "don't you dare tell anyone about Sharon. It's our secret!"

"Okay," he laughed, "but I'm on to you now. I'm going to watch you and Sharon real close. She is a fox! You're so lucky!"

Yeah, right. If you only knew, I thought. It was hard enough keeping my true feelings to myself and now, to make matters worse, I was going to have to make Sharon like me. How could I persuade her to be my girlfriend?

After we finished getting dressed, we put out the fire with lots of dirt. Jay looked at his watch and said we'd better get going. Before we left he made sure the cave entrance was well hidden.

I was real scared when we arrived back at the house. I had no idea what to expect. Jay looked at me and knew that I was feeling really uncomfortable. He assured me that the bad man was gone and that his father would be back to normal.

"How can you be so sure?" I asked skeptically.

"Just because. That's the way it always is!"

"This is way too crazy," I said. I felt trapped. I mean, I had no choice but to believe Jay and I couldn't run. Now I had to face Coach and be with him like nothing had happened. If I didn't, I would be killed. Of that I was absolutely certain.

As it turned out Jay was right. Coach was back to his friendly self. We picked Shelly up and made it to the Country Club with time to spare before the bridge tournament. Sharon and her parents never showed up. Thank God, I was off the hook for the time being. Jay and I spent the day playing water basketball and racing with the other guys. Later in the day we wrestled around in the water. Although I was still pretty sore, I focused on Jay, and tried to ignore what had happened that morning.

From that day forward, I worked to master what Jay had already conquered. He had this uncanny ability to not show people how he was truly feeling, no matter how painfully he was being treated or how sad people were making him feel. With this skill, I was able to face Coach and act as if nothing had happened. I could pretend that Coach still was the neatest man in the world, next to my grandfather, of course. Everyone knew that there was no one in the whole wide world who could compare with Grand pop.

It's funny, I thought, as I blankly stared at several photos of Jay and me, as hard as I had tried to suppress those memories, the more they came flooding into my conscious mind. I decided at that moment to finish this trip and — once finished — to burn each and every photo album exactly like Jay and I had burned our underpants so many years earlier. By burning the albums, I could perhaps burn away those terrible memories. I walked over to the fireplace and, despite the heat outside, lit a duraflame log. Once the fire was lit and brightly burning, I picked up the precious album and tossed it into the flames. Yeah, it was cathartic.

CHAPTER SIX

After a long pause I picked up the next book of pictures. The first few pages were more of the same, pictures of Jay and me and once in a while our friends at the pool. My mind had taken me back to that very volatile time in my life.

"Geoffrey," Mom called out to me, "Shelly is going to be here in less than thirty minutes to take you and Jason to the pool for the day." My eyes slowly opened and there Mom was standing in the doorway to my bedroom. Several days had passed since I had seen Jay. We had spoken on the phone several times, but Jay was too busy helping his mother prepare for the annual barbecue.

Mom, seeing that I was now awake, said, "Come on, get a move on it, sleepyhead." She hurried around my bedroom, packing my swim trunks and towel in my backpack. She was right, I had better get going. Shelly didn't like to be kept waiting. At least this time I knew that if I were a little late I wouldn't have to deal with

Coach's wrath because he was out of town on business. Nonetheless I was also aware that when Shelly was angry she was a force to be reckoned with. I jumped out of bed, got dressed, grabbed my backpack, put the book I was reading into it and flew past Mom to the front stoop to wait for them to pull up.

"You still have a few minutes for a bowl of cereal," Mom yelled.

"No thank you. I'm really not hungry," I lied as I ran outside.

Sure enough, Shelly was right on time. I grabbed my backpack, yelled goodbye to Mom and made a fast dash for the car.

"Good morning, Shelly. Hi Jay," I said happily.

"Good morning Geoffrey," Shelly said. "Ready for a fun day at the pool?"

"You bet I am," I replied, really meaning it.

Once we arrived at the pool, Shelly let us out and told us to be right here at four o'clock sharp when she'd be back to pick us up. Jay and I couldn't get into our swimsuits quick enough. We were out by the pool in no time. I breathed a sigh of relief after scanning the pool area and not seeing Sharon. Jay and I started to play catch with the beach ball he brought along. Soon a bunch of other kids joined in and we all played catch until Jay and I decided to go diving in the deep end. While we were waiting our turn at the diving board, I felt someone tapping me on the shoulder.

"Hello Geoffrey," the young girl said, standing there smiling at me.

"Hi Sharon," I replied rather tentatively.

"I was hoping you'd be here today," she said.

"Yeah, me too," I stuttered. "I was hoping to see you too," I tried to sound convincing when what I really wanted to say was, "I was really hoping to never see you again. Now I have to pretend I like you in front of all of these people."

Jay, who was in front of me spun around when he heard Sharon's voice, almost knocking me over. He smiled and winked at me not being at all subtle. He was in no rush for his turn on the diving board. He took his time climbing up the ladder trying to eavesdrop on Sharon and me. I figured if he was going to eavesdrop on us, I'd have to give him something

Kevin A. Carey

worthwhile to hear, no matter how much I would regret it later. "Oh Sharon," I said, "I've been thinking about you." Jay almost fell off the ladder he was laughing so hard. So that he wouldn't fall he jumped down and lost his place in line. Sharon and I stepped out of line too. I glanced over her way and saw this big grin on her face. God, you'd have thought I asked her to marry me. I couldn't stand it. I quickly changed the subject. "Sharon," I said, "Jay and I are going to race to the shallow end. Who do you think will win?"

"Well," she thought for a moment, "probably you, Geoffrey, you are the fastest swimmer in this whole pool and probably the whole world after all."

I grabbed Jay before he had a chance to make any snide comments and pushed him toward the edge of the pool. I knew Jay would be up for a race. He always was. Whenever Jay and I raced I almost always beat him. In fact, the only time he won was when I let him so that his pride would not be hurt and so that he would still talk to me. Jesus, what I wouldn't do to make Jay happy. I loved to see him smile. It made me feel so good inside.

"On your mark," Sharon shouted. "Get set. Go!"

Jay and I both dove into the water and swam as fast as we could to the shallow end. Sharon was already waiting for us there as I came in ahead of Jay.

"Oh, you are the fastest swimmer," Sharon loudly announced for all to hear as I climbed out of the water.

Jay winked at Sharon and told her that he let me win. Of course, Sharon knew better but let Jay keep his dignity and said nothing. Jay then discreetly swam off, although not too far away. He could not take his eyes off Sharon and me. It was time for a show. I swallowed hard as I leaned into Sharon, whispering, "Don't you think you should give the winner a kiss," hoping to God she would think I was crazy.

She, however, unhesitatingly planted a big, sloppy, wet kiss right on my lips. I tried not to look too grossed out, after all, I had to make this look as convincing as possible. I held my breath, turned to her again and kissed her back, only this time I held it a little bit longer. She was beaming. We both looked around the pool. As I had hoped, every single one of our friends, including, of course, Jay, was watching us. Every one

157

turned their heads away when they saw us looking at them.

"Oh Geoffrey, I pray for this every night before I go to sleep, and it was as wonderful as I had dreamed it would be," Sharon gushed.

Oh boy, what have I started? I thought. "Yeah, me too," I said trying to sound convincing, knowing that it probably was coming out all wrong.

"Boys," she said, still smiling at me and shaking her head.

"Well," I said, "I'm going to go and play catch with the guys now, okay?"

"Oh good," she said, "I want to play too. Can I be on your team?"

"But this is a guy's game," I said.

She began to pout, which I hated more than anything. "Sure," I said, really feeling guilty and showing it as I jumped into the water.

Jay's eyes were still glued on both of us. "Geoffrey's got a girlfriend!" Jay yelled as loud as he could. I turned red with embarrassment as all heads again turned toward Sharon and me. Oh well, I thought, at least it gets me off the hook with Jay. Now he can stop calling me a faggot all the time. It got quite annoying after a while. Sharon could not keep away from me. The scary thing was that I was actually starting to like her. Not as a girlfriend, mind you, more like a pal. Unlike most of the other girls at the pool, she didn't spend all her time sunning herself. She really did like to swim and play in the water. My summer vacation, which had started on a sour note, was shaping up to be a whole lot of fun. The search for Kenny had been called off and there was no news or speculation about his whereabouts. It was even reported in the Daily Dispatch, that Kenny had vanished off the face of the earth. Perhaps, the reporter speculated, aliens had taken him away for experiments or some weird shit like that, and would return him when they were finished. Some crazy people were actually starting to believe such a stupid, outlandish theory. When Mom read the article she commented that it was much easier to assume that aliens took Kenny away than it was to think that somebody might have hurt him. I guess, in a way, she had a point. I mean thinking about Kenny being "beamed up" by a spaceship was much better than thinking about him getting killed or something. Nevertheless, when we said our prayers at night we always said an extra "Hail Mary" and "Our Father" for his safe return.

A couple of days before the Independence Day barbecue, Shelly gave Jay and me an apple pie she had baked and made us take it over to the Mastersons. We were both nervous, but Shelly was adamant. When we got to the Mastersons' door our first instinct was to leave the pie on the little table on the front porch and run. Mrs. Masterson, however, answered the door too quickly. We both politely said hello and Jay handed her the pie. We hoped that she would take it and let us leave, but we were not that fortunate. She invited us in. She seemed anxious for the company. The time seemed to drag on and on. She showed us lots and lots of pictures of Kenny and told story after story about him. God, I thought, if Kenny knew his mother was saying such things about him, he would probably kill her. I know I would kill my mother!

She told us to wait a minute. When she returned she had a tray with three plates of freshly sliced apple pie. There were also three tall glasses of milk. I can still smell the aroma of Shelly's pies today. Boy, could she bake! After we finished the pie and milk Jay and I were finally free to leave. We politely said our goodbyes. Before we had a chance to get away Mrs. Masterson gave us each a kiss on the cheek. When we got outside and out of earshot we simultaneously let out a sigh of relief. We were both glad that it was over.

I looked down at a picture of Kenny with his mom and dad. It was taken at one of the Scotts' annual Independence Day barbecue bashes, when life was so wonderful and so carefree. They all looked so happy together. The only picture of Mrs. Masterson that remains in my head today, however, is the one that was never taken. It was the look of desperation and despair on her face when Jay and I were leaving after our visit. Mrs. Masterson was completely helpless and there was nothing Jay or I could do or say to change that. Her face, forever etched into my memory, still haunts me.

CHAPTER SEVEN

I returned from the kitchen with a cold beer and looked down at the photo album sitting open on the coffee table. The photos were of the Scotts' annual Independence Day barbecue. It was an event that much of the neighborhood waited for every year. All the mothers would make a covered dish of some kind and the Scotts provided all of the steaks, hot dogs and hamburgers you could eat. It was a feast. There was always a big volleyball and croquet tournament with the winning team members getting hand-made blue ribbons which Shelly had made throughout the year. The best part of the day was the fireworks display. Every year Coach got some really great stuff. He would set the fireworks off in the middle of the street when it got dark. No one ever stopped these illegal fireworks displays because Chief Baxter lived on the same block and attended the party every year with his wife and know-it-all daughter, Jill.

As I stared down at the pages, tears welled up in my eyes as the memories of that Independence Day flowed over me.

The day had started out nice enough as I recall. I got out of bed, had breakfast and called Jay. He had lots of chores to do before the party so he was not allowed to come out and play and he could not talk long. As usual, I spent the morning reading. I loved books, especially those about foreign people and the places they lived. I would read about a country and then I would daydream about what it would be like to live the lives of these people. The book I was currently reading was all about the Swiss Alps. There were lots of pictures of snow-covered mountains, chalets and skiers. My grandparents took Ben and me skiing every winter since we were six years old. We would go to various ski resorts in the Pocono Mountains. Someday, I pondered, as I read, I was going to be one of those skiers shushing down those Alpine slopes. Those mountains looked so big and so beautiful.

While I read, Mom was busy making tons of potato salad for the barbecue. She made the best potato salad I had ever tasted! Around two o'clock, Mom let us all know that it was time to start getting ready. "We need to get there by three. I promised Shelly that we would get there a little early to help out with the final preparations." Amazingly, everyone was ready on time. Dad put the lawn chairs and the cooler with Mom's potato salad and a case of beer in the back of the station wagon. Everyone hopped in and off we went.

There was lots of activity going on when we pulled into the Scotts' driveway. Jay and Coach were getting ready to set up the volleyball net in the side yard. Shelly was shuttling between the house and the backyard, hands full of various barbeque items. Ben and I helped put the net up while Mom and Natalie went in the backyard to help Shelly. Not that Natalie had any intention of helping anyone, but Mom wanted her close by so she could keep a sharp eye out for her as Natalie had a tendency to wonder off on her own when no one was looking. She brought Edgar with her.

I had this wild urge to grab him away from her as I watched his grass-stained tail drag across the ground. How could she let poor Edgar get all yucky like that? However, I kept my mouth shut because after all, Edgar was hers now.

It was chilling being around Coach. I was afraid to even look at him. I wasn't afraid that he would try to hurt me or something, because of all the people around. His mere presence, however, gave me the creeps. At least my emotions were well under control. Even though we were together in the same place, I managed to avoid looking directly at him. I glanced over at him every so often when I thought he wasn't looking at me. He was a beast, no matter what, and I was taking no chances.

People began arriving at about four o'clock. By almost five o'clock everyone except Chief Baxter had arrived. Jill and her mother were there. Mrs. Baxter made apologies for her husband telling everyone that he had been called down to the police station. There were so many people there. Sharon arrived with her family. Jay did his best to embarrass me by yelling

165

across the yard, "Your girlfriend's here, Geoffrey." I smiled, went over to Sharon and her parents and said "Hello". Jay was on top of us in a flash. I'm sure he didn't want to miss a single word.

Being the polite person that I am, I decided to put on a show for my best friends. I asked Sharon if she was thirsty and went and got us some lemonade. I couldn't help but feel everyone's eyes on me as I crossed the lawn with the two lemonades. "How cute," I heard Shelly say to my mother.

"I guess my little boy is growing up," Mom said.

Although I was red as a beet and hating all of the attention this little gesture of kindness was getting I was determined to make it look good. I kept on heading over to where Sharon was standing and gave her the drink. We heard her father joke with Coach, "He didn't offer me a drink." He and Coach laughed like it was the funniest thing they had heard all year. I then over heard Coach say in a serious tone to Sharon's father, "I wish Jason would find a nice girl like your Sharon." At least everyone was buying my little charade, even Sharon. My ploy to convince Coach and Jay that I wasn't a faggot was working.

The Mastersons were the last to arrive. Mrs. Masterson brought in this huge cake. It was giant, with three layers separated by these columns. It reminded me of a wedding cake. It was so elaborately decorated. Mrs. Masterson presented it to Shelly and told her that it was in appreciation for everything everyone had done during this very difficult time. Shelly helped place the cake on one of the many tables of food and gave her a big hug.

The party was just beginning to get going. The teams were all picked and the volleyball tournament was getting ready to get under way. From a distance we could hear the sound of sirens approaching. Police Chief Baxter came speeding up the block with another police car directly behind his. The side of the second police car indicated that it was from Folcroft, a couple of towns away.

Chief Baxter took his time getting out of the car and waited for the other officer before walking up to the party. The other officer had a manila envelope in his left hand. Both men had solemn expressions on their faces. Chief Baxter first gave his wife a hug and a kiss and then went over and talked to Coach and Shelly for a minute. Most conversation and gaiety had stopped dead.

Mr. and Mrs. Masterson had just come over to talk to Sharon, Jay and me before the police cars pulled up. It still felt awkward talking to them. As the police cars came into view with their sirens roaring I noticed both Mr. And Mrs. Masterson tense up. Neither of them, however, moved from where they were standing. Everything suddenly was like a movie being shown in slow motion. Shelly, Coach, Chief Baxter and the other police officer came over to where we were standing. Shelly put her arm around Mrs. Masterson and introduced Officer Burns to her. She told the Mastersons that he was Chief of Forensics for the Folcroft Police Department. "I am afraid there might be bad news," Shelly said. "There is a good possibility that Kenny's body has been found. These gentlemen need you to identify him. However, Jim thought it would be easier to do it with pictures first, in case it isn't him. We can go inside."

Before Shelly finished speaking, the expressions on the Mastersons' faces became one of shock. It was as if their breath had been taken away. Tears started to flow from Mrs. Masterson's eyes. "Honey, don't panic yet," Mr. Masterson said, trying to comfort his wife. "It might not be Kenny."

An eerie silence came over the partygoers as the small group made their way into the house. As soon as the door closed, whispered conversations and speculations about what had happened to Kenny and the renewed fears of the drug-infested park were recounted throughout the backyard. Jay and I were speechless. Kenny? Dead? Who would want to kill him? He could be a pain in the ass but he sure didn't deserve to die.

Ten minutes later Shelly came to the back door and delivered the bad news to the waiting crowd. She tearfully announced, "This morning a fisherman and his son found Kenny's body in the swamps behind the airport. It looks from the photos as if some sicko took an axe and chopped him up pretty badly. The police think he's been there for the past three weeks. As of right now, they have no clues as to who might have committed such a heinous crime. I know this is very difficult, however, Linda and David have asked that everyone please stay and enjoy the rest of the evening. They send out their regrets, but they are really not up to talking right now."

As Shelly was making her announcement, the Police Chief came out the front door with the Mastersons and escorted them into the backseat of his cruiser for the short drive to the morgue to positively identify Kenny's body. The once festive crowd was now very somber. Everyone's worst fears had been realized. Kenny Masterson was dead and for no apparent reason. Gradually everyone started to express his or her own theories about what might have happened.

Finally Coach came out of the house with Officer Burns. He said in a cracked voice, "Boys and girls, this is Officer Burns. He's a very nice man and he is going to stay with us for a little while. If any of you have any questions or need to talk to him, he is here to talk to you and to help you make some sense out of this terrible, terrible tragedy. Kenny is gone, and there is nothing more we can do for him, however, I ask that you pray for Kenny's mom and dad, It is very hard when a parent loses a child. Mr. and Mrs. Masterson will need your prayers and your help. Keep a stiff upper lip; Kenny would have wanted it that way. It is time for healing now." He then turned to Shelly and put his hand on her shoulder and openly wept. There wasn't a dry eye anywhere.

People stayed late into the evening but very little food was eaten. Shelly, Mom and some of the other women eventually put it away so it wouldn't spoil. It was decided that much of it would be given to the Mastersons. The annual fireworks display would not happen this year. Everyone was just too bummed out to enjoy them. By ten o'clock everyone made their way home. We were the last to leave. Our parents hugged each other and I even saw tears in Dad's eyes. It was the first time in my life that I had seen him cry.

We loaded into our station wagon and went home in silence.

The next couple of days were a very sad time for everyone. On Sunday, churches throughout the area memorialized Kenny's brief life and tributes were sent out to his family. Clergy of all denominations called upon the judicial system to apprehend and swiftly prosecute the individual or individuals responsible for this senseless act of violence. Although no one knew for sure if Kenny was anywhere near the park when this happened to him, there were renewed cries to permanently close and fence off the woods and quarries behind the playing fields. A petition was even circulated by some of the parents to be presented to the town council.

Four days after the bad news was received, Kenny's body was finally properly laid to rest. When we got to the church for the funeral, Coach was standing outside collecting kids from our little league team to sit in a special place of honor. He even had caps made for each of us. They were in our colors. They had blue with yellow lettering and they read,

"Kenny's Team." As the top of the hour approached, the entire team stood silently together with our hats on. The hearse and two limousines pulled up into the Notre Dame De Lourdes Church driveway. Several family members none of us recognized got out of the first limousine. Out of the second limousine emerged Kenny's mother and father and who we thought were both sets of Kenny's grandparents.

When Mrs. Masterson turned to us she broke down crying. She came over to us and told us how wonderful we all were and then gave Coach a big hug and said to him, "Peter, I don't know how to thank you, you have done so much for us already. Thank you for all of your support. You are a great inspiration to these young boys and girls."

"Thanks, Linda," Coach responded. "Kenny was such a fine boy and we are all going to miss him."

Under Coach's direction, we took off our hats and followed him into the church. We sat in the side pews, right in front. The casket was brought into the church and the funeral Mass began. About half way through the mass, Father Mulligan introduced the person who

173

would eulogize Kenny. He announced to the congregation, "Ladies and Gentlemen, I would like to introduce you to a man who is a pillar of this community. He is a civic leader, President of Chapter 107 of the Rotary Club, he has worked as a volunteer and headed up many charitable endeavors, he is a respected coach of baseball and football for the Black Rock Park Little League Association. Kenny, I am told, was especially fond of the man whom the kids simply call "Coach". Ladies and Gentlemen, I would like to introduce you to Mr. Peter Scott."

There was silence as Coach made his way around the alter and up to the lectern. After the things Coach had done to me, it sickened me to hear Father Mulligan saying nice things about him. Coach paused a moment to wipe a tear from his eye. He began, "Kenny was a good boy. Everyone loved him. He had a wonderful personality all his own and a smile that was infectious. I considered Kenny to be one of my own children as I consider all the kids whom I coach. Kenny will be missed by his family and all of his many friends. I will especially miss coaching him. He was a special little boy. Linda, David, you were so blessed to have him for the time that God gave you. As Father Mulligan told us earlier, Kenny is with God now, so I ask each and every member of this community to help Linda and David and their family to heal from this terrible tragedy. Thank you and God bless you."

I looked around and saw a sea of white hankies. Except for Jay, and me there was not a dry eye in the church. Just listening to Coach feed the congregation his line of bullshit was enough to make me sick. Thankfully the funeral mass came to an end. The pallbearers came up and took Kenny's body out of the church and back into the hearse for his final ride across town.

Once outside, I rejoined Mom and Dad for the ride to the cemetery. The funeral procession seemed to stretch as far as the eye could see. It was amazing how many people showed up, many of whom never met Kenny. It was nice that this many people cared enough to show their support for the Masterson family.

The ceremony at the gravesite was very brief. After Father Mulligan gave the final blessing over Kenny's casket, each member of our little league team took off his hat and placed it on top of the casket. We then went over to Mrs. Masterson and gave her a big hug and shook Mr. Masterson's hand. When it was my turn with the Mastersons, I didn't know what to say. I quietly and respectfully said, "I'm sorry."

Mrs. Masterson said, "It's okay Geoffrey. It couldn't have pleased us more that you were one of Kenny's best friends. He thought you were the greatest. Now, don't be a stranger, okay?"

"Okay," I smiled through glassy eyes. I slowly walked back to the station wagon where Mom and Dad were waiting. Mom put her arm around me and asked if I was going to be all right.

"Yes," I replied. I turned around and there was Coach, Shelly and Jay.

"Doug," Coach said, "I know that you, Jeannie and Geoffrey are planning on going over to the Mastersons' after the funeral, but how about if you, Jeannie and Shelly go. I'll watch the boys. That will give them a chance to get out of their suits and play.

"That would be wonderful," Mom responded, still with tears in her eyes. "We will take Geoffrey home and let him change out of his suit and into his play clothes. We'll drop him off in say about a half an hour?"

Coach smiled and looked directly into my eyes and said, "Then it's settled. Jason and I will see you shortly, Geoffrey." Both Mom and Dad gave Coach a nod and said their goodbyes. We all got into our respective cars and headed down the winding cemetery road.

Once we arrived back at the Scotts' house, Mom started in on me, "Now you be a good boy for Mr. Scott this afternoon. Don't you and Jason get into any trouble, is that understood?"

"There she goes again, doling out orders," I whispered so that only Jay could hear me.

"Geoffrey will be a good boy, Jeannie," Coach assured mom, cutting her off in mid-order.

I waved goodbye to Mom and Dad. They waved back and headed down the street for the half block walk to the Mastersons.

"Hey Geoffrey, I am setting up my Hot Wheels racetrack in the recreation room," Jay declared.

"I have a better idea," I whispered hoping Coach could not hear me. "Let's go down the park. It might be safer there. If you know what I mean."

"You boys will do no such thing!" Coach yelled to my dismay. "Obviously you two have not learned your lesson. One of your friends is dead probably because of that park! Do you want to end up like him? I can't believe you would defy the rules. Rules were made for a good reason. Get up to my bedroom, now. It is apparently lesson time!"

Oh fuck. What had I done? Because of me, Coach was angrier than ever and we were about to be put through hell again. "Oh shit," Jay muttered, "Now look what you've done." Without another word I followed Jay up the stairs. I had never seen Coach so angry, and I thought I had seen him at his worst. He was like a wild animal. He ripped Jay's clothes off of him, not caring this time whether they ripped or not. Although I wanted to stop him from hurting Jay, I was suddenly too paralyzed to do anything. I was powerless. Coach whipped his belt off of his pants which slid down to the floor by his side. He grabbed Jay and threw him over his knees and began to beat his bottom with the belt. He kept hitting him over and over and over again. He shouted, "You don't go into that park ever again without an adult. There are sick people who do sick things to young boys. I don't want that to happen to you."

I just could not stand it any more! Jay was pleading with his father to stop. Couldn't he see that Jay was bleeding! Exasperated, I finally screamed, "Stop it! Can't you see that you are hurting him?"

Before I had time to react Coach grabbed me and yanked my shorts and underwear down and in one swift motion rammed his huge penis up into my butt. The pain was excruciating and took the breath right out of me. Although I felt myself getting ready to pass out I somehow managed to stay conscious.

"You boys will listen to me and do as I say." Coach badgered us, turning into the bad man.

I looked over at Jay and momentarily forgot about my pain. I was horrified to see that there was not one inch of his butt that was not black and blue or bleeding. He was still lying on the floor where Coach had thrown him.

"This is your lesson today! To do as I say! I guarantee you boys won't ever forget it." As if Jay wasn't in enough pain, Coach grabbed him by his waist, picked him up from the floor and threw him across the bed. He then rammed his massive penis into Jay's butt and pumped him really hard several times. Unbelievably, though, it was over as quickly as it had started. When Coach was finally finished with Jay without a single word he grabbed his clothes and stormed off down to the recreation room.

I slowly crawled over to Jay and reached out to him.

"Don't touch me," he said weakly. "I am filthy, rotten garbage."

"Don't say that," I said sadly. Although I too was in a lot of pain, it was my turn to console him and to try to heal him. It took some doing but I finally convinced him to come into the bathroom with me. I ran warm bath water. We both got into the tub and soaked. I closed my eyes and drifted off to sleep.

I opened my eyes in a panic. I didn't know how long we had been soaking, but the water was now very cold and very dark red and my skin was all shriveled up. Apparently we had been in the tub for quite a while. I shook Jay, who had also either passed out or fallen a sleep. We quickly dried ourselves off and cleaned up the bathroom. We somehow managed to get everything back in place before Shelly and Mom and Dad showed up.

"Did you boys have a nice afternoon?" Shelly asked while we sat in front of the television quietly watching cartoons, as if we had been there the whole time.

"Yeah, we sure did," I lied.

The last thing I remembered about that horrible day was wanting to go over to Jay, give him a big hug and assure him that everything was going to be okay. Of course I did none of those things. I kept my feelings to myself and went home and cried myself to sleep.

CHAPTER EIGHT

The events which transpired that summer laid the ground work for who I would grow up to be; a hardened, disciplined, emotionless person. The rapes and lessons continued on a weekly basis through the rest of the summer. I grew to despise the man kids called "Coach" more and more each day. It even got to the point where I stopped using his name. I referred to him only as "him" or "that guy."

My love for Jay, on the other hand, grew with each encounter, or lesson as Coach preferred to call them. I knew he wasn't feeling the same way about me, and I knew I had to hide my feelings when we were not being "taught." However, when we were together at Coach's will, I put my all into it with Jay and made our forced sexual encounters very pleasurable and even very loving. I was so grateful for the time I got to be with Jay. It reinforced my feelings about my homosexual tendencies and even helped me to understand them. I was smart enough to know that what Coach was doing to Jay and me was wrong. I knew that the acts he performed on us were not sex or acts of love at all, but acts of violence and had nothing to do with the way two people express their love for each other.

It is ironic that such wisdom could come from those horrible lessons. I walked over to the fireplace and also tossed this photo album in.

The next album I opened was crammed full of photographs. I guess I was making up for lost time. For the first time this afternoon, I was enjoying flipping through the pages. Every opportunity I could get I took my camera to school. There were lots of pictures of my friends and classmates caught off guard doing all kinds of funny things.

Thankfully the "lessons" became less and less frequent during the school year, and even stopped during the Thanksgiving and Christmas holidays. I could tell just by the quality of the pictures that I had managed to separate the crap Coach threw at me from what life really was about. On those occasions when Jay and I had our so-called encounters with his father I managed to get through them by blocking out my emotions, by not being there, and having out-of-body experiences. I would only return to my body when Coach instructed me to perform some act of sex with Jay. I knew that sometimes Jay would remain disconnected from his body during our sessions, but I could not.

It was a very difficult time for me. As if my head wasn't messed up enough already, puberty was starting to set in which only confused things even more. Most young men have their first ejaculation in a wet dream. For Jay and me that was not the case. During one of our lessons in late May of 1971, I was being forced to put my penis into Jay's butt. On this particular occasion the tingling I felt turned into something very new. I was both scared and excited at the same time. At first I thought I was getting sick. I pulled my penis out of Jay's butt and shot strand after strand of this white gooey-looking stuff. Even though I felt ashamed at what I had just done, the feeling was absolutely incredible. Coach was ecstatic. He started laughing and said, "Geoffrey, today you have become a man and I am the one responsible for that. Congratulations."

Although I managed to hold my life together and appear to be just like the rest of the kids, my schoolwork suffered tremendously. I went from a straight "A" student to all "C's" and "D's" except for language classes in which I excelled. Mom and Dad were very concerned and lectured me on a regular basis on the virtues of a good education. My guidance counselor, however, convinced them that this was a common problem for many students. The transition from elementary school to junior high school was often very difficult. He suggested that they give it another semester before they pressed the panic button. He also suggested that since my strengths were in foreign languages, I should consider a concentration in them. At least the school year was ending and I would have the summer to think about what I wanted to do.

The final picture in the album was of Jay and me. We had our arms around each other, hamming it up for the camera. It was one of the few times we were that close to each other. Jay saw it simply as comradery; I saw it as much more. A tear dropped from my eye and landed on the picture. This time, however, it was a tear of joy rather than of sadness. I closed the album and placed it back in the box. How could I burn it after all?

CHAPTER NINE

I pulled the next photo album out of the box. On the cover was a wonderful panoramic view of Washington, D.C. at twilight, the moment right before the sun went down. The sky was a majestic orange and blue. I was quite proud of this particular picture. When my grandfather saw it, he took the negative, made a copy of it and put it on his desk at work. I was so surprised when he presented me with the photo album with the picture blown-up and embossed onto the cover. I remember feeling so special. Yeah, what a summer that had been, I thought to myself.

As the school year ended, I got some great news. My grandparents, who lived in Georgetown, Maryland, right outside of Washington, D.C., invited me to spend the summer with them. I overheard Mom telling my grandmother that she was worried about me, and that I just had not been my usual self for such a long time no matter how hard I was trying, and my poor grades reflected that fact. As a result everyone decided that it would be a good idea if I got away from my present environment. Therefore, I was going to get to spend the summer with my grandparents, whether I wanted to or not. Even though, I loved my grandparents and thought that my grandfather was the best person in the world, I was having mixed emotions about going. Going meant that I would be away from Jay and my other friends. Yes, I was finally going to be away from Coach, but Jay needed me, and I needed him. Although I raised some half-hearted objections, I knew that in the end I had no say in the matter.

School ended in late June. I had only a few days to pack and get ready. The day before I was to leave, Jay and I made one last trip to the cave. This time there was no need to go through our underwear-burning ritual. Coach was out of town. I made Jay promise to write everyday. I promised the same and that I would call him once a week to make sure he was okay. He assured me that he could handle his father and that he would be all right. I knew he was lying to me but there was nothing else either one of us could say or do that would make things any different.

That night, Mom and Dad took the family to a real nice restaurant for a farewell celebration. I was really happy when Mom said that Jay could join us if his parents permitted it. When we went to pick him up, Coach appeared at the door. I shrunk back in terror and then quickly straightened myself up, hoping that no one had noticed what I had just done. "Hi," I said. "I thought you were away on business."

"I came home early to see you off." As he put his arm around my shoulder, for all to hear, he said, "I couldn't let my favorite first baseman get away for two months without saying goodbye. We are really going to miss you. Oh well, I guess we are going to have to work extra hard when you come home. Won't we?"

I knew exactly what he was saying even if no one else got it, and I wanted the bastard dead right then and there. Finally, Jay came to the door working on a smile that I knew wasn't real. When he got into the rear station wagon seat reserved for the two of us I saw that he had this pained look on his face. I knew that he had just been severely beaten again. I whispered to him, "Jay, are you okay? Did your dad hit you again?"

189

"Shut up you fool. Do you want to get us both in trouble?" He replied in a hushed voice. He then turned to his mother and father and said goodbye and smiled and waved like they were the happiest family on earth. I, of course, knew better and felt so helpless. How could I leave my best friend to deal with his animal of a father all alone?

*****

The day to leave for my summer vacation had arrived and I had not packed my suitcases like I was told to do two days earlier. When Mom came up to inspect my packing job, she went ballistic and began running around my room ranting and raving like a lunatic. I was in a pretty bizarre mood and could not stop laughing no matter how hard I tried. I grabbed my camera and took several pictures of Mom on her little tirade. They were quite comical to look at; even now they made me laugh out loud.

Somehow we got to the airport on time. After we checked my luggage in and I got my seat assignment,

Mom started to cry. She kept giving me all of these stupid instructions, "Behave yourself," "Be a good boy," "Do exactly as you are told," "Watch your manners," She went on and on. Finally a stewardess came over to us and said that it was time to go. I didn't think I needed an escort, but it was apparently airline regulations that a stewardess accompanies children under the age of sixteen. Mom hugged me one more time and tried to go over her long list of instructions one last time.

"Don't worry, Mom, he'll be fine," the stewardess, whose nametag read "Monica" reassured her. I gave Mom one last obligatory kiss and hug and told her that I loved her. I shook my father's hand and simply said goodbye. I punched my brother one last time just for good measure. The stewardess took my hand and we walked out to the airplane. As we went up the steps of the plane, Dad called my name and I turned around. He snapped a picture, "For your mother," he shouted. I lifted my camera to my eye and snapped a picture back at them.

Kevin A. Carey

My first time in an airplane was really neat. Monica introduced me to the other stewards and stewardesses and even the pilot who gave me my very own set of wings to pin on my blazer. In no time at all we were in Washington, D.C. I was the last person on the plane and the last person off of it. I could not wait to see my grandparents. I had only seen them once since they moved to Washington, D.C. almost two years before. As I stepped out of the plane with Monica holding my hand, I saw them standing at the gate. I pulled free from her and bolted down the steps and over to where they were standing. Monica, who had become my new friend, was surprised and apparently a bit shaken up. When she caught up to me she told me how dangerous it was to do that, and not to ever do it again. I paid little attention to her. I was so happy to finally see my grandparents, especially my grandfather. They both gave me a big hug and kiss. We talked and talked all the way back to their house in Maryland. Grand pop took a little detour through Washington, D.C. He pointed out all of the big monuments. We drove past the White House and the

Capitol building. My grandfather was so smart. He knew everything. We had so much fun. I could not wait to get home to write to Jay and tell him all about my first airplane ride and all of the wonderful and fascinating things Grand pop had shown me.

When we finally arrived at their house, I could not believe how big and beautiful it was. Grand pop, still in tour guide mode, explained that it had been built in the old Victorian style, like many of the houses in England. Grand mom took me up to the room that I would be staying in. It was great. We climbed two long flights of stairs. My room was at the very top of the house and it was huge. It even had its own bathroom. When you looked out of the window you could see the Washington Monument way off in the distance.

After I got settled in, we called Mom and Dad to tell them that I had made my journey just fine. I told them all about the great plane ride and how I was made a pilot and had the wings to prove it. Although Mom tried to sound like everything was great, I could tell by her voice that she was not going to stop worrying until she saw me again in the flesh. Grand mom cooked dinner and served it in the dining room instead of the kitchen. She said that this was a special occasion, which called for using the good china. They had this humongous dining room table that seated sixteen when all the leaves were added. For dessert she made my favorite, bread pudding. It was so thick and creamy! I was in heaven. As we were finishing dessert, the phone rang. Grand pop excused himself and left the room to answer it. He returned a short time later and announced that he had to leave right away to go to an emergency meeting.

"Not again," my grandmother protested, "Your grandson just got here."

Grand pop shot her a look. She backed down and said, "I know, I know. Now please try and not be too late."

He smiled, leaned over and gave her a little peck on both cheeks. He then turned to me, "Be sure you get to bed early. You've got a busy day ahead of you tomorrow and you will need your rest."

I jumped up from the table, ran over to Grand pop, gave him a big hug and promised him I would do just that. He was the absolute best and I would do anything for him. My grandfather was a very important person. He worked for the United States government. I was not real sure what he did though, because whenever anybody asked him what he did for the government, he always somehow managed to change the subject before anyone could figure out what it was he did. The only thing I did know was that his office was in the White House, that he worked directly for the President of the United States and he got to travel a lot as part of his job. I mean he really traveled. He was always flying here and there. Sometimes he would tell stories of some of his adventures. It sounded so wonderful. I guess that's how I got my interest in traveling. I remember one time when I was only five. It was before they moved to Georgetown. It was in November 1963. I remember it like it was yesterday because it made such an impression on my life. My brother and I were staying overnight. A big black limousine pulled up in the front of the house during the night. Some men in blue military uniforms got out, came to the door and talked to Grand pop. He told Grand mom he had to go to work. He took the suitcase that he always kept packed, out of the living room closet and went with the men. I've always remembered that night because of the grave and serious look on his face and what Grand mom said to him. She said, "Please be careful and come back safely to me you crazy man."

I figure her plea must have worked, because when he returned home he surprised her and finally took her on a long-overdue vacation to Niagara Falls. He barely gave her time to pack. Unfortunately their vacation only lasted two days. President Kennedy was shot and killed the day after they left. It was a terrible time for the country. Mom and Dad had to go to the airport to pick Grand mom and Grand pop up. Of course the whole family went along. When they got off the plane they both looked so sad. When Grand pop saw my mother he went over to her, gave her a big hug, he started to cry and said, "This didn't have to happen. John was my friend." At first I didn't know whom he was talking about. In fact, it took a few years before the light bulb went off inside my head. The John he was talking about was President John F. Kennedy.

I admired my grandfather all of my life. I even dreamt of growing up to be just like him. I decided to tell him just that very thing the next night at the dinner table. After he came home from work I said, "Grand pop, you are the greatest person I know and I want to grow up to be just like you someday and do the same thing you do, whatever that is."

His reaction to me was the last thing I had expected. He first smiled at me and then this serious look came across his face. He said, "I would love for you to follow in my footsteps, but I understand that you were having some problems with your school work this past year. Is there something wrong?"

I got all flushed and turned beet red. I lowered my face to my plate and lied, "No, nothing is wrong. Seventh grade was just too hard for me."

Unfortunately, Grand pop could see right through me. "This is not your mother you're talking to. She might buy that line, but I don't."

There was no way I could tell him that Coach was doing unspeakable things to Jay and me and that it made it hard to concentrate so I continued to insist that there was nothing wrong.

"Okay," he said, "go ahead and keep lying to yourself and to me, but, let me warn you young man that those kinds of grades will not get you very far in life, especially if you want to be like your grandfather. You have to be at the very top of your class. Anything other than number one and you will be useless, you will be a nobody. I know you can do it. I've seen you do it."

I was devastated. His words pierced right through my heart and soul. The pain I felt was worse than any physical pain Coach could have ever inflected on me. I could not look at the man I adored and aspired to be like. With my gaze still focused on my plate, I asked to be excused, ran up to my room and slammed the door. I retrieved Mr. Rabbit from his secret hiding place in the bottom of my backpack and began to cry. Fear was ripping through me. I had failed my own grandfather.

Later that evening, Grand mom came up to my room to talk to me. When she knocked on the door, I quickly tossed Mr. Rabbit under the bed. She came in and sat down on the edge of the bed and said, "Your grandfather only wants the best of everything for you. He loves you very much and he is so proud of you, and he knows that you have it in you to be the very best."

I was feeling so humiliated and ashamed.

Grand mom continued, "Your mom told us that you did real well in your experimental language classes. She said you got straight A's in French, German, Spanish and Latin. If you had to pick one, and only one language, which one would it be?"

I never really thought about it until now. I liked them all. After giving it a little bit of thought, I responded, "German, yeah, German, because you have to make all of these neat guttural sounds with your throat."

Grand mom smiled and said, "Good, then how about if you and I go to the international book shop tomorrow and buy you a couple of books; one on how to speak German and one about Germany. Let's show Grand pop that you can be the best and be someone that he can be proud of and show off to his friends."

I turned to Grand mom and smiled at her.

"I take that smile to mean you like that idea. Good. Well, it's time for bed." She kissed me on the forehead, got up and shut the door behind her. I slept like a log that night. I didn't even need Mr. Rabbit. He stayed safely tucked under the bed the entire night.

*****

At dinner the following evening, Grand pop was apparently still mulling over the previous evening's conversation. He asked me if I had given any thought to what we had discussed the night before. With a big grin on my face I looked over at Grand mom who was smiling too.

"Okay," Grand pop questioned, "what do you two have up your sleeves?"

Grand mom told me to go get the stuff we had bought. I got up from the table, ran into the living room, got my bag and quickly returned to the kitchen and pulled up a chair right next to Grand pop.

"What do you have there?" he asked.

I pulled out my new picture book of Germany, a history book about Germany and a beginning German language book. I proudly told him that I really wanted to learn how to speak fluent German so that I could travel to foreign countries just like him. I watched as a smile came across his face. I was so glad to be back in his good graces. He looked at me and said, "This is great, your mother told us you did well in your language classes and I know how much you like reading about geography and history. Yes, indeed, this is great news." He got this serious look on his face again. He said, "I can't tell you what it would mean to me for you to follow in my footsteps. But, remember Geoffrey, you have to excel in all of your subjects."

"I know," I said, "and I promise I will do better next year and every year after that."

Grand mom let out a sigh of relief and we all smiled. Grand pop and I went into the living room with my picture book. I sat next to him on the couch and listened to him as he told me some of his favorite stories about some of the places we were looking at in the pictures and he even taught me some new German words. By his own admission, Grand pop was not fluent in German, but he knew enough to get along if he ever had to.

I said to him, "I hope one day I will be able to go to Germany and to travel to distant and far off lands."

"You will, Geoffrey. I promise you," he said.

We spent the next couple of weeks visiting all of the historical sights in Washington and the surrounding area. We visited Monticello, where Thomas Jefferson lived, and Mount Vernon, where George Washington lived. When we weren't sightseeing, I was curled up outside in a comfortable lawn chair reading about Germany and its fascinating history. I tried to spend at least an hour a day with my language book, but it was so hard when you didn't have someone to tell you if you were pronouncing the words correctly. The little bit of German I had taken in school last year was not enough to know whether or not I was speaking properly. Grand pop tried to help me when he could.

I really missed Jay. I faithfully wrote him a letter every night. I think my grandmother was tired of giving me a stamp every morning, but if she was, she never said anything to me. On Sunday nights, Grand mom let me call Jay for fifteen minutes. It was never enough time. I could hear the pain in his voice. He could never hide it from me. I tried to comfort him as best I could from so far away. He was always trying to think about my feelings by telling me not to worry, that at least I didn't have to put up with it too. I had to admit that, despite the nightmares that refused to go away, my mind was much clearer. As much as I missed Jay and my friends at the pool I was doing pretty good and having a great time with Grand mom and Grand pop. I even fantasized, despite Coach's parting words to me, that once I got home the abusive behavior wrought by him would simply stop and Jay and I could finally go on with our lives.

I looked up from the photo album feeling really good. There were so many wonderful memories, however, no matter how hard I tried, the tragic memories always overshadowed the good times.

CHAPTER TEN

I could not believe how many photos I had taken in such a short period of time. I closed volume one of my summer vacation and gingerly placed it back in the box. I could never destroy these albums for they reflected some of the best times of my young life. Volume two was of my thirteenth birthday celebrations. Yes, I celebrated my birthday for two weeks straight. I became a teenager in grand style. It was so special, holding lots of promise for the future. If only the rest of my life could have been as wonderful.

Mom, Dad, Natalie and Ben were coming to visit for the last two weeks of my summer vacation. I was looking forward to seeing them, though, I had to admit, I really didn't want to have to share my grandparents with anybody right at the moment. The day before their arrival Grand mom and I spent the entire day cleaning the house. We did not stop until after 11pm when Grand mom gave the furniture the final white glove test of the day. She finally declared the place fit for company.

The day of Mom and Dad's arrival began with one last white glove inspection. Finally, I heard a car horn out in the driveway. It was Mom and Dad. Grand mom looked down at her watch in a panic. She shook her head back and forth, looked around the room and said, sounding somewhat perturbed, "Oh no, they are an hour early. I'm not ready. This house is a mess. Geoffrey, take your books upstairs right now."

Of course the house was not only fine; it was perfect. You could eat off the floor, that's how clean it was. I did as I was told and ran the books up to my room and threw them on the bed. I was so excited; I had to go to the bathroom. The bathroom window faced the front of the house. I peered out the window and could not believe what I was seeing, or should I say, whom I was seeing: there was Jay standing on the front lawn. I almost lost it right then and there. I threw open the window and called out to him.

Grand mom looked up at me and yelled. "Close that window this instant, young man, the air conditioning is on. You're wasting expensive electricity."

"God, Grand mom," I yelled back, "relax, you're going to give yourself a heart attack!"

I closed the window and ran down the stairs and out to the front lawn and made my way to where Jay was standing at the bottom of the driveway, completely oblivious to the rest of the family. Before I could reach Jay, Mom grabbed me and gave me a big hug and kiss. She said, "Surprise! I knew you guys missed each other, so Mr. and Mrs. Scott gave their permission for Jason to spend the whole two weeks with us."

I was speechless. The only thing I could say was, "Wow, I can't believe this."

"Believe it," Jay said. "My dad has been real busy at work and he has been pretty stressed out, so when your mom invited me to come with them to see you, they jumped at the idea and decided to take a vacation of their own, by themselves, at home."

Afterwards everyone exchanged greetings. There was a lot of small talk. Jay and I unloaded the station wagon. Jay would be sleeping in my room, so we took his backpack and his suitcase upstairs to my bedroom. "Gosh," I told Jay, "this is going to be the best vacation ever!"

We could not stop yapping. He told me about all the kids at the pool. He even made it a special point to tell me how much Sharon missed me. "I know," I said, "she keeps sending me these yucky letters. Look at them!" I pointed to the stack of envelopes on the top of my dresser. "They have this gross smelling perfume and lip marks that say 'Sealed With a Kiss.' Christ, I have to put up with my grandmother's smartass comments every single time I get one of these things."

"Oh, that is gross. I'm glad it's happening to you, and not to me. Could you imagine if my dad saw those letters? It scares me to even think about it."

"Speaking of the asshole, how are you doing, really? And don't sugar coat it for me. You can tell me everything."

"Oh, you know how it is. I hate him. He hates me. But he is my dad, so there's nothing I can do about it. You know perfectly well what he would do to us if either of us ever told anyone. Now, I'm here to have a

207

good time, so let's not talk about it, or even think about my asshole of a father for the rest of the vacation."

"Okay," I said, "it's a deal." We both spit on it and headed downstairs. We spent the afternoon outside on the back porch sipping lemonade and catching up. Grand mom prepared a special birthday dinner, which we sat down to when Grand pop got home from work.

I got lots of neat presents. Mom and Dad gave me the usual clothes, Jay gave me two brand spanking new matchbox cars, and his parents gave me a new shirt and a really nice tie to go with it. It was a real tie, not a clip on. "Somebody is going to have to teach me how to tie this thing."

My grandfather piped up and said, "I can do that. You're going to need it next week. I have a surprise for both you and Jason. Next Wednesday I have arranged for the two of you to have breakfast with President and Mrs. Nixon."

The room got real quiet. Mom finally broke the silence and said, "Isn't that wonderful! You boys will have so much to talk about after this summer is over."

"Thank you Grand pop, you're the greatest," I said.

"Yeah," Jay said, "thank you Grand pop. Boy, I sure am lucky to be Geoffrey's friend."

My grandfather was beaming. I'm sure he was truly enjoying all of the attention he was getting. He paused a moment and said, "Oops, I almost forgot. Grand mom, where is our present for Geoffrey?" She reached behind her chair and pulled out a big nicely wrapped box and handed it to me. "Happy Birthday!" she said.

"Wow," I exclaimed, "What a big box. What could be in there? Hopefully not the usual stuff like more clothes. I have enough clothes to last me forever, and then some."

Mom began to chastise me for the rude comment, but she let it go when Grand pop gave her a nasty look.

I was so anxious to see what it was that I dove right in and began tearing the wrapping off. Everyone laughed at me. I must have looked pretty comical. Inside was a brand new reel-to-reel tape recorder and yet another wrapped package.

"Wow," I said with a big smile on my face, "my very own tape recorder. I've never had my own tape recorder; they are so expensive."

"Geoffrey!" Mother scolded me. "That's not nice either."

"Sorry, Mom. I just got a little too carried away."

Grand pop, I believe was as excited by all the goings on as I was. "Well, go on and open the other package."

I, again, tore off the paper. It was a book and lots of tapes. The title of the book was "The Department of Defense Foreign Language School Training Manual-German."

I just looked at it, not really comprehending what I was holding in my hands. Grand pop couldn't have been happier. He was grinning from ear to ear.

"Now you can learn German, and any other language you want to learn, the proper way. This is the way the Defense Department teaches its field agents how to speak foreign languages so that we can better understand people of all nationalities around the world. One day the world will be a better place to live. A world where people can live in harmony with each other, all because of people like you, who have a special talent for learning foreign languages. I like to think of people who speak foreign languages as goodwill ambassadors to the world."

Grand pop ended his grandiose little speech by asking me what I thought. I was in complete awe and so very happy, and quite frankly, I didn't understand even half of what Grand pop was trying to say.

"Me, an Ambassador?" I pondered out loud. "Wow!" Everyone laughed and applauded. I turned my attention back to the tape recorder. "This is so cool," I said. "Now I can hear how to pronounce the words right, instead of just guessing how they sound. Thank you, Grand pop and Grand mom. I love you both."

"So, we're going to have a linguist in the family," dad said as he shook my hand and wished me a happy birthday.

Grand mom got up and directed everyone into the dining room for the singing of Happy Birthday and the cutting of the cake. Grand pop gently grabbed my shoulder and we lagged behind the rest of the others.

211

He whispered into my ear, "Geoffrey, if you want to follow in your grandfather's footsteps, those tapes are the key, and of course, good grades."

I looked him in the eye and said, "I've always dreamt of being just like you."

He smiled and gave me a big hug. "That a boy!" He paused for a moment. "Whenever you need more tapes on German, or any language, ask me. You can't buy these in any bookshop. They are very special programs designed only for people who work for the government."

Well, I thought, as I looked up from the many photographs, I didn't quite become a goodwill ambassador, but I certainly did become a language specialist. Although people always said that I had an ear for languages I had to admit that the Defense Department tapes and the intensive specialized language training I received certainly made it easier. I can now fluently speak German, French, Spanish, Russian, Polish and Japanese.

The next series of pictures were mostly all repeats from the first batch I had taken. The only difference was there were different people in them. We all had so much fun. This time I got to play tour guide and explain all the sights to everybody. At the end of the first day of sight seeing, my grandfather turned to my mother and said, "I am so impressed with Geoffrey, he has the mind of an elephant. He doesn't forget a thing I tell him. He has remembered everything I've told him, down to the minutest of details and, believe me, we've seen and done a lot."

I just loved being the center of attention. My ego was soaring for the whole two weeks. Everyone seemed to be having so much fun. We toured and shopped and then toured some more. There was so much to see. Jay and I especially liked going through the Smithsonian Museum. There was so much history in that one place.

At night, Grand pop would sit all of us kids down in the living room and tell us his famous Wild Wild West stories. He was the best storyteller ever. We would laugh until it hurt.

Kevin A. Carey

*****

Our big day had finally arrived, and the excitement was building to a fever pitch. Jay and I were going to meet the President of the United States of America. We were going to have breakfast with, as Grand pop put it, "the leader of the free world." I think Mom was more excited than either Jay or me. It was eight in the morning and she had already been up two hours ironing both Jay's and my clothes. Grand mom even joked about the fact that mom was ironing creases into creases.

While we got ready Mom bugged us the whole time, "brush your teeth, don't wrinkle those pants, I just ironed them, comb your hair, Oh Geoffrey you need a haircut. My goodness, that hair of yours is much too long. I know the President isn't going to like it one bit."

My beautiful shoulder-length blonde hair was the last thing that anybody was going to fuck with. It meant a lot to me. "No way," I angrily snapped, "I am not getting a haircut. Not even for the President of the

United States." Mom, knowing that she lost this argument every time we had it, just shook her head, sighed, and walked away.

When it finally came time to leave, Mom started in with her usual list of instructions. "Be good," she bellowed, "Watch your posture, and don't eat your food in a rush."

Jay and I just chuckled and nodded our heads in agreement. Grand pop pulled the car out of the garage and we made a mad dash for it. We almost made a clean get away, but then Mom came running out of the house.

"Oh what can it be now?" I said disgustedly.

"Geoffrey, you forgot to give your mother a kiss," she sheepishly said.

"Oh Mom," I said, turning red.

"Now, Geoffrey," Grand pop said, motioning me to get out and kiss her goodbye. "Don't worry. We will wait for you."

I got out of the car, gave Mom a quick peck on the cheek and got right back into the car. The scene on the front lawn must have looked pretty comical to any onlookers. It was like we were going to be gone for days. Mom and Dad, Ben and Natalie and Grand mom were all on the front steps waving at us. It reminded me of the opening scene of "The Beverly Hillbillies." We waved back as the car drove out of sight.

Grand pop was in a super good mood. He turned to us and asked, "Are you guys excited? We have a great day planned for you, starting with a special tour of the White House."

Jay, still in awe of the whole thing, said, "Wow, we're really going to visit the President of the United States. I still can't believe it!"

"I can't believe it either," I added.

Grand pop asked us to remember something that he felt was very important. He said, "Don't be nervous. Remember even though Mr. Nixon is the President, he is still a person. Don't treat him like a celebrity or a god. He wants to be treated like you guys would treat your friends."

"We can do that," I said.

"Are we going to meet his dog, too?" Jay asked.

Grand pop laughed, "Willie is his name. I am sure you'll get to meet him too."

Jay had so many questions. He next asked, "Will we get to meet Mrs. President Nixon, too?"

Grand pop obviously thought that was hysterically funny. He could not stop laughing. I shot a look back at Jay and said, "You dope, she's not the President, he is!"

Jay sneered back, "I know, you jerk, what do you think I'm stupid or something?"

"Boys, boys," Grand pop laughed, "I don't want any fighting from either of you. To answer your question, Jason, yes, you are going to meet the First Lady. But please, call her Mrs. Nixon, although I'm sure she'd get a kick out of being called, 'Mrs. President Nixon.' But seriously, don't call her that."

"I won't," Jay said, "I promise."

Grand pop turned to me with this serious look and said, "And that goes for you too, young man." I knew he wasn't reprimanding me or anything, but I always hated it when he made a cross remark to me. No matter how innocuous the remark was, it always made me feel

217

inferior. I changed the subject by asking, "Is it okay if I tell the President that I am learning German and I want to be just like you when I grow up?"

"Yes, I'm sure he would like to hear that."

Jay laughed at me and said, "Next thing you're going to say is that you want to be the President of the United States of America. Give me a break."

"Now Jason," Grand pop interjected, "you boys can be anything you want to be, and do anything you want to in life just as long as you put your mind to it, and study hard and get good grades."

After fighting the morning rush hour traffic, we finally arrived at the Northeast Gate of the White House. I couldn't believe it. I had heard that security was extremely tight at the White House and that they searched everything before you could even get through the front gate. The car in front of us stopped at the gate and a guard came out with a big mirror on wheels and searched the underbelly of the car for anything suspicious. After they had fully inspected the car, we drove on and Grand pop pulled up to the guardhouse. A marine wearing a blue uniform and white gloves stepped alongside the car. He looked really young. He peered into the driver's side window, saluted Grand pop, and waved us on through without a second look. Grand pop returned the salute and drove through the gate. Jay and I were both in awe. "Wow, Grand pop," I said, "How did you do that? You must be really important."

"They all know me here. This is where I work," he said nonchalantly.

After Grand pop parked the car, he opened his briefcase and handed us each our very own security badge. They had our pictures on them and our names. He pointed out that the Presidential Seal was embossed on it. The badges were attached to chains so we could wear them around our necks. Jay and I felt really important.

Another guard met us in the parking area. He also saluted. Jay and I were mesmerized by the man whom we simply thought of as Grand pop. We knew that he had a great job and knew lots of important people, including the President of the United States, however, we had no idea of the magnitude of it all. Jay leaned into me and whispered, "Man, I knew your grandfather was important, but I didn't know he was that important."

"I didn't either," I whispered back.

The guard and Grand pop spoke briefly but we could not hear them. We then began walking towards the South Portico of the White House itself. Jay and I stopped dead in our tracks. There on the steps waiting for us was President and Mrs. Nixon and Willie. We still couldn't believe what was happening; yet there they were, in the flesh, waiting for us. As we approached them, Grand pop murmured to us, "Remember gentlemen, just be yourselves and act natural."

"Good morning, Dick. Hi Pat." Grand pop cheerfully greeted them as he shook hands with the President.

President Nixon smiled and said, "Good morning gentlemen."

"I'd like to introduce you to my grandson, Geoffrey Brooks, and his best friend, Jason Scott."

President Nixon shook my hand first and then Jay's. I was in shock, but I did as I was told and held my emotions in check, which was not all that difficult. Good old Coach had taught me all too well.

Next I shook Mrs. Nixon's hand. Boy did she have a strong handshake, even stronger than the President's.

"Hello boys, welcome to the White House," Mrs. Nixon proudly announced to Jay and me. She had the warmest smile.

"May I pet Willie?" I politely asked.

President Nixon laughed, "Yes, of course you may. Say hello, Willie."

Willie barked a friendly bark right on cue and brought his paw up to meet my waiting hand. "He loves children. I mean young men such as yourselves," President Nixon said, changing his phrasing, hoping he had not offended us.

"Wow, what a smart dog. Did he have to go to school to learn that or did you train him real well?"

Mrs. Nixon answered, "Although Mr. Nixon did a wonderful job of training him, Willie learned how to do that in charm school. All pets, before they live in the White House have to go to charm school, because they have to meet many important people everyday. Just like the President."

Grand pop just smiled and said, "Didn't I tell you guys how important education is, even Willie has one."

President Nixon finally said, "Gentlemen, we have a special day planned for you. Mrs. Nixon has pretty much cleared her schedule for the day. Call it a vacation day for her," he laughed jovially, and continued, "Your grandfather and I have some important business to attend to upstairs but we'll be back for breakfast and I'll be checking in on you from time to time. Mrs. Nixon will give you a tour of this great house. If you have any questions whatsoever, ask her, she's the expert. She can tell you anything and everything about this house. Can't you, honey?"

She blushed, "He exaggerates just a little bit, but yes, it's my job as the First Lady to know it's history so that I can explain it to visiting dignitaries and VIP's like yourselves."

"Did you have to go to school to learn everything?" I asked.

Everyone laughed. Mrs. Nixon answered, "In a way, yes I did. I listen to the tour guides who give the tours, over and over again. I also read everything I can get my hands on concerning this fascinating building. Reading is such an important part of studying."

"I love to read," I boasted.

"Does he ever," Jay added. "I think he likes his books more than his friends. When we are in school, at lunchtime, while everyone is playing stickball or out on the playground equipment, Geoffrey sits in the grass and reads. Don't you think that's odd, Mr. President?"

"No, no, not in the least bit. But Geoffrey, you need to interact with your friends, too. You should play sports. It makes you a well-rounded person. I played a little football at Whittier, as an undergrad, and I was pretty good I might add."

"He was more than good!" Grand pop interjected.

The President laughed again. Boy, he really likes to laugh a lot, and I bet he likes kids too, I thought to myself.

"Okay, okay, enough already," the President said. William, we have some work to do. If you will excuse us gentlemen, we will catch up with you in about an hour for a nice big breakfast, which I am certain you will thoroughly enjoy. We have some of the best chefs in the world right here in our kitchen.

"Have a good time guys," Grand pop called out to Jason and me as he quickly followed after the President.

"Gosh," Jay again whispered to me, "your grandfather is so important."

I couldn't believe it myself. I just stood there and stared at them as they disappeared around a corner. I was still rather awestruck.

"Boy, I'm glad they're gone," Mrs. Nixon said. "We have a little less than an hour before the public tours begin at ten. If we don't finish, the tourists will have to wait, because you men are our special guests today. If you have any questions, please stop me and ask. If I can't answer your question, then I will ask one of the tour guides. They are well trained and quite capable of answering any questions you might have, no matter how odd or strange you might think your questions are. Believe me, they've heard it all over the years."

We turned and entered the White House for the first time. It was awesome. The ceilings were so high. The first room Mrs. Nixon showed us was "The Blue Room." She explained to us "that an architect by the name of James Hoban won a contest for the best design of a house for the President of the United States. Work began in 1792. Mr. Hoban designed the Blue Room in the shape of an oval at the request of President George Washington, however, George and Martha never did get a chance to live in this grand house."

I was fascinated at all the information Mrs. Nixon was sharing with us. Our private tour of the White House continued. We saw the Red Room, the State Dining Room, the Green Room and the East Room. It was so amazing that there could be so much history in one place.

Next, we took an elevator marked "PRIVATE" down one flight to see the historical rooms on the first floor. They included the Map Room, the Diplomatic Reception Room, the China Room, the Vermeil Room and finally the Library.

When we entered the Library, it was already a bit past ten o'clock and the first tour was waiting outside the open Library doors. Someone noticed the First Lady and called out from behind the velvet rope. Mrs. Nixon graciously acknowledged the gentleman and posed for a picture. Then she put her arms around Jay and me and told us to smile. Dozens of flashes went off in our faces. I was blinded. Mrs. Nixon gave one last wave as we left the room through the opposite doorway. The crowd of on-lookers cheered as we walked away. Jay and I were now celebrities!

We walked out of the Library and into the Entrance Hall. The Entrance Hall in itself was absolutely fabulous. The walls as well as the floors were marble. The row of columns, or colonnade, as Mrs. Nixon described it, took my breath away. We proceeded through the Cross Hall and entered an elevator where yet another guard was waiting to escort us up to the private living quarters.

As we exited the elevator, Mrs. Nixon said to the guard, "Thank you, Rudi. Could you please go upstairs and tell the President that breakfast will be served in ten minutes?"

I leaned into Jay as we entered the living room and said, "Now this is more like it. I mean it looks more like a home up here. It's filled with antiques, but it is definitely more cozy."

Mrs. Nixon continued our tour. "I'd like to show you the Lincoln Bedroom. Now boys, did you know that President and Mrs. Lincoln never slept in this room? This room was named the Lincoln Bedroom because it was the room that President Lincoln was brought to after he died the night he was shot in Ford's Theater, which isn't too far from here. The doctors did the autopsy right here in this very room."

"Wow, that is so neat," I said. "We visited Ford's Theater just yesterday."

Mrs. Nixon added, "They say that President Lincoln's ghost along with a host of other ghosts still roam these hallowed halls today. Although I must admit, I still haven't run into any of them yet. People who have seen these spirits say they are friendly sorts."

Jay and I stared at each other, wide-eyed. "Oh Wow! The White House is haunted," Jay blurted out with a modicum of excitement.

Mrs. Nixon laughed, and reminded us that even though there were ghosts living with them they were friendly and not haunting anybody.

We left the Lincoln Bedroom, both secretly hoping to see Abraham Lincoln's ghost, or any other ghost for that matter. We were following Mrs. Nixon and giggling about the ghosts. For a brief moment Jay and I thought our wish of seeing a ghost was going to come true. We were so lost in the fun we were having that we didn't hear the elevator doors open behind us.

All of a sudden I felt this tap on my shoulder. I glanced over at Jay, who was staring straight ahead and asked, "Did you feel that?"

"I sure did," he answered. I continued, "When I count to three, turn around real fast. One, two, three..."

"Boo!" The president yelled. Jay and I jumped about ten feet into the air. Both Grand pop and the

President could not stop laughing. My heart was racing a mile a minute. "Thank goodness you're not the ghost," I sighed.

"So," the President said, "Mrs. Nixon has been telling you some of her ghost stories."

"Yeah," Jay said, "Have you seen Abraham Lincoln's ghost yet, Mr. President?"

"Well Jason, see that portrait of Mr. Lincoln at the end of the hall by the stairs? They say that if you watch his eyes they follow you up and down the stairs and down the hall."

"Oh man," I said, "so he could be watching us right now?"

"That's right," Grand pop said. "Now, young men, there are 32 bathrooms in this house, find one and wash up for breakfast."

Mrs. Nixon pointed down the hall and said, "Third door on the right. We will be waiting for you in the living room."

Even the bathroom was amazing. It had gold handles on the sinks and white marble basins. They were whiter that Grand mom's, if that were possible.

The wall was papered with presidential seals like the ones on our badges. We returned to the living room as a servant was announcing that breakfast was being served. We were escorted into an enormous dining room. The table alone sat over twenty people. It was magnificent. The candelabra in the center of the table was so beautiful. There were lots of flowers arranged throughout the room, making the room smell so pretty. We stood by our chairs at our appointed spots. There were gold engraved name cards at each of the five place settings. We waited until we were told to be seated by the President.

As we sat down he told us, "Pat and I usually sit at opposite ends of the table, however, for your visit today, we will make an exception to that rule and we will all sit together."

How crazy is that? I thought. I mean, they would have to yell at each other just to have a conversation. After we all sat down, Grand pop was appointed to say grace. After grace was said, President Nixon picked up a little crystal bell, which was strategically placed next to his place setting, and rang it. Two servants immediately came in and poured fresh squeezed orange juice and doled out some fresh strawberries from a large crystal bowl. A third servant appeared and asked each of us how we liked our eggs and what side dishes we wanted.

When breakfast was served, everything was done in such a professional manner. It was a great meal. We had lots of fun talking about the tour of the White House, school, and summer vacation. I told the President how I wanted to follow in my grandfather's footsteps even though I had to admit to myself I still had absolutely no clue what it was that he did when he went to work everyday.

I quietly mused to myself, "Man, how neat is that? I know some adults who have no idea where they want to work, and I know already, and I'm only thirteen years old." Grand pop and President Nixon smiled. Grand pop was smiling the broadest though.

After we had all finished eating, the President rang his crystal bell again and the plates were immediately removed and more tea and coffee was poured.

The President then announced, "Gentlemen, we have another treat for you. Your grandfather is taking you up to Capitol Hill where Vice President Agnew will be meeting you and giving you a private tour of the Capitol, including the Senate and House of Representatives, which are presently in a rare late summer session."

"Wow, the President and the Vice-President too!" Jay exclaimed.

"We promised you boys a full day of surprises," the President said, "there is still one more big surprise after that. You will have to wait until after your tour of Congress is over for that though."

Jay and I were so excited. We just could not believe it. First we met the President and the First Lady, and then we got to see the White House. I had read all about the White House, but it was so incredible to actually see it in person. Now, to top it all off we were going up to Capitol Hill to meet the Vice President of the United States. My mind could barely absorb it all. What could be bigger than all of that?

It was almost noon when we left the White House. After thanking President and Mrs. Nixon and saying goodbye, we boarded the second floor elevator and went to the sub-basement. We entered a little train station-like area where this open-air tram was waiting for us.

"This is unbelievable," I said to Jay, "The President's own subway system."

"That's right," Grand pop said, "this is one of the most secure subways in the world. It runs between here and the Capitol and other important government offices around town. It makes it much safer for the President to get around town."

We stepped in the tram and off we went for a short ride to the sub-basement of the United States Capitol. As we pulled into the station, Jay and I both recognized the person standing on the platform before us. Jay leaned in to me and whispered so that only I could hear him, "Jeez, he's a lot shorter than he looks on television." We both laughed, but immediately straightened up hoping that Vice President Agnew did not hear us.

We went through another round of formal introductions and greetings. Grand pop turned to us and said, "You guys have a good time, and behave. I'll see you later. The Nixons will be bringing you home this evening. Actually there is a very special dinner planned for the entire family. See you later boys," he called out to us as the tram car pulled away.

We just stared at Grand pop with our jaws down to our knees as the tram disappeared back into the tunnel from which it came. "Wow!" I muttered. "President and Mrs. Nixon are coming to Grand mom and Grand pop's house. How cool is that?"

Before anyone had a chance to answer, the Vice President cleared his throat and began, "Gentlemen, welcome to the Capitol, the seat of the United States government..." And so the tour began. We saw so much. Even though the Vice President stayed with us throughout the entire tour, several different guides explained the rooms and their history. I noted to myself that Mr. Agnew was not as nice or as fun as Mr. And Mrs. Nixon. The tour itself was kind of neat. Each time we went into a different room, the public was cleared out first and then we got to go in for our private tour. It was a really long tour and at times really boring. It took over two hours, but we saw and learned so much.

After the tour was over, the Vice President took us into the Senate Chamber. He explained to us his job as the leader of the Senate. He told us that whenever the Senators voted on a new law and there was a tie it was his job to break that tie. Apparently that didn't happen very often in history though. Next, he took us up to his desk positioned high above the rest of the Senate Chamber where he could oversee everybody. He let us sit in his chair. I could not help myself. I don't know what came over me. I picked up the gavel sitting on what Mr. Agnew called the dais and banged it down on the wooden block several times. The room got real quiet. The Vice President quickly grabbed it out of my hand. I could tell he wanted to yell at me but he simply said that I could not do that while Senate was in session. He even tried to look stern, but he was smiling. He announced to all present to carry on and to ignore the disruption. Everyone in the Chamber

235

laughed. The guy who seemed to be running the proceedings from a dais directly below the Vice President's gave the Junior Senator from Massachusetts an extra five minutes of time.

After spending a bit more time observing the proceedings, we came off the dais. The Junior Senator came up to us and shook my hand, smiled and said, "Thank you, young man, I was floundering around and getting nowhere. You gave me a minute to gather my thoughts and five extra minutes to explain them. Please feel free to distract me anytime. It gets a little dull around here at times."

Vice President Agnew introduced us to Senator Edward Kennedy, the Junior Senator from Massachusetts. The man needed no introduction. He was a Kennedy after all. I smiled at him and said, "Anytime you need me to help you out just call, my Grandfather has the number, he works for the President at the White House, just like I will someday."

Mr. Agnew explained to Mr. Kennedy that I was Bill Schuster's grandson. Mr. Kennedy's smile broadened as he told me what a great man my grandfather was and how much his brother, President Kennedy, had relied on my grandfather's knowledge and wisdom.

Jay and I were again rendered speechless. Man, I thought to myself, Grand pop must really be somebody special, somebody very important.

Our last stop was the floor of the House of Representatives. We walked around meeting congressmen from all over the country. My arm was so sore from shaking so many hands. I was glad when it was over. Finally, Vice President Agnew gathered us into an elevator that took us back down to the tram station. "Boys," he said, "it has been a pleasure meeting you both. Good Luck with everything and may all of your wishes come true."

We thanked him for the wonderful afternoon, and I apologized for using his gavel. He laughed and said, "Let's keep that incident between us, I don't think your grandfather or the President would have as much of a sense of humor about it as Mr. Kennedy did."

We waved goodbye as our tramcar pulled away. The guard who was escorting us back to the White

Kevin A. Carey

House barely said two words to us. We returned to the White House tram stop where Willie and Mrs. Nixon were waiting for us. "So how was your afternoon, boys?" Mrs. Nixon asked.

Jay said, "We had a great time, and Geoffrey even..."

I stopped him in mid-sentence with a good swift kick in the pants.

"Ouch!" Jay squealed.

"Boys, boys, now what are you two fighting about?"

"Oh nothing," I answered, "we're just fooling around."

"I guess boys will be boys. I wouldn't know. I only had girls."

We went up the elevator to the private living quarters. Mrs. Nixon had a plate of various cakes and glasses of cold, fresh lemonade waiting for us. The four of us, including Willie, went outside to the balcony and enjoyed the view. We all talked like we had known each other forever. After a short time a smiling President met us on the balcony. He gave Mrs.

238

Nixon a kiss on the cheek and shook our hands. He took two cakes off of the tray and put his hand with one of the cakes in it to his side. In a flash Willie was by his side gobbling up the cake. Mrs. Nixon shot him a disapproving glance, and we all laughed. Mr. Nixon was such a nice man. I truly was looking forward to the day when I would be working here in this great house.

"Where's Grand pop?" I asked.

"I sent him home early today, so that he could pickup the rest of your family to meet us for dinner later in Baltimore."

Jay was looking over the balcony rail at the parking area. "But Geoffrey, isn't that your grandfather's car still parked over there where we left it this morning?"

"Yes, it is," Mr. Nixon quickly replied. "Since we will be celebrating Geoffrey's birthday tonight I sent him home in one of my limousines. The driver will be bringing everybody in one car to the restaurant. It's a lot easier that way."

I thought a minute, being the geographical expert I considered myself to be, and asked, "Baltimore? Isn't that pretty far from here?"

"Yes, you are a very bright young man. You do know your geography, just like your grandfather said you did." He continued, "When you are President of the United States you get certain privileges." Mr. Nixon paused a minute as if he heard something off in the distance. Sure enough he had. "Here comes our ride now," he said with a smile.

Jay and I watched as a huge helicopter came into view with the presidential seal on the side. I recognized the helicopter from many of the books I had read about the presidency. It was "Marine One," the President's helicopter and it landed on the lawn right in front of us.

"Our chariot awaits," the President quipped.

I could tell by the expression on Jay's face that he was thinking the same thing I was. I think we both spent the whole day in a perpetual state of awe and shock. We finally snapped out of it and tried to compose ourselves. A servant appeared out of nowhere and took our glasses and the tray of cakes. Rudi was waiting for us at the elevator bank. He escorted us downstairs. We exited through these huge glass doors into the Rose Garden. It was so incredibly beautiful. As we walked towards the helicopter, there were several reporters behind a rope and they were shouting all kinds of questions at the President. Many of the questions seemed, at least to me, to be really mean. President Nixon completely ignored those stupid reporters, telling us not to pay any attention to them, that they didn't know what they were talking about. Without another word, we all boarded the helicopter and yet another marine helped us into our seats and made sure our safety belts were securely fastened. We were then each fitted with a headset and microphone. The marine explained that the noise from the blades of the helicopter was very loud and this was how we could talk with each other. After everyone was comfortably strapped into his or her seats and headsets securely in place, the helicopter lifted off. The view from the air was magnificent. Mr. Nixon commented to us, "This view never ceases to amaze me. Isn't it beautiful? It is like poetry in motion. Mr. Sparks, I'd like you to give Geoff and Jason the VIP helicopter tour of Washington, D.C."

"Yes, Sir, Mr. President," the pilot replied. He took over the intercom system and showed us Washington D.C. and its surrounding area from the air, replete with all of its splendor and history. About an hour later we landed at a small heliport on the water's edge of Baltimore's Inner Harbor. The presidential limousine was waiting for us. There were several other cars filled with, as we learned later, Secret Service Agents. They seemed to be everywhere. The President said, "Don't let all of these Secret Service Agents bother you. Being the President, one can never be too careful. He began to laugh and confided, "especially in today's political climate."

We arrived at "Schaeffer's Seafood House", a well-known seafood restaurant in Baltimore's Inner Harbor. Another presidential limousine was parked out front of the restaurant. The President said, "Everyone else must be here already."

I noted that there were no other cars in the parking lot. I asked, "Where are all of the cars? Two weeks ago when Grand mom and Grand pop and I were here this place was packed. I was told that this place is always packed."

Mrs. Nixon said, "Whenever the President goes out for dinner the Secret Service closes the restaurant to the public. It is for the President's protection, and the service is so much better."

Jay looked at me in astonishment and said, "Can you believe it? They closed the whole restaurant just for you. I mean, it is your birthday."

"No you silly head," I said, "they closed it because the President is here. He's the important one." Then I whacked Jay in the head. He whacked me back. It was pretty embarrassing when the President came up from behind us and grabbed us both by our shoulders and told us to behave or else he was going to have to report it to my grandfather. We both sheepishly apologized and pleaded with him not to do that. He smiled and said, "Both apologies are accepted. Your grandfather does not need to know a thing. Does he?"

Kevin A. Carey

"No," we both replied in unison. We proceeded into the restaurant. As we made our way into the dining room, everyone stood up and began singing a rousing chorus of "Happy Birthday," President Nixon put his arm around me and said, "Happy Birthday, Geoffrey." Although I was red as a beet, I was on top of the world.

Mom came over to me and gave me a big hug. "How was your day?"

Before either Jay or I could open our mouths President Nixon said, "I believe these two young men had a terrific time today. Didn't you boys?"

"We sure did!" I said.

"Well isn't this the perfect ending to a perfect day?" Mrs. Nixon smiled.

President Nixon said to Mom, "Mrs. Brooks, you should be proud of these fine young men. I must compliment you, your husband and Jason's parents on how well these boys have been raised. Please send my best regards to Jason's mother and father, as well."

"Thank you, ah, very much, ah, Mr. President. I will, ah, make it a point to call Shelly. Ah, that's

Jason's mother. I'll, ah, call her first thing in the morning. Or should I, ah, do it when we get home tonight?" Mom was blushing and stuttering. I saw a nasty look pass between her and Grand pop. She instantly straightened herself out, stopped stuttering and said, "I am very proud of both of them. Please allow me to introduce you to the rest of my family."

Introductions were made all around. Of course Grand mom and Grand pop knew the Nixons very well. I overheard Grand mom say to Mrs. Nixon, "Hi Pat, it's been too long."

"Yes, I know, Emma, but my duties as the First Lady keep me quite busy these days. I am planning a luncheon at the White House next month. I do hope you will be able to attend."

My grandmother replied, "I would be honored."

We all sat down to a wonderful dinner. I got to have my favorite, steamed lobster. It was served with clarified butter; a piping hot double stuffed baked potato and broccoli. The meal was terrific, and Mrs. Nixon was right, the service was impeccable. Glasses were never empty and the table never cluttered.

After dinner was over the headwaiter brought out my favorite cake, German chocolate and all sang another chorus of "Happy Birthday". I looked over and saw the president make a gesture to one of the Secret Service Agents posted at the front door of the restaurant. The Agent came over to Mr. Nixon and handed him a small package. Both he and Mrs. Nixon stood up and presented me with that package.

President Nixon said, "On behalf of Mrs. Nixon and myself, we would like to wish you a very happy birthday and much success in the wonderful and adventurous life you have ahead of you. No matter what your career goals are, whether it be following in your grandfather's footsteps or being a teacher, it doesn't matter what it is. This goes for all you boys and girls. Always remember, even though we might think the next kid is smarter than we are, studying and hard work makes the difference." He then presented me with the small, elegantly wrapped gift.

Everyone applauded and the evening was over. We said our goodbyes. Both President and Mrs. Nixon hugged Jay and me and wished us both well. "Keep fighting," Mr. Nixon said to all of us as they left the restaurant. Minutes later we heard the loud noise of helicopter blades as "Marine One" whirled by overhead on its way back to the White House.

I could not wait to open my gift. I carefully took the wrapping paper off and opened the pretty blue velvet box. Inside was a hand carved penknife. The inscription on the blade simply read, "United States Senate." How apropos, I thought, especially after the debacle I had caused earlier in the Senate chamber. Grand pop explained that the penknife was a special limited edition piece made for each of the one hundred members of the United States Senate. He told us that only one hundred and twenty-five were made and that I was one of the lucky twenty-five non-senators to receive such a special gift. He said, jealously, that he didn't even own one. Then he pulled out another velvet box identical to the one I had just received and presented it to Jay. "The President wanted you to have one also as a small token of your visit."

"Wow," I said, "matching penknives." I then turned to Grand pop and with a smile and tears in my eyes, said, "I promise I will cherish it forever."

"Me too," Jay added as he stared down at the treasured gift.

When we got outside there was a long line of people waiting for the restaurant to reopen to the public. A private stretch limousine into which we all piled in, with plenty of room to spare replaced the presidential limousine, which brought the rest of the family to the restaurant.

I still reminisce often about that summer. It was so special. The penknife was now proudly displayed in a small shadow box on the mantle above the fireplace. I went over to it, as I often did, and opened up the blade. United States Senate - how appropriate. Amazingly, Senator Kennedy still remembered the incident on the dais some ten years later. We met briefly at a national security hearing a couple of months ago. He was a member of the investigating panel. I was sent to observe and see what I could learn. After the proceedings were over for the day I approached Senator Kennedy and reintroduced myself. He began to laugh before I could finish. He said, "How could I ever forget you. You saved my ass that day." After glancing down at my credentials, which were dangling from around my neck, he said, "So you've done it. You've made your dreams come true. Congratulations. Wouldn't it be great if all of America's youth could be motivated by someone to make their dreams come true?"

My keen sense of perception, which I had so diligently been developing and honing over the past several years, told me that he was cooking up some crazy political scheme in his head, and he had decided that I was going to be his poster boy. I stopped him and reminded him that, as my credentials indicated, I was a National Security Agency Trainee, and as such no publicity of any kind was allowed.

Ted Kennedy was right though. I had made it. I was working for the National Security Agency just like my grandfather had, and I was genuinely happy. There was no doubt I had worked very hard for this, shed a lot of tears and even some blood. Was it all worth it? Yes! Of that I had absolutely no doubt. I placed the penknife back in its place of honor in the shadow box on the mantle and closed the photo album. I carefully placed the album back in the box with the previous album to be savored another time.

CHAPTER ELEVEN

I opened the final volume of pictures of "My Summer in Washington, D.C." Instead of flying back home I went back with the rest of the family. The ride home, although under four hours, felt like four days. We were a weary bunch of travelers by the time we pulled into Jay's driveway. As tired as we were, however, Jay and I were riding high and itching to tell all of our other friends about our day with the President and Vice President of the United States of America. We had not stopped talking about it since that incredible day. I think Mom, Dad, Natalie and Ben were getting sick of hearing the same stories over and over again. Each time the stories seemed to become grander and grander. Somehow one of the stories evolved to the point where Jay and I had actually seen President Lincoln's ghost. Of course we had not, but it made for a great story.

The story about how I single handedly stopped the governmental process for even the briefest of moments did not remain a secret for long, thanks to my best

251

friend. He told everybody before we got home from dinner with the President that night. Luckily everyone, including Grand pop, laughed about it. The next day, in fact, Grand pop came home from work with all kinds of stories that were circulating around the floor of the United States Senate, about how Geoffrey Brooks stopped the governmental wheels from turning for the first time in one hundred and ninety-four years.

About half way home, Mom called Shelly to give her our estimated time of arrival. Shelly spared Mom from having to prepare a meal when we got home by inviting us all over for an informal barbecue. Once we were at Jay's house he and I completely monopolized the conversation. Finally Ben had had enough and yelled, "Haven't we heard enough! It's not like you're the first person to ever visit the White House, tons of people do it everyday."

"That's not nice," Mom scolded Ben.

"But Mom, the two of them haven't shut up since last week and I'm sick of it!" Ben retorted.

I yelled back, "You're just jealous because you didn't get to go!"

"I am not," Ben shouted, "Besides, who wants to visit the White House, only brown nosing faggoty boy scouts do that."

There was complete silence as Mom got up from the table and grabbed Ben by the scruff of his neck and dragged him to the back of the yard where a rather heated discussion ensued. When they finally returned to the table, Mom said, "It's been a long day and everybody is tired. Thank you for a wonderful evening, Shelly, but I think it's time for these kids to get some sleep."

"Yes," Shelly said, "I think you're right. Geoffrey, will you be joining us at the pool tomorrow?"

I looked at Mom before I answered to make sure it was all right. Without me having to say a single word, Mom said, "Of course you can go."

"And," Mrs. Scott added with a knowing smile, "your little friend, Sharon, keeps asking Mr. Scott and me when you will be returning."

As I turned ten shades of red Jay and Ben started singing, "Geoffrey and Sharon sitting in a tree, K-I-S-S-I-N-G…"

"Shut up!" I yelled.

Dad finally intervened and said, "I think it's time to go."

Mom started to gather plates and stuff, but Shelly grabbed her arm telling her to leave it, that she would take care of it after we left. We all piled back into the station wagon minus Jay. I rolled my window down to say goodbye. Coach peered into the open window and said, "See you tomorrow morning at the usual time. Won't it be fun getting back to the usual routine and seeing your friends again?"

Jesus Christ, the man was relentless. I knew it was all too good to be true. Vacation truly was over. I gave a sort of half smile and waved as we pulled away.

*****

I had a very restless night knowing what the day was probably going to bring. Even Mr. Rabbit, who had been hidden away the whole two weeks Jay and I were together, could not serve as much of a source of comfort. I tossed and turned and had that same nightmare over and over again. At one point during the night I even woke up in a cold sweat. Thankfully Mom and Dad did not hear me and make a fuss.

Like clockwork, at precisely 8:30, Coach pulled up in the driveway and honked his horn. Mom handed me my backpack and I made my way out to the car.

"Good morning, Geoffrey," Coach said as I got into the front seat and buckled myself in.

"Good morning, Coach," I wearily said.

As we drove away Coach reached over and started to rub his hands up and down my leg. My whole body jerked when he touched me. I knew what I had to do, so I put on my best happy face and let him stroke my leg.

"It's been a long time. I hope you haven't forgotten everything I've taught you."

I smiled and agreed with everything he said. I assured him that no, I hadn't forgotten a thing.

"Good boy," he sneered.

He took his hand off of my leg when we pulled into the driveway. Even though I was not at all looking forward to what was about to happen with Coach I was excited about being intimate with Jay. Yes, it had been too long. Even though we had slept in the same bed while visiting Grand mom and Grand pop nothing ever even came close to happening.

We walked into the living room where Jay was watching TV and waiting for us. I said hello to him and he said hello back. Without a word or a command or anything, we made our way upstairs where Coach was already laying down some old sheets he had taken from the back of the closet. After he was done covering the bed, he came over to us and as usual, he took off all of our clothes. Seeing Jay naked always made my penis get an erection, however I was no longer embarrassed. After we were both completely naked, Coach proceeded to take all of his clothes off.

"Geoffrey," Coach snickered, "you should go first this time."

Before I had a chance to lie down on the bed, Coach picked me up and threw me down on the sheets that he laid on top of the bedspread. In the blink of an eye his penis went up inside of my butt. Before I had a chance to get out of my body, I felt a tinge of excruciating pain piercing throughout. I finally retreated to the ceiling, where I waited for Jay to join me.

"Boy, is he mad at you!" Jay said when he finally floated up to me.

"Why do you think that?" I asked.

"Weren't you paying attention?"

"Fuck no," I said, "Why do you think I escape up here?"

Jay couldn't argue with that one. He said, "Okay, anyway he is really pissed off at you for intentionally going away for so long. He said that he was forced to halt lessons and now we are behind and how are we supposed to learn anything if you deliberately go away for long periods of time."

"No offense, Jay, but your father is fucking nuts!"

"Tell me something I don't already know," he said.

It was again lesson time so Jay and I returned to our bodies. Jay was right; Coach seemed awfully pissed that I took an extra long vacation. Like I had a choice! Give me a fucking break.

Coach expressed his anger in the lesson he was trying to teach us. "Today's lesson," he announced, "is how to discipline your girl when she disobeys you. This is done by slapping her on the butt not too hard and not too soft, but just enough for her to get the point, and then screwing her without the usual foreplay that I taught you. This leaves no marks and really humiliates her."

Holy shit. It sounded so gross and disgusting. Did he ever do that to Shelly? I wondered. The twist to this lesson was that Coach was the one who spanked each of our butts really hard and then Jay and I had to fuck each other. Our lesson for the day ended with Coach ejaculating in our underwear as usual. We quickly got dressed. Coach stood there and laughed and laughed and said, "It's so good to see you again, Geoffrey. We've missed the pleasure of your company." He then turned his head in Jay's direction and said, "Haven't we, son?"

Jay sheepishly bobbed his head up and down and said, "Yes, Geoffrey we missed you."

"Oh and Geoffrey, if you or your family ever try to take my boy away from me again even for a little while, you will all have me to deal with."

Coach dismissed us and we ran down the stairs and out of the house. We headed straight to our secret hiding place in the park without a word passing between us.

Jay was much more agitated than usual. Once we were safely inside the cave he started yelling, "Who the fuck does he think he is? Telling you how to run your life. I tell you, I'm going to kill him someday. I just won't be able to help myself."

"I know you're upset, Jay," I said as I tried to calm him down, "but if you did that you'd get caught and they'd put you in jail. You remember what that asshole said? No one would ever believe us and they would take us away from our friends and family forever. You don't want that to happen, now do you?"

"No, I know, you're right," Jay agreed.

In solemn silence we burned our underpants, put the fire out and headed back to the house for our ride to the pool. When we got back to the house, Coach was waiting for us in the car. It was as if nothing had happened less than an hour before. Coach was his old self again. It was so unbelievable.

We picked up Shelly at the beauty parlor. When we got to the pool Sharon was waiting for us by the front gate. When she saw the Scotts' car she started madly waving her arms back and forth desperately trying to get my attention. Coach could not stop laughing. "It looks like someone has an admirer," he said, winking back at me. I could not believe it. He pulled right up next to her, rolled down his window and gave her the same wink he had just given me.

"Hello Mr. and Mrs. Scott. Hi Jason. Hi Geoffrey," she said, full of a lot of nervous energy. "Geoffrey, why didn't you call me when you got home yesterday?"

I hated it when she made me feel guilty, no matter how trivial it was. I lowered my head and said, "Oh you know, we got home late and then my mom got on the phone and talked forever with God knows who about God knows what. I really did want to call you. I hope you understand?"

"You know I do," she said. "I just missed you, that's all."

I turned four shades of red when Mrs. Scott commented, "Oh, how sweet."

Jay saved the day when he grabbed my arm, pulled me out of the car with our backpacks in tow. "Come on Geoff, let's get into our swim suits so we can play water basketball with the other guys." I thoroughly hated water basketball. Some of those guys could be so rough and so mean. If that were what it was going to take to stay away from Sharon for even a little while then I would gladly play.

When Jay and I walked out of the locker room Sharon and her girlfriends were waiting and ambushed us. "Girls," Sharon announced, "This is the cute guy I've been telling you about all summer. Some of you, of course, remember him from last summer. This is my boyfriend, Geoffrey. He is so wonderful. Why he and Jason got to spend a whole day with the President of the United States and they even got to go for a ride in his helicopter."

Oh great, I thought, now she's going to tell everyone all about my business. Why doesn't she just get the letter I wrote her about it and read it out loud to all of them!

"Oh Geoff," one of the other girls said as she grabbed my arm, "tell us all about it!"

The look on Sharon's face was priceless. If looks could kill this girl would have been dead. Jay thankfully once again saved the day. "Come on," he said, "We need another person for water basketball. The sides are uneven."

I turned back to Sharon and promised her that I would be over later to race her and tell her all about my trip. Even though I had written her all about it she was still insisting that I fill her in on every last detail. As I walked away from the group of girls, I heard Sharon growl at the girl who grabbed my arm. She snarled, "If you ever touch my boyfriend like that again, I'll rip your head off." Boy, was I glad to be out of there. Even though I hated water basketball, and some of the guys were real jerks, I played longer than usual just so I could avoid Sharon and her friends as long as possible. The game finally broke up a little over an hour later. Sharon, who had elected herself head cheerleader for the game, met me at the edge of the pool. "Geoffrey, you were great. You were so much better than the rest of those bullies!"

"Thanks," I replied. When I looked over to the grassy area where everyone laid out their towels to get some sun, I noticed a boy whom I had not seen before sitting by himself and reading a book. I walked over to where he was sitting and introduced myself, "Hi, my name is Geoffrey Brooks. Are you new here? I've never seen you here before."

"Hi," he said, "my name is Kurt Lewis, and it's you who appears to be new here."

"Oh yeah," I said feeling a bit embarrassed. "I've been on vacation in Washington D.C. for the past seven weeks."

"So," Kurt said, "I noticed you playing basketball in the pool. You're pretty good."

"Thanks. I really don't like the game that much, but the sides were uneven. So what are you reading? If you don't mind me asking?"

Kurt smiled and said, "No, no, not at all. It is a book about the life of Jean Harlow. She is my absolute favorite movie actress of all time. My second favorite is Norma Shearer. Do you like old movies?"

"I'm not a big movie fan," I admitted. "I like to read about foreign places and then pretend in my mind that I go to those places. It's so much fun."

"That sounds so romantic in a way," Kurt said adding, "My dream is to go to Hollywood so I can see where all the classic movies were made and where all the famous movie stars live."

"That sounds so glamorous," I replied. It felt so good to talk to someone who really seemed interested in things other than sports and girls. I really wanted to get to know this guy better, however, before I had a chance to say anything Sharon barked at me and grabbed my arm pulling me away, "Come on," she said, sounding somewhat annoyed, "the racing is about to get started and we need you."

I looked back at Kurt as I was being dragged away and yelled to him, "Come and join us, it'll be fun."

"No thanks," he said, "it looks like you have your hands full with your girlfriend. It was nice to meet you Geoffrey. Talk to you later."

God, how I longed to stay and talk with him. "It was a pleasure," I shouted back so he could hear me. "I'll talk to you later."

Once we were out of earshot of Kurt, Sharon decided it was time to read me the riot act. "What is your problem? You've been acting strange all day. First with that little bitch, Samantha, and now you're talking to that creepy guy. Nobody likes him, you know. They say he stares at the boys all the time. Johnny says he's a faggot. You'd better not get too close to him in case, you know, it rubs off or something."

"Oh Sharon," I said, "don't be ridiculous. He seemed like a perfectly nice guy."

She retorted, "I'm serious, if I see you talking to him again, I'll break up with you! Now, I talked to my mother this morning and asked her if you and Jason and Lisa could come over next Saturday for a camp out in the backyard. She said that it would be fine if it's okay with you guys, and your parents of course. I already talked to Jason and his mom and dad while you were talking with that jerk, and everything is cool. Jason said he would come if you were going. So what do you say?"

Jesus Christ, I thought to myself. Now she is planning my life. I didn't want to go, but I knew that would cause more grieve than it was worth. "Okay," I said resignedly, "if it's not a problem with my parents." In Sharon's mind the issue was settled and next Saturday was a definite. Right now, however, I had other things on my mind, like Kurt. Was he gay like Sharon said he was? And, how could I find out without causing a scene? If Sharon got angry enough and broke up with me over a guy everyone perceived as being gay I would be in big trouble, especially with Jay and Coach, even if he weren't. The debate waged on inside of my head. But what if he's gay? God, what must he think of me? Water basketball, racing, and girls. I'm sure he's already got the wrong impression. But what are my choices? How do I let him know how I really feel without alarming everyone else? And then there was always the question, What if I'm wrong? What if everybody's wrong? What if he is straight and just being friendly? I had never felt so alone and so confused before. Although it probably was not the right thing to do, I made the decision to play it safe for now and to leave well enough alone where Kurt was concerned.

When we were far enough away from where Kurt was sitting Sharon looked into my eyes and asked rhetorically, "Do you truly want to be my boyfriend? If you will recall in my last letter to you in Washington D.C. I told you that if I were going to be your girlfriend we would have to act like boyfriend and girlfriend and hold hands. I want you to kiss me and treat me like a lady. No more of this elementary school bullshit!"

I felt like I had just been slapped hard across my face. I saw everything I had worked so hard to create crumbling before my very eyes. As the panic built up inside of me I decided first to play her game, no matter how painful it would be, and second, to get this kissing thing out of the way. Not for Sharon's sake, but for

Jay's sake, so that he could see for himself that I meant business with Sharon and that I was not gay. I thought about it a minute. This will be easier than I thought. The plan was perfect. As long as Kurt stays right where he is, we can go behind the locker rooms at the other end of the pool. This way all of Sharon's and my friends, including Jay, could watch and we could pretend that we thought we were hidden enough so that no one could see us. I grabbed Sharon by her waist and told her that I had a big surprise for her. She looked at me and smiled and said, "Ohhh Geoffrey. You're so big and strong. Where are we going you big brut?"

The girl talks too much. I just had to keep my cool and all of this nonsense would be over soon enough. I took her to the spot behind the locker room. I waited a couple of seconds for the troops to get into position for a peek, pretending, of course, that I had no clue that Sharon and I were not alone. Sharon was smiling at me and shaking with apparent anticipation. I took a deep breath and leaned in and kissed her. It was very awkward at first. Her metal braces cut my upper lip and drew blood but I kept kissing her as if I felt nothing. In between breaths she tried to apologize, but I would not give her that chance. I drew from Coach's lessons and kissed her like she had never been kissed before. It was even overwhelming for me. When I finally let her go she gasped and asked, "Wow, where did you learn how to do that?"

With a smug look on my face I simply said, "I guess it's a guy thing, it just comes naturally."

Sharon had this great big smile on her face and although she was trembling like I had never seen before, she enthusiastically exclaimed, "Well, it was great! Let's do it again."

Although I had accomplished my goal I kissed her again and put up with the cut lip. The entire time I allowed my mind to wonder away from Sharon and fantasized that I was kissing Kurt. Although I had plenty of experience kissing Jay I knew that kissing Kurt would be somehow different. Kurt would return the passion, unlike Jay who couldn't wait for it to be over.

When Sharon and I finally made our way back to the pool hand in hand, as she had requested, everyone turned their heads and went about their business as if they had not been intently watching us. I'm sure they were all jealous. I looked around and didn't see Kurt anywhere. That was a good sign. I hoped and prayed that he was unaware of the madness I had just perpetrated to save my reputation. I walked over to the concession stand to get some ice for my now throbbing lip. There he was in the line next to mine. Our eyes met briefly, and it was obvious in that instant, at least to me, that he knew who I really was and how I really felt. His eyes pierced right through my heart and into my soul. When he was right next to me he leaned in to me and said, "I saw that ridiculous little show you put on for your so-called friends. Just remember you can't fool everybody. I feel so sorry for you. I hope that someday you will accept who you are and learn how to be yourself, your true self." With that, he purchased his drink and disappeared from my life forever. Rumor had it that his father was transferred back to Dallas. The only memory I have of him was a snapshot I had taken of him earlier that day, completely unaware at the time of the impact he would have on my life. I learned a lot about myself that day. Now there was no doubt in my mind about who or what I was. The problem was that I knew that I could never be as vocal and open about as Kurt was. I was being forced by my family and friends to live a life of lies and deceit. I sat at the edge of the pool, holding a towel full of ice cubes to my fat lip and openly wept for the person I could never be.

CHAPTER TWELVE

I turned the page of the photo album to the pictures from Sharon's camp out. Of course Mom and Dad said yes. However, in the end nobody else but me showed up. Jay called earlier in the day apologizing that something very important had come up and not to worry that it had nothing to do with his father. Sharon's best friend, Lisa, also canceled at the last minute. I knew that Sharon was looking forward to this little backyard adventure all week so when she called me to see what I was doing, I told her that I would definitely be there and that I wouldn't miss it for the world. She sounded so happy over the phone. Thinking back now on the whole incident I would bet that I was set up. I suppose that was not so terrible. Sharon was actually a lot of fun to be with, even though, putting it mildly, she was a bit too bossy. She was always trying to persuade all the guys to race against her in the pool. After a while most of the guys would turn her down, not because she was a girl, but because they knew she would beat them. Sharon had big plans to not only be on the swim team at school but to be the captain. Her mother, on the other hand, was not so keen on the whole swimming thing. I vividly remember that one day at the pool she said to Sharon, "Why can't you be like the other girls and spend the day getting a nice tan?" Sharon looked at her mother like she had two heads and yelled, "No way, I'm not like the rest of those girls." I tried not to laugh as Sharon defiantly turned her back on her mother and stormed away in a huff.

The mini camp out turned out to be a lot of fun. Mom spent all morning packing my stuff. I couldn't believe all the shit she was packing into my little backpack and duffle bag which Grand mom had bought me in Washington to carry home all of the extra stuff I had accumulated during my stay there. "But it's only going to be for one night," I protested.

"I want you to be prepared," she responded.

"Prepared for what?" I asked.

"You just never know. Now please go and make sure the back of the station wagon is cleaned out so that we can put your camping gear in it."

When we pulled up in front of Sharon's house, she and her father were working in the garden pulling up weeds. "Hi Geoffrey," Sharon called out excitedly. I jumped out of the car and went over and gave her a hug. Her father stopped what he was doing, took off his gardening gloves, and walked over to the car and graciously helped Mom out of the front seat. "Good afternoon Jeannie," he said, "Long time no see. How are you doing? I heard from my little girl here that you had a terrific vacation."

"Yes, thank you. It was wonderful and quite spectacular. Geoffrey really got to see and do a lot of fascinating things." Mom then turned to me and said, "Let's get your gear out of the car. I can't really stay today. I have so much to do before the sun goes down."

Sharon and I started pulling all of the stuff Mom had packed from the back of the station wagon. Even she could not believe how much shit there was. "It's only one night, not a week!" Sharon quipped.

"I know. I know," I laughed, "I told Mom that exact same thing."

"Okay, let's get this stuff in the backyard," she chuckled, appointing herself camp counselor. I almost had to run to keep up with her as she led the way to our designated campsite that was situated in the back of her very spacious backyard.

When we came around the corner to the backyard I stared in wide-eyed amazement. "Wow," I said, "I didn't know you had a built-in pool, and it's huge. Why do you even bother going to the club?"

"Because all of my girlfriends and you are there, silly," she smiled.

Trying to be nice, but being more interested in the pool I said, "That's so sweet, but do you get to use it much?"

"Oh yes. I'm out here every single morning, except when it rains of course. I told you. I am going to be an Olympic champion some day and win a gold metal or two."

The scary thing about that statement was that she meant every word of it. We set all my stuff down and walked back around to the front of the house to say good-bye to Mom and to get a few more loose items.

Mom was talking to Sharon's parent's non-stop. I finally got a chance to cut in on the conversation to ask her if she had packed my swimsuit, because I had no idea just what she had packed. Still in mid-sentence she turned to me and said, "It's at the very bottom of your backpack," then she went back and completed whatever she was saying before I cut in.

Mom finally said her goodbyes, set a time to be back tomorrow to pick me up and then she started in on me, "Mind your manners, and…" Before she could say another word I cut her off and told her not to worry about a thing. She actually left without barking out another order.

Sharon took a hold of my hand, "Okay Geoff, let's get your tent put up. Now, Dad said we can't start a bonfire, but later on, after dinner, we can use the hot coals from the grill to roast marshmallows and make smoores." We finished making camp. I clicked yet another picture. We were having a good time. It was nice to be with Sharon without having to look over my shoulder.

Everyone in the yard suddenly stopped what they were doing trying to figure out what the incredibly loud music coming down the street was all about. Sharon gasped, "Aunt Addie?" Sure enough, coming down the street, headed right for us was a bright fire engine red Mercedes convertible with a woman behind the wheel wearing a faded wedding dress. In one fluid motion she screeched to a halt, turned off the radio, shut off the engine, and gracefully climbed out of the car, maneuvering this wedding dress with a long train like it was no big deal. Sharon and her parents had the strangest looks on their faces. They were expressions that ranged from shock to horror to surprise to mild amusement. Everyone was speechless as they watched Aunt Addie gracefully make her way up the driveway. I quickly decided that this was one opportunity I could not let pass me by. I got my camera ready. Aunt Addie looked at me smiled and struck several poses while I clicked off about five pictures. Then she grimaced, turned around and began to cry. She sobbed, "Today is my tenth wedding anniversary and Paul was called out of town on business again. Every single year, on our anniversary, he gets called out of town and I am to spend the day *and* the night alone. Don't you find this business trip nonsense on our anniversary kind of strange? I know I do."

"You are so right Addie, there is no reason why you should be alone today or tonight," Sharon's mom said, obviously going out of her way to avoid Aunt Addie's personal marital issues. Sharon's mom continued, "Sharon and her friend, Geoffrey, are having a camp out in the backyard. Why don't you join in the festivities?"

Sharon eagerly said, "After dinner dad is going to let us roast marshmallows and make smoores over the coals of the grill. I wanted to build a bonfire, you know, to make it like a real camp out, but Mom insisted that it would be a fire hazard and she didn't want to be responsible for burning down the neighborhood."

"Now that sounds like fun, but I'm not quite dressed for the occasion," Aunt Addie said, wiping the tears from her eyes. She reached into the passenger seat of the car and pulled out a half empty bottle of champagne. Sharon's mother almost tackled Aunt Addie, grabbing the bottle from her hands. "There are children here, Addie. Think about the impression you are making on them. I don't think it's a very good one. Let's get you upstairs and out of that dress while Sharon brews up a fresh pot of coffee. I'm sure I have something for you to wear."

"Geoffrey," Sharon said, "why don't you change into your swim suit so we can race in the pool? Aunt Addie can be the judge."

Fifteen minutes later, Aunt Addie was sitting by the pool with a hot cup of coffee ready to judge the swim races. We swam six very close races. I was so worn out. The score was tied at three wins each. I kinda thought that I had won at least one of the races Aunt Addie claimed I had lost and Aunt Addie was being biased, but it made no sense to argue about it. Sharon was now insisting on one more last race to see who was the best. Being the nice guy that I am I let her win, but only by a little bit. Of course she gloated about it the rest of the day.

One thing about Sharon, she had more energy than anyone I knew. We had barely dried off when she announced that it was time to play croquet. She recruited both of her parents and Aunt Addie. She approached the game with the same vigor and seriousness that she did everything in her life. Aunt Addie, on the other hand, preferred a much more relaxed game and appeared to be getting annoyed at Sharon's constant outbursts. Whenever anyone's ball did not go where Sharon thought it should she would correct that person by showing them the proper technique. Everyone tried to keep their cool. Sharon's mother constantly reminded her that it was only a game. Sharon, of course, paid no attention whatsoever and continued to shout out pointers when she felt they were needed. The croquet game, thankfully, was cut short by an unexpected rainstorm. It came from out of nowhere, and in a matter of minutes tiny raindrops turned into a heavy downpour. Everyone scattered in all directions. Sharon's parents ran about the yard cleaning things up while Aunt Addie raced to put the top up on her car. Sharon and I put all of the now soaking wet camping gear in the garage. The tent appeared to have gotten the worst of it. It was going to take forever for it to dry. That gross wet canvasy smell was already permeating the garage.

We spent the remainder of the day and evening playing monopoly and other assorted board games. It really was a lot of fun. I spent the night in the guest bedroom. It definitely beat sleeping outside on the ground in a damp, smelly tent. Whenever I was with Sharon I had a good time. It, however was not what I craved in life. I knew exactly what I wanted, even at the tender age of thirteen. First and foremost was to work for the United States government using my language skills. The second thing I wanted from life was to be myself. The reality was that if I were to choose the life that I so desperately wanted I would have to forever hide who I really was. As the summer drew to a close I made the decision to sell my soul, my very being, to the devil for what I believed to be a glamorous life, which I as yet, truly did not understand.

*****

The new school year had begun and Jay was already insisting that we go to the school dances which were held every other Friday night. My father offered to drive us to them. He even offered to pick up Sharon who lived some twenty minutes away. He was really pushing hard for me to have a girlfriend. Inside I truly resented him for it, although outwardly I pretended that it was okay. The other thing Jay was insisting on was that we try out for the basketball team together. As much as I cared for him and wanted to be with him, there was no way I was going to play basketball. My grandfather was even insisting that I be on a team in the winter term and the spring term. Because I knew that I had to keep my grandfather appeased, I finally opted for wrestling. I actually enjoyed it once I got into it.

My grandfather also intervened on my behalf when it came to course selection. He insisted that I take two languages and that I be advanced one year in mathematics and in science. My guidance counselor was skeptical to say the least, considering my performance the year before. My grandfather, however, would not take no for an answer and went right to Mr. Strand, the superintendent of the school district. I got the classes he wanted me to take. They were challenging, but I was on a mission. The rest of my friends who were my age, were talking about experimenting with their sexuality. They yakked incessantly about their supposed conquests with this chick or that chick. I, on the other hand, had already experienced many facets of sex. I had knowledge far beyond my thirteen years. It made it very difficult to interact with guys and girls my age. I felt more comfortable around adults than I did around my own friends. At least I had Sharon as my shadow, which kept the guys at bay.

My grandfather saw to it that I excelled in all of my classes. He continued to supply me with Department of Defense language materials. Of course, he always made me promise not to tell a single soul about the tapes. He didn't have a thing to worry about. I was a real pro at keeping secrets.

I struggled with the advanced algebra class I was taking. I pleaded with my grandfather to take me out of the class. "Put me in something I can handle. I hate math." He told me that it was important to be challenged; that life was full of challenges. He then went out and hired a private math tutor to work with me three evenings a week. Ronnie Grant was his name. He was a senior and a really cool guy, and really good looking too. I enjoyed listening to him explain math problems. His voice was so easy to listen to. He gave me that tingling feeling all over, although I knew I had to continue to hide that. It wasn't long before I was excelling at math.

I was busy all the time. I had wrestling practice everyday after school except Fridays. Ronnie came over to the house to tutor me three nights a week. To add to all that, Grand pop arrived out of the blue one day, with a guitar in hand. He gave it to me with free lessons. Although I strongly objected, telling him I had no time, I started taking guitar lessons. He said, "Geoffrey, you need to be well rounded. You need to get involved in as much as you can. It's good for the mind and soul."

I had very little free time to spend with my friends. I hardly even had time to relax. I guess it wasn't such a bad deal. When I wasn't studying or practicing I was still always thinking about Coach and the pain. As hard as I tried, I couldn't get it out of my mind. I also could not stop thinking about Jay and my love for him. I just wanted to be with him all the time, even though I knew full well that he did not feel the same way about me.

I continued to see Sharon about every other week and talked with her on the phone almost every day. As promised, Dad played chaperone and he picked her up before every school dance.

Jay had a new girlfriend every couple of weeks. My dad would pick up one girl one week, another the following week and yet another the week after that. None of their names were worth remembering, because they were in and out of Jay's life like a revolving door. He never seemed to be satisfied with any of the girls he was going out with. "All the girls in this school are so immature," he would complain to me. I remember one incident in particular. He asked Sandy (the girl of the week, as I liked to call them) if he could touch her

285

breasts. She got mad at him and slapped him right across the face. "Jesus Christ!" he yelled at me. "When are these girls ever going to grow up? I can't wait to show them what real sex is."

"God Jay," I stated in a disgusted tone, "you are just like the rest of them, only worse. A little knowledge can be dangerous."

With so much going on the school year flew by. The days seemed to blend into one another. I managed to finish the school year at the top of my class. I also had an undefeated wrestling record. I put my all into everything I did. I should have been on top of the world, however I was miserable. Throughout the school year Coach continued to order Jay's and my presence for his "lessons." My hatred for him grew deeper and deeper each time he forced himself upon me. The bastard lied to me from the very beginning. He promised that the pain would not be so bad "the next time." Of course the intensity of the pain never subsided. The saving grace to it all was that I was able to disconnect from the pain each time he abused me. I had to try with every ounce of my being to hide that pain. I succeeded quite well in doing that.

The simple feelings of joy and happiness which I felt each time Jay and I were forced to perform sexual acts on each other, although quite perverse from an outsider's point of view, brought me great satisfaction. Of course, I could never share my real feelings with anyone. There was no one who would have understood. I didn't need advice; I just needed someone to listen to me and to truly love me.

My only other close friend was Sharon. Even though I had trouble dealing with her being my girlfriend, she had become a fast friend and I felt safe talking to her. One night about a month before school let out I finally got up enough courage to tell her my true feelings, thereby risking destroying the illusion I had so carefully built over the past several years. I told her that as much as I cared for her it was other boys that actually attracted me. After I told her, we sat there and stared at each other for a very long time not saying a single word to each other. She finally drew real close to me. A tear fell from her cheek as she said, "I don't understand, but I think I've known ever since I saw the way you acted at the pool with that weird guy. I just didn't want to believe it, but Geoffrey, it's okay. You are still a beautiful person. You are very confused right now and I want to be the one to help you find your way, no matter what way that is."

Those words pierced through my soul and I began to cry. This girl had wisdom far beyond her years. I told her that despite what I felt in my heart I could never reveal these feelings to anyone. Once I explained to her why I could never tell anyone she sadly said, "Believe it or not I do understand where you are coming from. Your secret is safe with me." From that day forward Sharon and I put on a show for all to envy. Everyone who knew us was amazed that teenage love could last so long and seem so wonderful.

Yes, I thought, as I stared down at the picture of Sharon and me smiling and peering into each other's eyes, I had, without a doubt, mastered the art of deception. I closed the album and tossed it into the flames of the fire.

CHAPTER THIRTEEN

The next photo album in the pile brought tears to my eyes even before I opened it. The first several pages were wonderful, for this album covered the summer Aunt Vivian came visiting all the way from Salem, Oregon. I can still remember the happiness and anticipation in Mom's voice when she announced to the family that Aunt Vivian was coming. It could not have come at a better time. It was the last day of school and Jay was having dinner with us. Mom was in such a great mood. You could tell that she was bursting inside, just dying to tell us something. We all sat down to eat and Mom finally blurted it out, "I've got the best news! I spoke with Aunt Vivian this afternoon and she is coming to visit us. She will be here for the Independence Day Barbecue."

Mom was right; this was great news. Aunt Vivian was the coolest grown-up on the planet. She was so much fun. She wasn't like all the other adults. She loved to do all kinds of neat stuff with us. She would take us to play miniature golf, to the movies, and in the evenings after dinner she would take us to Dairy Queen for ice cream. She would let us order anything, even a banana split if we wanted it.

I turned to Jay. "You remember Aunt Vivian. She visited us a few summers ago."

Jay began to chuckle. Of course he remembered who she was. Once you met Aunt Vivian you never forgot her. I looked over at Jay and knew that he was remembering the same incident that I was. During one of her visits a few years back, while she was relaxing in our backyard, Jay and I decided to tie her to the lawn chair she was sitting in and make her our prisoner. We quietly snuck up from behind and began tying a clothesline to her legs and the bottom of the chair. She pretended not to notice that we were tying her up but her uncontrollable laughter eventually gave her away. She was laughing so hard by the time we tied the last twine of rope around her upper arms that you could hear her throughout the entire neighborhood. We didn't let her go until she promised to take us to Dairy Queen for hot fudge sundaes!

Aunt Vivian was a schoolteacher so she had the whole summer off. This summer she was planning to visit each and every member of the family, a family that had managed to spread themselves all around the United States, from Seattle to New York and many points in between. In typical Aunt Viv style, she told Mom that she would be here in five days, in time to make the Scotts' annual barbeque. Although it was very short notice, Mom didn't even do her usual freak out; in fact she was elated.

That evening after dinner, Mom called a family meeting and demanded everyone's complete cooperation. She told us that there was much work to be done before Aunt Vivian arrived. I had to not only clean my room, but I also had to clean the spare bedroom in the basement, where I was going to sleep while Aunt Vivian was here, because she was taking my room. I really didn't mind at all. At least I was two floors away from people so they didn't have to hear me if I was having a nightmare or something. Plus, if I wanted to read or study my German or French I could stay up as late as I wanted to and not bother anyone.

291

Jay and I barely saw each other that week. The one day we did get together and go to the pool Jay was in better than usual spirits. His father had been called out of town to Texas on business. He would not be back until the day before the barbecue. It was the first Saturday after school let out, the first big day at the pool, and I wanted to go with Shelly and Jay. I wasn't sure if Mom was going to let me though. Aunt Vivian was due to arrive the next day and Mom kept ranting and raving that the house was still a mess and she had so much to do and there was no way she was going to be ready in time. Thankfully Mom couldn't get rid of me fast enough. She thanked Shelly and told her, "It would be much easier without the kids around." Ben was spending the day with some of his friends, and Dad, who oftentimes worked on Saturday, took Natalie to the office with him.

Shelly dropped Jay and me off at the pool, deciding not to stay, muttering under her breath that she could not show her face there without her husband who seemed to be working a lot of weekends lately and out of town frequently.

Jay and I changed and joined a group of our friends who were already there. Everyone was happy to see each other. I heard stuff like, "boy, you haven't changed a bit," or "look how much you've changed since last summer." To me it was the same old bullshit — the same cast of characters doing basically the same things, just on a different day nine months later. My attitude really sucked, but for some reason I felt that I did not fit in with these people anymore. Sharon, who always got to the pool when the gates opened at ten, came running over and gave me a big hug and a kiss right in front of everybody. I suppose I should have been used to it by now, but I wasn't and she was embarrassing the crap out of me. She said to me, "I am so glad that school is over, now you can concentrate on me, instead of those stupid books."

"Yes, dear," I said. We sounded like an old married couple. I was getting into this role-playing thing. It could be a lot of fun and it appeared to be working. I added, "I promise to spend more time with you, but don't forget what I told you. I really need to bone up on my language skills, because I am being skipped up to both German 3 and French 3 next term."

"Oh Geoffrey," she whined, "you have all summer for that." Then her tone of voice suddenly changed and she became much sterner, "Besides, if those books are more important than me, then you had better find yourself a new girlfriend." Everyone within earshot of our conversation gasped and turned their heads and walked away as if they had not heard anything so unthinkable. She even threw me for a loop. I wasn't sure if she was acting for the benefit of our friends or if she was serious. Whatever it was, she sure was convincing. Perhaps this was just her way of letting go and moving on so she could meet guys who could give her what I could not. I selfishly thought, if she dumped me she'd mess up everything. I made a mad dash over to where she was standing. "Wait Sharon," I yelled out loud enough for everyone to hear me, "I promised I would pay attention to you." Then I lowered my voice so that only she could hear me. "Are you trying to blow my cover?"

She looked into my eyes and said, "Oh Geoffrey, I am so confused. Of course I want to help you, but you have to help me too. I want to feel important. I know we're not really boyfriend and girlfriend, but the only thing I ask is that if we are going to play this game let's play it together. Treat me like your girlfriend, not a thing you can toss aside and reel back in when it's convenient, like most guys do. This is a fairytale relationship…please treat it like one."

I recognized her need and the wisdom of what she said. I promised to treat her like the princess she indeed was!

She looked over at me with a smirk on her face.

"What?" I asked.

She started to shed a few crocodile tears and whispered, "But first let's have our first fight for our fans." Then she tried to make a frown, raised her voice and yelled, "Don't ever yell at me like that again. I deserve better!" She then turned away from me and prissily stormed off. I had to pinch my arm until it hurt. It was all I could do to contain my laughter.

As I turned to march off in the opposite direction Jay grabbed my arm and started yelling at me, "Go after her, fool. Tell her you're sorry and that you love her. You know the drill!"

"Oh yeah," I said, angered by the remark, "taught by that asshole father of yours." I wanted so badly to take the remark back, but it was too late. I could tell Jay wanted to take a swing at me, no matter how much he knew my statement was true. Before either of us had time to react, I focused back on the matter at hand, Sharon. "I promised to spend more time with her. Now she has to meet me half way. I'm a person too. She's not the only one in this so-called relationship!"

Jay gave me a dirty look and yelled back at me, "But you yelled at her, and that's not very nice. Now you go over there and apologize right now."

"No, I refuse. Now leave me the fuck alone."

"Okay, big shot, do it your way!" he scowled as he walked away from me and over to the side of the pool where Sharon was sitting and put his arm around her. I could not believe what was happening. Jay was putting the moves on Sharon. If it weren't for Sharon's look of desperation I might have let it go to see how far Jay would go, but I couldn't risk loosing my cover! I went over to where they were sitting, grabbed Jay's arm and took it from around Sharon's shoulder. "Nobody steals my girl, not even my best friend…"

When all was said and done it must have been one hell of a performance. Jay apologized. The fairytale relationship between Sharon and me was still intact, and it gave the rest of the gang something to gossip about for weeks to come. Later Jay and I did a couple of races, with Sharon as the referee and judge. Jay and I wrestled around in the water after the races and he spent the whole time lecturing me on what an asshole I would be to let the prettiest girl at the pool slip away.

At the appointed time, right before it was time to get ready to go home, Sharon and I slipped away to the back of the locker rooms. We always pretended to make it look like it was a big secret, but we always made sure that everyone knew exactly where we were going and what we were doing. She loved the attention and it helped me to stay in Jay's good graces. We would do some major french kissing and I would run my hands over her breasts. I hated doing that most of all. Every time we had one of our little encounters, whether it be at the pool, or behind the school whenever there was a dance, it was always Jay I was thinking about, not Sharon.

All of Sharon's girlfriends looked up to her as the "experienced one." She talked a good game to her friends. The guys often reported back to me the things she was telling her girlfriends, in the strictest of confidence, of course. Boy, did Sharon have one hell of an imagination. Although I was thrilled that she was doing this for me I still could not understand it. I mean, by helping me she was hurting herself, unless she honestly believed that we still had a chance. I hoped that those thoughts were not going through her mind.

CHAPTER FOURTEEN

The next section in the photo album showed lots of happy faces. It was simply titled "Aunt Vivian." I can still remember that Sunday morning before she arrived. I woke up to the sound of the vacuum cleaner running in the hallway. Mom was making final preparations for Aunt Vivian's arrival later in the day. As I glanced over to the window I noticed it was dark outside. Maybe it was raining or something. I rolled over and stared at the alarm clock in disbelief. It was 6:00 in the morning. She's out of her fucking mind, I thought. Mom popped her head into my room briefly and said, "Oh good, you're awake. We're going to eight o'clock mass today. Aunt Vivian is arriving from Salem on the 12:30 flight this afternoon. There is still a lot to do and I'll need your full cooperation. You're the oldest and I'm counting on you."

"Okay," I mumbled.

The morning seemed to drag on forever, but finally we were at the gate where Aunt Vivian's plane was arriving. We all watched in anticipation for her to exit

299

the front door of the plane. Most of the passengers had exited before Aunt Vivian finally emerged. She was yapping away and laughing with one of the stewardesses. Aunt Viv was such a neat lady, I thought, she made friends with everybody. As she and the stewardess came down the steps from the airplane she looked up into the terminal windows and saw us all madly waving at her. She smiled and pointed us out to her new friend. They both waved back. In a few short minutes they came up the stairs and into the terminal building. Aunt Vivian let out a boisterous hello to everyone. She was beaming with excitement. She then introduced us to Jackie Olsen, one of her former students. Aunt Vivian told us how proud she was of her and what a great student she was and how nice it was to see that women really could make something of themselves in this "all male world." She wished Jackie well; they exchanged phone numbers, and promised to have lunch together in the fall, back in Salem, Oregon, when their schedules permitted.

We headed to the baggage claim area with Ben on one side of Aunt Vivian and me on the other. Our arms were tightly wrapped around her waist. She told us all about her flight and the nice people she met on board. Aunt Vivian sure was a talker. She rarely let anyone get a word in edgewise. We gathered up her suitcases while Dad brought the car around to the arrivals entrance. We loaded everything and piled in. I'm sure it was uncomfortable for her, but she insisted that she sit in the middle of the back seat with her two favorite nephews on either side of her.

Mom had planned a big dinner for later in the day. Aunt Charlotte, Uncle David, and my cousins Jeff and Stephen, were coming over. In spite of this, and Mom's repeated objections, Dad decided to take us to Ruby's Diner for lunch. Aunt Vivian exclaimed loudly, "Oh Jeannie, I really miss the Northeast, especially a Ruby's burger and fries. Nobody, anywhere in the entire US of A makes a better burger than Ruby's, and I've traveled this wonderful country of ours from east to west and north to south and back again." Well, how could one argue with that? Mom stopped her griping and gave into the wishes of Aunt Vivian and the rest of us. We all clapped and cheered and off we went to Ruby's.

*****

Aunt Vivian's first week in Swarthmore was a whirlwind of activity and fun. Twice she took Jay, Ben and me to play Chip and Putt. She said that we were too grown up to play miniature golf. Aunt Vivian was an avid golfer with an eleven handicap, which apparently was considered pretty phenomenal for an amateur. She took it upon herself to teach us how to play. She bought each of us, including Jay, a chipping iron and a putter. She was great! When we weren't at the Chip and Putt, she took us to a neighborhood park to practice our chip shots. We lost more golf balls to the woods and the stream, but nobody seemed to care. "It's all part of the learning experience," Aunt Vivian told us.

To give Natalie equal time, Aunt Vivian took her to the miniature golf course and they spent at least an hour everyday playing with Natalie's Barbie dolls.

While Natalie and Aunt Viv played dolls I studied German and French.

Sharon continued to call every single day. I didn't doubt that she would grow up to be another Aunt Vivian. Sharon could also talk your ear off about the stupidest, most mundane stuff. First, she would gossip about all of our friends, then she would tell me about this outfit or that outfit that her mother was buying for her and what was wrong with it. Next, she would tell me all about how good of a swimmer she was becoming and how she couldn't wait to race Jay and me because she was sure she would win every time. No doubt about it, she was an exceptional swimmer. Boy, was that girl driven! Finally, either my mother or her mother would come along and say something like, "You two lovebirds have been on the phone long enough, time to say good-bye." She would try to stay on the line until her mother would have to pry the phone from her hands or my mother would start stomping around me in anger. Once we said good-bye I was free for another day.

*****

303

Saturday, July 3, 1971, came and went without incident. We didn't go to the pool because there was so much preparation going on for tomorrow's barbecue. Coach was still in Texas and wouldn't be home until later in the evening. Mom and Aunt Vivian volunteered to give Shelly a hand since she was all alone. It was actually kinda fun for Jay and me. While the three women worked in the kitchen we got to taste everything. Our job was to make sure the yard was in perfect condition. Of course that wasn't too difficult, considering the gardener did most of the work the day before. Nevertheless Shelly could always find something not quite right, and off we would go to take care of it. Finally she gave us the tedious task of untangling the volleyball net. Every year, no matter how careful people were, it always managed to get tangled up when it was put away.

Everything was finally ready by about seven o'clock that evening. Mom called Dad to come and pick us up. Just as we were leaving, Coach arrived home in one of those airport limousines. As I passed him in the driveway he winked at me and said, "Good evening Geoffrey. I am really looking forward to tomorrow. How about you?"

I tried to smile and look happy, but I knew exactly what he meant by the comment. The last week had been wonderful without him. I finally looked up at him and lied, "Yeah, me too."

Coach then smiled and said, "Take a picture of your good ol' Coach." Everyone else appeared amused but I was not. I reluctantly snapped the picture. It turned out to be the last photograph that I would take for a very long time.

CHAPTER FIFTEEN

I had intentionally left the rest of the photo album empty except for a couple of postcards from friends and relatives on vacation. Even though the bulk of the album was devoid of pictures, I could still vividly recall the events that my camera lens did not capture…

I heard my name being called from far away. It took me a minute to get my bearings. It was Mom waking me from a sound sleep. "Good morning, sleepy head. Today must be your lucky day! You don't have to go to church with us."

I must be having a dream because I couldn't be hearing her right. She continued jabbering, "Shelly called and asked if you could come over and help Jay with some last minute things. Now get dressed. Peter will be here in a few minutes to pick you up after he drops Shelly off at the beauty parlor. Louise is coming in special to do her hair for the barbecue."

Oh fuck, I thought as I got dressed, what is today's lesson going to be. I hurried so I'd be ready before

Coach arrived and avoid his wrath as much as possible. As I finished putting my sneakers on I heard the car pull in the driveway. Heading out the door, I vaguely heard Mom shouting things at me from behind. I even thought I heard her say that Aunt Vivian wasn't going to mass either, that she was finishing up her famous Waldorf salad.

"Right Mom," I said as I got into the back seat of the car.

"Hey Geoff," Jay greeted me. "How's it goin, man?"

"Great," I answered. "I can't wait for the party later."

"Me either," Jay cheerfully acknowledged.

"Hey, Coach," I said as I flashed him a big bright smile, "are you going to have the best ever fireworks display, like you always do?"

He looked back at me with a friendly smile and said, "Why thank you Geoffrey. Of course they're going to be the best yet. I can't disappoint my boys, now can I?"

I could not believe the incredibly good mood that Coach was in this morning. It put me on my guard even more. I was absolutely certain it could not and would not last.

Before we went back to the house we had to make a stop first at the grocery store and then the butcher shop to pick-up hot dogs, hamburgers and fresh steaks. I couldn't believe how much the steaks cost. Money didn't appear to be an issue, but it took a lot longer than Coach had expected. Jay and I gave each other a glance, because we knew that he was getting agitated at the long lines. "It's Sunday, for goodness sakes, what are people doing out shopping? Aren't they supposed to be in church praying or something?"

I tried to make light of it. I said, "It's a holiday and nobody wants to miss your famous fireworks show. That's why they are all shopping now."

Coach was not very much amused by my attempt at humor and only became more impatient as we waited in line. It took almost twenty minutes before we finally made it to the cashier. All the while I could see Coach's mood getting darker. When we finally paid and got out of the shop he was so upset that he screeched out of the parking lot. There was total silence all the way home. Thank God we were there in no time. As Coach turned the car off and took the keys out of the ignition he looked down at his watch and annoyingly stated, "Shit, look how much time we wasted."

He then took the bags of meat out of the trunk of the car and marched into the house with the two of us right behind him. Once we were all inside, he tossed the bags on the couch and growled at us, "Get upstairs now! We don't have much time. That bitch at the beauty parlor is just going to have to wait until we're finished here."

Without any hesitation, knowing full well what the consequences would be if we disobeyed the order we started up the stairs. As we crossed the room I noticed that the front door was not completely closed. I was going to say something but I was too scared at that moment to open my mouth.

It had become routine by now. Jay and I got undressed as Coach pulled sheets from the back of the closet and draped them over the bed. He quickly tore his clothes off and stood in front of us with a raging hard on.

"Okay you bitches, it's been a long time and I can't wait any longer. Now which one of you is going first?" Without waiting for a response, he continued, "Yes, Geoffrey it should be you. Or should it be you, Jason? No, I think it should be both of you together. Get over here, both of you, and start sucking my cock and balls."

Like robots, went over to where Coach was standing and knelt down in front of him. I took Coach's massive hard on in my hands and slid my tongue up and down it. Jay worked on Coach's hairy balls. At least for the moment neither of us was getting fucked and that was good. The whole time Coach was shouting out obscenities. He loved to degrade us and call us sluts and whores, telling us how much we deserved "whatever he could dish out."

Suddenly, Coach stopped ranting and raving and pushed us away from him. I turned around and there stood Aunt Vivian holding her salad. For a second she stood there and didn't do or say anything. The expression on her face was one of utter shock. I grabbed one of the sheets off of the bed and wrapped it around me.

Coach shouted at Aunt Vivian, "What the fuck are you doing here, bitch?"

I yelled at her, "Run, before he hurts you. Run!"

Aunt Vivian came out of her semi-trance and started screaming at the top of her lungs. In her panic she dropped the bowl she was carrying. It shattered, sending glass flying everywhere along with the green marshmallowy Waldorf salad.

As Aunt Vivian ran down the stairs, I heard her calling out, "I'm going to call the police!" And then I heard her say, "Oh Thank God you're home."

There at the bottom of the stairs stood Shelly. "How the fuck did she get home from the beauty parlor?" Coach said to no one in particular. I watched in slow motion as Shelly rushed up the stairs past Aunt Vivian. She calmly, yet deliberately looked into Coach's eyes and said, "Peter, get the hell out of here and take your God damned clothes with you."

Like a timid little mouse, Coach quickly gathered up his things and slithered out of the room past Aunt Vivian who was now standing in the doorway. He stepped on some glass and let out a shriek, but kept on going.

Now it was Aunt Vivian's turn to try to take control of a situation that was beginning to spiral out of control. "Where is he going?" she demanded.

"Oh don't worry," Shelly yelled back at her, sounding a bit put out. "He's not going far, just down to the recreation room to compose himself."

Aunt Vivian could hardly believe what she was witnessing. Shelly was acting like this kind of thing happened all the time. As the light bulb inside of her brain lit up, Aunt Vivian began to tremble. Her face turned white as a sheet. "You mean to tell me he's done this before to these boys?" She asked, hoping against hope that she was wrong.

"Oh no, of course not. He does have a temper though. This is the only way I know to defuse it," Shelly said matter of factly as she stepped over the broken glass and globs of salad and came over to us. "Are you boys alright? Did daddy hurt you?"

We were both shaking and told her "no."

Aunt Vivian was completely astounded, "I don't believe what I am seeing or hearing," she said as she walked over to the side of the bed and picked up the phone on the nightstand.

Shelly moved towards Aunt Vivian and said, "Now Viv, I wouldn't do that if I were you. We don't need to get the police involved in this. This is a family matter."

Aunt Vivian shot back, "Bullshit, this is not a family matter. I am calling Geoffrey's parents right now. They should be home from church by now."

Shelly put her hand on the phone, not letting Aunt Vivian pick up the receiver. Aunt Vivian looked Shelly squarely in the eyes and said firmly, "Get your fucking hands off that God damned phone."

Jay and I sat there in complete silence as Shelly backed away and Aunt Vivian dialed the phone, reaching Mom. Aunt Vivian made sure we couldn't hear what she was telling my mother. She slowly hung up the phone and announced that Jeannie and Doug were on their way over. The expression on Shelly's face was turning from cool collectedness to obvious fear. Jay and I grabbed our clothes and ran to the bathroom to get dressed.

"Jay," I said once we were safely behind the bathroom door, "What's going to happen to us now? My father is going to kill me. He is going to send me away forever, I just know it."

"Oh stop it! You know my mother will take care of it, she always does."

"You're right. I just don't want to be taken away," I whined.

"Stop being such a cry baby, I told you my mother will handle this. Now let's go," Jay said, sounding rather sure of himself.

We exited the bathroom where the two women were waiting for us. It was a very awkward moment for everyone. For the first time in a very long time, I began to cry. I went over to Aunt Vivian and started muttering, "I'm so very sorry."

"It's alright now," she assured me. "Your mom and dad are on their way and we will get to the bottom of this." She darted a nasty look towards Shelly.

Shelly started to clean up the salad and glass. "And on my nice white carpet. I hope it won't stain it."

Aunt Vivian was dumbfounded by Shelly's callous disregard for Jay and me. There was a knock at the front door. Shelly stopped cleaning up the mess and we all stepped over the glass and clumps of salad and made our way down the stairs to the front door. Shelly let Mom and Dad into the house and asked them to have a seat.

Mom looked terrible. She said, "What the hell is going on? What is so urgent, Vivian? Is everybody all right? Where's Peter?"

Shelly started in again with her soothing tone, "Calm down, Jeannie, everything is just fine. Peter is down in the recreation room."

Aunt Vivian quickly cut Shelly off and snapped, "Everything is not fine. I caught Peter molesting these boys."

There was complete silence. Mom and Dad's faces turned ashen. "What are you saying?" Mom asked as she began to shake all over. "What exactly did you see?"

"You want me to describe it to you?" Aunt Vivian asked sarcastically.

"I don't know what I want you to do," Mom said, trying not to get hysterical. She then turned to Jay and me asking us if we were okay.

"They are just fine," Shelly said.

"Be quiet Shelly. I'm not talking to you!" Mom barked.

I cut in, "We're okay, Mom. I'm just scared that you are going to have us put away."

"Why would we want to do that, Geoffrey?"

I broke down and started to cry uncontrollably. I couldn't help myself. Two years of pent up fear were pouring out of me.

Aunt Vivian interjected, "What is it with all the questions? Can't you see these boys need to get to the hospital right now! That thing in the basement needs to be arrested, locked up. God knows what he's done to these kids."

Shelly, in her demure voice said, "Now Viv, that won't be necessary. The boys said they are just fine. Now let's let it go."

Dad finally spoke for the first time, "No, Shelly, Vivian is right. A doctor needs to examine these boys right away."

"Oh Doug," Mom said, "I agree with Shelly. The boys aren't hurt after all."

Aunt Vivian was livid, "So you're just going to let this go, like nothing has happened? You're going to let Peter get away with this?"

You could see two separate alliances forming: Mom and Shelly versus Dad and Aunt Vivian. A compromise was finally reached which satisfied everyone. Dad decided that we were going to the emergency room to be examined. If the doctor determined that some kind of sexual abuse had taken place then they would deal with Peter. I was relieved that I didn't have to answer any questions, because I had no idea what I would tell them. I had to get Jay alone so we could get our stories straight.

"Come on boys," Dad said, "get in the car. I'm taking you to the hospital."

I could see that Mom was crying now. Jay remained completely stoic and emotionless throughout the whole ordeal. We silently got up from our seats and went out to the car. The adults remained behind to plan what they were going to do.

We were finally alone. "Okay," I said, "Let's get our stories straight. What are we going to tell the doctors?"

"That's easy," Jay said now sounding like his mother. "We tell them nothing, except that Dad was angry today and made us do this to him. Besides, we don't exactly know what your Aunt Vivian saw, now do we? What the doctors and everybody else for that matter don't know won't hurt them, or us."

Aunt Vivian and Dad came out the front door. Dad told us that Mom and Shelly would come to the hospital after they called everyone to cancel the barbecue due to a little family emergency.

The ten-minute ride over to Taylor Hospital seemed endless. Nobody uttered a word the whole time. I went over my lines in my head at least a million times. I was as ready as I could be for those doctors.

Being a Sunday morning, there was not much activity in the emergency room. I heard one of the nurses comment that "This must be the calm before the storm. Every year there are tons of firecracker-related injuries. Won't those people ever learn?"

Dad and Aunt Vivian went to the admitting desk to sign us in. It was less than five minutes before we were swept away to separate examining rooms. Oh fuck. I thought. This is not good. In fact it could be really bad. We need to be together to keep our stories straight. I unfortunately, was powerless to do anything.

A nurse came in and took my temperature and blood pressure. How absurd I thought. I'm not sick. Maybe she didn't know that. She said that it would be a few minutes that the doctor could not examine me until a detective was present.

"A detective?" I asked. "Why is a detective coming?"

"A sex crime has been committed. A detective is required to be here while you and your friend are being examined."

Oh shit. Things were not looking good, I thought. I could only hope that Jay could keep his story straight. I sat in this little examining room full of all kinds of breathing machines and surgical equipment. I waited alone for what seemed like an eternity. Finally a whole entourage of people entered the room. There was Mom and Dad and even Aunt Vivian. She had apparently insisted on being present. Then I was introduced to Detective Marks of the Ridley Park Police Department, the town the hospital was located in. Dr. Sherwood was the examining physician, and Dr. Weinstein, the staff psychotherapist, was also present. It was intimidating to have all of these people around me, but I was ready. I had rehearsed the story in my head at least a million times. They were not going to trip me up.

Dr. Weinstein began as Detective Marks flipped open his little notebook, "Geoffrey, why don't you tell us in your own words exactly what happened this morning."

"Well," I said, "I don't really know. I mean it was really weird. We came back from the grocery store and the butcher from picking up the meat for today's barbecue. Coach was in a bad mood because we had to wait in line for so long, plus he said the he had a really difficult business trip and he was under a lot of pressure to get some project finished. Anyway, he just snapped. He ordered us upstairs to his bedroom and made us take off all of our clothes. I know how angry he gets sometimes, so I knew I had better do what he said. He took his clothes off too and grabbed our hair and forced our faces, well you know?"

"No we don't know, tell us," the doctor said calmly.

Mom shouted, "Do we really need to hear this? He's already told you what happened!"

"Relax, Mrs. Brooks, your son has been through a very traumatic ordeal and Detective Marks needs to make a determination as to whether or not Mr. Scott needs to be picked up and arrested, or if perhaps there was some kind of consent on your son and his friend's part."

I thought Aunt Vivian was going to have a hemorrhage right then and there. "We're talking about thirteen year old boys here. This, this monster forced himself on these kids. How can you even think for a moment there was consent on their part?"

"Excuse me, Miss," Detective Marks interrupted, "It may not be clear to you now why it is so important, however, a man's reputation is in the balance here. It is very important that we get all the facts and we get them right."

I could see that Aunt Vivian was clearly agitated. I only hoped that Jay was having a better time at it than I was. Although I thought that I was doing a great job and not showing any emotion, I was quickly coming to realize that this was not going to be as easy as I initially thought it would be.

Dr. Weinstein continued to question me. "Did Mr. Scott hurt you in any way? By that I mean did he hit you or beat you or make any kind of physical contact with you?"

"No sir," I answered.

"Did you ever see him strike his son?"

"No sir."

"Did he threaten you?"

"Well, in a way he did, I guess."

"Please explain what you mean, Geoffrey. It's okay, nobody is going to be mad at you if you tell us something you are supposed to keep a secret."

"Coach said that if we told anyone about this that we would both be in big trouble."

"What kind of trouble?" Doctor Weinstein asked.

I think my fear was beginning to show. "Oh, I don't know exactly what kind of trouble, just trouble."

"No, I don't understand, explain to me what you are afraid of. Are you afraid he is going to hurt you if you tell?"

I hesitated. This questioning was going in a very bad direction. I tried to evade the question by steering the conversation in a different direction. "If my grandfather finds out about this, I know what will happen."

"What will happen?" Mom asked.

"Oh, you know, Mom. He won't let me work with him and I probably won't get to see him ever again."

"That's ridiculous son, your grandfather loves you," Dad said.

I began to cry again. Dr. Weinstein had this confused look on his face. He continued, "Geoffrey, I know this must be very difficult for you. You must understand that we are only trying to help you. Let me ask you a very difficult question, "Has he done this to you before?"

I completely lost it, so, I lied and answered, "Absolutely not!"

"It's okay, Geoff," Dr. Weinstein said. "It's apparent you're not ready to talk about it yet. That's okay."

He turned to the other people in the room and asked everyone to leave so that Dr. Sherwood could continue the medical examination. Everyone left the room except for Dr. Sherwood and Detective Marks. The doctor made me take all of my clothes off down to my underwear. He examined every spot on my body. I guess he was looking for any signs of being beaten by Coach. There were none.

Then came the moment of truth and probably one of the most embarrassing moments of my entire young life. The doctor laid me face down on the examining table. He explained to me that he needed to pull my underpants off and examine my rectum. He apologized for the pain and the embarrassment, but insisted that this was a necessary part of the examination. "It will only take a couple of minutes," he assured me.

He then slowly lowered my underpants and took them off. "That's good." He turned to the detective and said, "There are no external signs of beating like there was on the Scott boy."

Oh shit, I thought, that's why the questions about Jay. I tried to watch what the doctor was doing next, however it was pretty difficult from the position I was in.

"If I'm right," the doctor continued talking to the detective, "this scope will slide right in."

After a brief hesitation I felt a small tube slide up my butt. I stayed completely still.

"Does that hurt?" The doctor questioned me.

"No sir," I answered.

I heard the detective mutter to himself, "Damn."

"You had better have someone pick Mr. Scott up right away. I've seen enough," Dr. Sherwood told the detective.

The doctor finished up and had me get dressed. Even though it was summer outside, the air conditioning inside was freezing cold on my body. Dr. Sherwood said to me as he walked toward the door, "Sit tight, I'm sure Dr. Weinstein will want to talk with you again."

I was lost in my thoughts. There was no way they could know anything unless Jay told them. Maybe the doctor was just trying to scare me into talking. I sat there alone for another eternity when finally the entire entourage of people, including Dr. Weinstein, clamored back into the examining room. Thank God for Aunt Vivian. She brought me a nice big strawberry milk shake from the hospital cafeteria. It tasted so good. I could tell that Mom had been crying and was trying to compose herself in front of me.

Dr. Weinstein said, "Geoffrey, before you told us that today was the first time Mr. Scott approached you in a sexual manner."

"Yes," I said.

"We would like you to rethink your answer, remembering what I told you. No one is going to hurt you. We only want to help you, but you have to help us for us to do that."

I almost cracked, but I needed to know one thing first. "What did Jay tell you?"

"Jason hasn't told us anything. Besides, he is not our concern right now; you are."

I couldn't hold it back any longer. "What did that fuckhead tell you? He made me promise not to tell. He promised that his mother would take care of it."

Dr. Weinstein put his arms around me and said, "Calm down son. Everything will be all right. Now, please, tell us what's going on?"

"What makes you think anything else has been going on?" I shouted, pushing the doctor away from me.

The tension in the room couldn't be any thicker. Before the doctor got a chance to answer my question my mother screamed, "What does Shelly have to do with this?"

"Nothing, Mom," I answered. Then to reinforce my answer I said, "I promise."

Dr. Weinstein looked deeply into my eyes and said, "Son, I am so sorry for all that you have been through. It must have been terrible. Let me reassure you that it is all over now. We are going to help you. Let me first tell you that the police have already arrested Mr. Scott, so you have nothing to fear. You are safe now."

The doctors had Mom, Aunt Vivian, even Dad in tears. Detective Marks just kept on taking notes.

Dr. Weinstein continued, "Second, the examination which Dr. Sherwood just performed on you found that you have had some pretty serious damage done to your rectum. He told us that not only is there recent damage, but there is also a lot of scar tissue. This would indicate that something terrible has been going on for quite some time. Are you ready to talk to me now? Do you want everyone else to leave the room so we can talk alone?"

I truly didn't know what I wanted at that moment. I could not believe that I had been found out. How was I going to explain things so that Mom and Dad wouldn't think that I was some kind of a freak. I had pulled off one charade after another for almost two full years. Could I do it again? I certainly hoped so. I just started talking with everyone in the room. I spoke in a monotone voice. The emotion of everything had left me a very long time ago. "I honestly can't remember right now when it all began. I think it was the weekend a couple of years ago when we went down the Shore for Jay's Pop-pop's birthday."

Mom gasped and muttered, "I knew I shouldn't have let you go."

"It wasn't my fault. I mean, I didn't want him to do anything to me. I just could not stop him." I paused for a moment. Dr. Weinstein draped his reassuring arm across my shoulder, "It's okay son. It's okay."

I went on with the "Reader's Digest" version of my story, "Before I had time to think Coach pulled my pants down and stuck his thing inside my butt. It hurt an awful lot, but I was okay."

Dr. Sherwood asked, "You said you were okay. Didn't you bleed?"

"I suppose I did. But just a little bit," I lied remembering back to the blood on the shower stall and the plastic and especially the blood on Shelly's bedspread and her horrible screaming.

Dr. Weinstein continued pushing on, "Was Jason or anyone else present when this happened to you?"

"No. It was just Coach and me."

"This was not the only time Coach did these things to you, was it?" Detective Marks interjected.

I hesitated and finally shrugged my shoulders and said, "Well, no, but it wasn't so bad all the other times."

Mom let out a shriek and suddenly became the inquisitor. "All the other times? What exactly do you mean, Geoffrey? How often did he do this to you? What do you mean that the other times were not so bad? Did you like what he was doing to you?"

Finally my father grabbed her by the arm and demanded that she stop right now. Although she stopped yelling I could tell just by looking at her face that she was angry with me for what happened.

With a blank stare on my face I took a deep breath and tried to start answering some of mom's questions. "I don't know how many times. There were too many to count. The reason it wasn't so bad was that Jay was with me after that first time."

Dr. Weinstein continued with the questions. "Why didn't you and Jason tell anybody what Mr. Scott was doing to you?"

"He threatened us."

"I know this is difficult for you Geoffrey, but you must understand how important it is that we get all of the facts. How did he threaten you?"

"He said he would tell everyone that we were lying and then we would be taken away."

"That's all?" Dr. Weinstein asked sounding puzzled.

"Yes," I lied.

This line of questioning seemed to go on forever. Mom sobbed the whole time but managed to keep quiet. I continued to give short answers, hopefully offering very little information.

Before Dr. Weinstein finished with his myriad of questions he asked me about my relationship with Jay. "When was the first time the two of you had a sexual experience together with Mr. Scott?"

I thought back and answered, "It was about two weeks later." I went on to explain that Coach was teaching us how to please women by using each other as examples.

"Oh how sick!" Aunt Vivian screeched.

I tried to comfort Aunt Vivian. I said, "Aunt Viv, don't worry, it was okay, because I care for Jay. So I really didn't mind it at all."

"Are you telling us that Mr. Scott forced you to perform sexual acts on each other?" Dr. Weinstein asked.

"Yes," I smiled for the first time, accidentally letting my guard down. But it was suddenly so easy to answer these questions. The fears that I had been harboring inside of me for so long seemed to be melting away.

"So you enjoyed being sexual with your friend?"

"Yes, it was great!" I enthusiastically answered, completely carried away by the thought of Jay and me together.

"Do you think Jason enjoyed it too?"

"No," I answered sadly, "not as much as I did. He would tell me so. But that was okay."

"Geoffrey, your mother tells me that you have a girlfriend."

"Well, yeah, sort of. Her name is Sharon. Her dad is the president of the same accounting firm that Coach works for."

"What do you mean when you say 'sort of' your girlfriend?"

"Oh, you know, she's a girl."

"Have you and Sharon ever had sexual contact with each other?"

"Oh no," I answered hoping I wasn't getting her in trouble too. "Although all of our friends think we have, but it's not Sharon that I'm interested in."

"Whom are you interested in then?"

"Why Jay, of course," I responded rather matter of factly.

There was suddenly some commotion in the room but Dr. Weinstein raised his arms in the air and quickly quieted everyone down. Then he asked the question I had most been dreading, "Geoffrey, do you understand what it means to be gay?"

I again took a long pause. I now had myself convinced that I was going to be taken away so it didn't much matter what anybody thought. I answered, "Yes, I think so." Even I could not believe what I was saying.

"Do you think that you might be gay?" Dr. Weinstein calmly asked over Mom's loud sobbing.

I tried to brush off the obvious answer to the question with a simple, "I don't know. I don't think so."

Mom sat there shaking but tried to keep quiet.

"So you didn't stop what was going on because you enjoyed it?"

"Well, I didn't like it much when Coach forced himself on me. However, I enjoyed time I could be with Jay. It felt good and we were gentle and didn't hurt each other."

That was the straw that broke the camel's back for Mom. She couldn't hold it in any longer. She burst into tears and started ranting, "Oh my God, oh no! My son is gay. He likes having sex with boys. That's not right! He'll go to hell for eternity. God will punish him for his homosexuality."

Aunt Vivian had also had enough. She grabbed Mom by the arm, looked her dead in the eye and hissed, "Enough of this bullshit, Jeannie. Your God may be a God of damnation, but that is only your sick and prejudiced opinion. Can't you see that your son has been victimized, raped, yes raped, by this evil man? How dare you make your son an outcast, and you call your God a loving God?"

Dr. Sherwood had heard enough and without another word grabbed both women by their arms and escorted them out of the examining room. When he returned a couple of minutes later he said to Dad, "I think the boy has had enough for one afternoon. This has been a very trying day for all of us, especially little Geoffrey here." He then turned to me and said, "Son, you've been through a very traumatic ordeal and for that I am so very sorry."

"Detective Marks," the doctor continued, "I think we're done here, don't you?"

Detective Marks readily agreed, reminding us that he still had many more questions which would wait for a later time.

Dr. Weinstein looked down at me with a very sad look on his face. "You can go home now and get some much needed rest. I'm going to give your mother some medicine. It will help you too," he paused for a moment and said, "Relax, and perhaps get a good night's sleep." As we walked out of the examining room, Dr. Weinstein said to me, "Take care of yourself, son. I look forward to talking to you again real soon."

Mom and Aunt Vivian were sitting next to each other, both staring into space, not speaking to each other at all in a now very crowded waiting room full of people with assorted maladies. As I approached them I kept my eyes focused on the floor. I didn't see Dad anywhere. I was sure he was already making arrangements to have me shipped off.

"Mrs. Brooks, may I speak to you for a moment?" Dr. Weinstein asked.

"Yes, of course," Mom answered.

"Your son has been through a great deal today." He handed Mom a small envelope of pills. "Please give him two of these when you get home, and then two again tomorrow morning."

Mom took the small envelope from Dr. Weinstein. She didn't even ask what they were or what they would do. She then hesitantly asked, "Doctor? What if he is, you know, homosexual? Is there anything that can be done to cure him?"

"Don't you worry about that. Your son needs a lot of love right now. If we later determine that he is homosexual, we will deal with it then. I will tell you this; homosexuality is a very much-misunderstood disease. It has been observed that people who have it have no control over their feelings and emotions.

Perhaps in Geoffrey's case, years of sexual abuse with people of the same sex have conditioned his mind into believing that he is homosexual because that is the only thing he knows. That is why we have psychotherapy, to recondition his mind to think what is right and normal."

"Oh thank God," Mom said, letting out a sigh. "Thank you so much doctor; you have been wonderful."

Aunt Vivian started to open her mouth, but decided that it would be fruitless to argue with Mom. She turned her head and muttered in to the air something to the effect of "I am appalled how ignorant supposedly intelligent people can be."

I was confused by it all. Maybe I was sick. Maybe the doctor was right. If he were then maybe I would not be shipped away while the doctor tried to make me better. I looked around the room for the first time and realized that I hadn't seen Jay or Shelly anywhere in the emergency room waiting area. "Where is Jay?" I asked. "I need to talk to him."

"No," Mom said. "I think you see too much of that boy as it is. We are going to have to limit your contact with him."

"No!" I shouted back at her. "You can't do that to me! You don't understand."

Dad stepped in from nowhere and firmly took a hold of my arm, pulling me away. "Don't you ever talk back to your mother, young man! Now apologize to your mother right now."

I was quickly shaken back to reality and tried with all the strength I could muster not to cry, however, the tears began to flow. Dad was making his feelings known for the first time and I didn't like what I was hearing. "Jason is a very bad influence on you. Look what his animal of a father has turned you into. I don't want to hear his name ever again!" With that he let go of my arm and stomped out of the emergency room.

A couple of minutes later Dad pulled the car up to the entrance. We all quietly got into the car. The silence was deafening. It was Aunt Vivian who broke the silence. She offered to treat us to Ruby's hamburger and fries since none of us had eaten all day and it was already after six o'clock.

Mom just gave her a disgusted look and growled that the only thing she wanted right now was to get home to her other children. Aunt Vivian looked over at me and saw that I was shaking. She put one of her hands into mine and with the other she stroked my hair. For the first time that day, I saw a tear roll down her cheek. She quietly said to me, "It's okay, Geoff. It's over now. No one can ever hurt you like that again. You've got us to protect you now."

Thank God for Aunt Vivian I thought. Hopefully she can talk to Mom and Dad and convince them not to send me away. We pulled into our driveway at about 6:15. I saw Aunt Charlotte and Uncle David's car parked at the head of the driveway. Before we got out of the car, Mom turned to me and said, "Geoffrey, I would appreciate it if we don't talk about this incident in front of your brother or sister, or anybody else for that matter. We will deal with it privately. There is no need to get anyone else involved. Besides, you don't want everybody to think bad things about you, now do you Geoffrey?"

"Jeannie!" Aunt Vivian shouted, "Geoffrey has done nothing wrong! It appears to me that you and I need to talk."

"Maybe you need to stay out of this, Vivian," Dad abruptly cut in.

"It seems that you are placing all of the blame on Geoffrey, when you should be making sure that Peter will never do this sort of thing again to Geoffrey or any other innocent young boy," Aunt Vivian said.

Dad got out of the car and slammed his door shut. He stormed into the house. Mom scolded Vivian for offering her opinion when it was not called for.

"I cannot believe the ignorance you've displayed today," Aunt Vivian retorted. "Your mind is brainwashed with that bullshit Catholic doctrine."

Mom would hear no more of Aunt Vivian's tirade on the Catholic Church. She rushed out of the car and into the house. Aunt Vivian and I followed.

Ben was waiting for us at the door all excited. "Hey, everyone, guess what happened today, guess!"

"What Ben, what? I can't guess," Mom said trying to give Ben the attention he was demanding.

"The police went to the Scotts' house and took Coach out in hand-cuffs. Isn't that neat? Nobody knows why, though. I promised all my friends that I would find out for them."

"My goodness," Mom said to Ben. "I can't imagine why they would want to take him away. He must have done something really terrible."

"Oh no, not Coach, he's way too nice for that. He's the greatest. He's teaching me how to be a pitcher. He's the best."

I noticed Mom wince at the thought of Coach even being around another of her children. She said to Ben, "Okay Ben, that's enough. I tell you what, as soon as I know what happened, you will be the first person I'll tell. Maybe later you and me need to sit down and talk about Coach Scott. What do you think?" she then winked at him.

That seemed to appease him, at least for the time being. Aunt Charlotte and Uncle David were right behind Ben. They had come over to watch Ben and

Natalie after Mom called them and apparently told them that they were taking me to the hospital with severe stomach pains. Aunt Charlotte came over to me and gave me a big hug and asked if my stomach was better. I was about to ask her what she was talking about, but I knew that for my own good I'd better play along with this latest charade.

Mom answered before I could, "It's getting better. It was just a touch of food poisoning. Nothing too serious. The doctor gave him some medicine to make him feel better." She doled out two pills from the small envelope, put them in my hand and told me to take them and go downstairs and lie down for a while so that I would feel better.

Evidently Mom had no intention of telling Aunt Charlotte and Uncle David the truth. As I turned to go downstairs I heard Aunt Charlotte say to Mom, "You had a phone call right before you walked in the door. It was a Detective Marks from the Ridley Park Police Department. He said he was from the Sex Crimes Unit and that you needed to call him as soon as you got in. Now, Jeannie, what is this bunk about food poisoning?

What is really going on? I want some answers and I want them now. This is my godson we're talking about."

Aunt Charlotte looked at me and noted that I was lingering and listening to her little speech. She stopped and waited for me to walk out of the room. I willingly took the pills and went down to my room. It wasn't long before I was fast asleep.

*****

Although it was only around seven in the evening when I went to sleep, I ended up sleeping soundly through the night. When I woke up I found that someone had changed me into my pajamas and I was tucked in under the covers. Boy, those must have been some powerful pills. The doctor wanted me to take two more this morning? There was no way. I mean, I slept enough already, more than I've slept in a really long time.

I lay there for a few minutes, deciding whether or not to get out of bed or if I was safer right where I was.

I heard footsteps coming down the stairs to my room. I recognized the sound of the flapping slippers. It was Mom. I closed my eyes and pretended that I was still asleep. I felt her sit down on the side of the bed.

"Wake up sleepyhead," she said.

Please God, I thought, don't let her take me away. Please, Aunt Vivian, tell me you've talked to her and made things right. I opened my eyes and rolled over.

"You must have really been tired. How are you feeling today?"

"I don't know," I answered honestly.

She just started talking. She must have spent the entire night composing the speech she was now delivering. I could see that she was agonizing over her words and fighting back tears. "Geoffrey, I am so sorry for being so hard on you. You're my baby and I love you. I will always love you, no matter what. I want you to know that I'm here for you and I will always be. I don't understand what is going on inside of your head. I don't even think you understand it. You are so young. I only wish that you had come to me with this in the beginning."

345

I took a chance and reached up and gave her a big hug. I started to cry and said, "I'm sorry, Mom. I'm so sorry. I was too scared to come to you. I was so afraid that he would hurt me."

"I know honey, I know." She was now holding on to me for dear life. "You don't have to worry about him hurting you ever again. Your father is down at the police station right now taking care of that."

"Mom?" I asked. "What about Jay? Is he okay?"

"Yes, he is going to be staying with his grandparents for a couple of weeks. As much as your father and I are against it, Aunt Vivian thinks it would be a good idea if you'd call him later."

"Thank you, Mom. You know he's not to blame. He's my best friend ever and Coach hurt him real bad too."

"I know he has, but considering everything, don't you think it's a good idea if you stay away from him for a while?"

I was devastated. Mom really didn't understand. I had come this far so I decided to protest. "But Mom, he's my best friend. You don't understand."

"No, you're right, maybe I don't understand, but I still think it's best." She paused for a moment and then continued. "I do have some good news for you. Grand mom and Grand pop are on their way here. I spoke to them last night and they are taking an early flight and renting a car so that they can get here as soon as possible. We have an appointment with Detective Marks. Grand pop wants to go with us."

"Oh God." I started to cry again. "Grand pop must hate me. What am I going to do?"

"No, honey. Don't even think that. He doesn't hate you. He loves you very much. He is coming to help us, to help you. He has a better knowledge of the legal system and how it works."

I couldn't stop crying. I was sure that the future that I was working so hard for was gone. Me and my fucking big mouth. I just wanted to die. I finally said, "Don't make me answer anymore questions. Please, no more."

"I know, honey, and I am so sorry, but you will have to. Don't you want to cooperate with the police?

You don't want Coach to do this to you or anyone else ever again, do you?"

"No," I whispered.

"Good, now get dressed. Oh, Sharon has called several times. She is worried about you. I told her that you have a severe case of food poisoning and that you would be calling her real soon when you felt better."

Mom got up and went back upstairs, her slippers flapping behind her. I leisurely got dressed contemplating how I would answer all of the questions they would throw at me. I went upstairs and went into the dining room where everybody was just sitting down, getting ready to have breakfast. Before Aunt Vivian had a chance to sit down I went over to her and gave her a big hug. I whispered to her, "I'm so sorry. Thank you."

"You're welcome," she said. "What have I done?"

"You know," I said.

"Yes, I think I do," she smiled. "Now enjoy your breakfast."

*****

After breakfast I called Sharon. You would have thought I had died by the way she was acting. Before I hung up with her, she asked, "Have you talked to Jason since yesterday?"

"No, why?" I asked.

"Well, first the Independence Day Barbecue got abruptly canceled, then my dad got this strange phone call from Mrs. Scott. She told him that Mr. Scott was in jail. After he got off the phone, he told us about the jail thing and then went flying out of the house. What's going on? Do you know? My dad refuses to tell me no matter how hard I try to push him."

"No," I lied, trying to act surprised. I told her that the only thing I knew was that Jay was staying with his grandparents for a couple of weeks, but he wouldn't tell me why. Before she got a chance to ask anything else I quickly changed the subject. I explained my food poisoning ordeal to her again in great detail. She quickly forgot about Mr. Scott.

"Oh, Geoffrey. You are the best. I don't know what I would do without you."

"Oh now stop it!" I gushed.

I heard a car pull up in the driveway. I looked out the window and saw Grand mom and Grand pop getting out of it. "I have to go now, my grandparents just got here from Washington."

"Wait a sec, you didn't tell me your grandparents were…"

I cut her off. "Sorry, I gotta run! Bye!"

"Call me later Geoffrey?"

"Okay, I will." With that I put my finger on the disconnect button on the phone, disconnected the call, but continued to hold the phone to my ear and pretend that I was still talking to Sharon. The anxiety level inside of me was so high at that instant that I just wanted to bolt. I wanted to run out the back door and never come back, knowing full well that it would accomplish nothing and probably make matters even worse. I did my best to pull myself together and I decided that my best approach was to remain emotionless because it was my emotions that were always getting me into trouble. I pretended that I was still on the phone when they walked in and they tiptoed past me. I waited until they were in the living room before I yelled into the phone receiver, "Okay, Sharon, talk to you later. Bye."

I walked into the living room and said, "I was just talking to my girlfriend." I babbled on quickly about the phone call before Mom said, "Geoffrey, can't you say hello to your grandparents. You haven't seen them since Christmas."

I apologized and said "hello." With that, Grand mom came over to me and gave me a big hug and a kiss. Grand pop came over and shook my hand and asked me if I was okay.

"Oh yeah," I answered, "just a little food poisoning. No big deal. Right mom?"

The look on Grand pop's face was that of disturbed confusion. "What do you mean?" Grand pop asked. "I didn't hear anything about any food poisoning." Grand pop asked.

Mom's face was all red. She sent Natalie and Ben outside to play then turned back to Grand pop and said, "Dad, I can't tell people what really happened. What would they think?"

Grand pop thought about it for a moment and after a brief pause said, "Yes, perhaps you're right. That was very smart of you. What time is our appointment scheduled for?"

"One o'clock."

"Good, that gives us a little bit of time to talk."

Mom and Aunt Vivian left the room for a few short minutes. I took the initiative to talk incessantly while they were gone so that I didn't have to confront Grand pop about the situation. I told Grand mom and Grand pop how well I had done in school this year, even though they had heard it all before. I also went on about how much I was enjoying my language tapes and how it was almost time for more. Mom and Aunt Vivian finally returned with a tray of coffees for each of the adults and a glass of milk for me. Mom also brought the other two pills with her. After she gave everyone their coffee she handed me the glass of milk and the pills. Instead of putting up a fight I took the pills from her. Almost like a professional magician I pretended to take them, but instead palmed them. They eventually made it down into my pants pocket for disposal later. It was a great feeling to pull off such a trick right in front of all of these adults. As I slipped the pills into the back pocket of my pants, Dad walked in the door holding up a folder full of papers. "I got it!" He said triumphantly. Mom seemed exceptionally pleased at whatever Dad had brought home with him.

I half smiled and asked, "What did you get, Dad," praying to God that it was not my deportation papers. My heart skipped a beat or two anticipating the bad news.

"This is the restraining order from the judge."

I was so relieved. I didn't quite know the legal meaning of a restraining order, but I did know that it was not a deportation order.

It was Grand pop's turn to preen his feathers. He sat back in his chair and said, "I woke the judge up at 6:00 a.m. this morning. He assured me that he would sign it as soon as it came across his desk, and I see he did."

That little grandstand performance took the sails right out of my father's mood. You could tell that it irked him that Grand pop had intervened. His face turned several shades of purple, but he didn't say a word. Mom turned to him and smiled sheepishly, "Don't worry dear, you know Dad has connections. He's just trying to help."

Pretending this little power play was not taking place Grand pop put his right hand out and said, "Doug, let me see it please."

Dad reluctantly handed the manila folder over to Grand pop. The animosity between the two men was frightening. I was glad that Dad wasn't an aggressive man. Otherwise I think there would have been much more of a confrontation right there in the middle of the living room. After several anxious moments, everyone settled back in their seats. Grand pop began to speak as his eyes scanned through the restraining order. "Geoffrey, it's a terrible thing that is going on here and we need to get to the bottom of it, and the only way we can do that is with your full cooperation."

I nodded my head in silent assent.

He continued, "I spoke at length with Dr. Weinstein last evening. You and I can speak like two adults even though some people in this room think that you are still a child. Considering everything that has transpired, there is no doubt in my mind that you should be treated like an adult, as you deserve. Now, Dr. Weinstein relayed some very disturbing observations to me. He told me that he has personally never seen two rectums as severely damaged and mutilated as yours and Jason's. Based solely on the physical evidence he even questioned how the two of you have managed to survive all this time. I told him that was an easy one, at least on your part. I told him it was your lineage," Grand pop smiled, but quickly got serious again. "What is important is that you did survive and to ensure that this does not ever happen to you or anyone else ever again. That is why we need your full cooperation. We need you to tell us everything you can about the Scotts. I don't mean just Mr. Scott, but also Mrs. Scott and," he hesitated, "your friend Jason."

Boy, oh boy. I thought. Grand pop sounds like a cop now. Was whatever he did for the President of the United States so powerful that he could boss around judges and anybody else he wanted to for that matter?

From here on in I was really going to have to be on my guard. One screw-up and Grand pop would deport me and he had the power to do it.

"So, Geoff, please tell us what happened, from the beginning."

After a few minutes of looking down at the floor and drinking my milk, I carefully thought out my words and said, "It's like I told the doctor yesterday. The first time Coach, well, you know, put his thing up inside my butt, was when we went down the Shore to celebrate Pop-pop's birthday."

"When was that?" Grand pop asked.

Mom answered that one for me, "It was the weekend of June 13th, two years ago. The reason I remember it so well is because that is the very same weekend that the Masterson boy disappeared." Mom began to cry, but continued, "Thank God it wasn't my baby, maybe this is a blessing in disguise. Oh how terrible."

Dad put his arm around Mom and tried to comfort her. After a brief period of silence Grand pop continued with his questions. "Was Jason there when this happened to you?"

"No," I answered, "Coach got me alone."

"Did he threaten you in any way?"

"Yes. He told me that no one would believe me and that I would be taken away if I told anybody."

"But, did he actually threaten you with bodily harm?"

"Yes."

"Yes, what?"

"Yes, he said he would hurt me."

"The doctor said that there was a lot of damage inside of you. Do you remember ever bleeding?"

"Well, yes, but it wasn't bad," I again lied, trying to keep my story consistent.

"When was the next time that Mr. Scott got you alone?"

"It was a couple weeks later. It happens whenever Shelly, Mrs. Scott, has an appointment at the hairdresser. That way he knows that we will be alone."

"Is Jason usually present?"

"Yes."

"What happened when the three of you were together?"

"Well every time he would first stick his thing in Jason's butt and then in mine."

"Didn't you have a choice? What I'm asking is, if you knew he was going to do this to you, why did you go over there?"

"It wasn't that simple. I had no choice. I was afraid that he was going to hurt me."

"But wasn't he hurting you when he was doing this terrible thing to you?"

"Yes, a little bit, but it didn't hurt much, honest." There was no way I was going to tell him about Jay's and my out-of-body experiences.

"You told the doctor yesterday that you and Jason had sexual relations. Tell me about that."

Okay, I thought, be careful, he's trying to set a trap.

"Coach, he called it lessons."

"Lessons?"

"Yeah, you know, he was teaching us how to be around girls."

"By having sexual relations with each other?"

"Yes."

"Who played the girl?"

"We had to take turns."

"Yesterday you told the doctor that you, for lack of a better word, enjoyed it."

"You know what I meant."

"No, I don't. Explain it to me."

"Well it was better to do it with Jay than it was to do it with Coach. With Jay it didn't hurt at all."

"So all of that stuff yesterday about looking forward to being with Jason on an intimate level was nonsense?"

"Yes," I lied, "I was scared and confused and didn't know what I was answering "yes" and "no" to."

"That makes perfectly good sense to me. I think the way things were handled yesterday was terrible. I'm sure it must have been worse for you."

"Yes," I answered.

"Now let me ask you about Mrs. Scott. You said yesterday that Jason promised you that she would make things right. What did you mean by that? Did she know what was going on between the three of you?"

"Oh no, absolutely not! It's just that Shelly, Mrs. Scott, always seemed to know the right things to say to make everything better." Although I could tell that my answer did not completely satisfy him he thankfully decided not to pursue it.

"I guess that's everything." Grand pop finally said, "Now, let me explain this restraining order to you. It says that Mr. Scott is not allowed within 50 feet of you at all times. You cannot go to the Scott home and he cannot enter your home. If this order is violated, Mr. Scott will be sent back to jail."

"Back to jail?" I questioned.

"Yes, he was released late last night to the custody of Mrs. Scott. However, he begins a thirty day inpatient psychological evaluation tomorrow if all goes well."

"Oh my God! What about Jay? He's still in danger."

"No, he's okay. The court has placed him in the protective custody of his grandparents for the time being. You will get to talk to him later, after you tell Detective Marks everything you just told us."

Grand pop then took a deep breath. "I have also arranged something which, I am sure you will agree with me will help you to understand what is going on inside of you. In order to help you to deal with everything that has happened to you, your Mom and Dad and I feel that you need to spend some time alone and speak with Dr. Weinstein."

"But why?" I protested.

"You may not understand it now, but someday you will thank us for it. I know that your Dad's insurance will not cover this, and besides we need to keep this quiet. So here is what I have proposed and what all concerned parties have subsequently accepted. I have promised the Scott family that Mr. Scott will not be prosecuted and the matter will remain quiet as long as he meets the following conditions: 1. He fully complies with the restraining order: 2. He pays all medical costs incurred on your behalf; 3. He spends thirty days in the state mental institution for a full psychiatric evaluation; and 4. He not molest Jason ever again. I know that one will be difficult to enforce, but that is where you come in Geoffrey. If Jason ever tells you that his father has laid even a single finger on him it is your duty to tell Dr. Weinstein or me.

With that, Grand pop got up and went to the phone. I heard him ask for Detective Marks. Unfortunately I didn't hear anymore of their conversation. After a few minutes Grand pop hung up the phone. He went back to his seat and picked up his briefcase, which he had placed next to his chair when he came in the house. From the briefcase he produced the next installments in the German and French language series as well as a set of beginning Russian tapes. My face began to beam. Grand pop had not lost the faith he had in me after all. I thanked him and reassured him that I would one day make him very proud to be my grandfather.

"I know you will, son. Now, we need to get ready to go."

Grand mom was given the job of babysitting Ben and Natalie while we were out. Over Mom's vehement objections Aunt Vivian also came along insisting that she was too involved not to participate.

Upon arrival at the police station, we were all directed to a conference room, except for Grand pop, who was taken two more doors down the hall to Detective Marks' office. Except for the large oblong table and overstuffed chairs, the room was completely empty. There was nothing on the stark white walls. When you spoke you could hear a faint echo. I needed to go to the bathroom, so I asked the woman who showed us in where the men's room was. She pointed down the hall and to the left. As I moved down the hall I heard muffled voices coming from one of the offices. It was Detective Marks' office. I stopped short of the door, looked around to make sure I was alone in the hallway and listened in on Grand pop's and Detective Marks' conversation.

Grand pop said to Detective Marks, "So, did you find out anything?"

"Yes. Plenty," Detective Marks replied. "I spoke with Shelly Scott's mother. She remembers the weekend in question quite well. Apparently a big birthday party had been planned for her husband at their summer home in Cape May, New Jersey."

"What do you mean 'had been planned'?" Grand pop asked.

"Interestingly enough, the only people to arrive at the party were Shelly and Jason Scott. According to Shelly's mother, Mr. Scott was called to go to Texas for his job, which apparently was a common occurrence."

"So where was my grandson through all of this?" Grand pop anxiously asked,

"Wait, I'll get to that. There are a few more facts you need to know."

"Go on."

"I called Mr. Scott's firm and spoke to a woman in the Human Resources Department to find out if they kept any attendance records for their executives. The woman, Sylvia Ott was her name, was more than helpful. She informed me that indeed such records were kept. Apparently Mr. Jones, the president and CEO of the company, insisted on knowing exactly where his key personnel were at all times. He also, to our advantage, has a compulsion for retaining such records. The man has kept every piece of paper, every record since he established the company over fifteen years ago. Well, she checked her logbook for the time in question. Peter Scott did in fact have that weekend off, however, the number he left was not that of his parents in Cape May, New Jersey: It was his home phone number. Finally, I have one more interesting little fact. There is a notation in the records that Mr. Scott called in sick that following Monday."

Grand pop pondered what he had just heard and said, "So, it sounds like there's a whole lot of lying and covering up going on around here. Let me ask you this, Detective Marks. Doesn't it strike you as odd or is it just a coincidence that the same weekend this whole bizarre thing happened with my grandson, that young lad — who was a close friend of my grandson — disappeared. And more coincidentally the boy lived on the same exact block as the Scotts. I do know one thing, Geoffrey was with Mr. Scott that weekend and I'm betting that he knows a lot more than he is telling us."

Detective Marks went over to a file drawer and pulled out a thick folder. "You may be on to something. Kenny Masterson was the boy's name. However, I am afraid to push your grandson too far today. He has apparently been through one hell of an ordeal over the past two years and if he does know anything about the Masterson murder if we push him too hard he may never tell us."

Grand pop sighed and said, "I have to agree with your assessment of the situation. Don't bring up the Masterson murder today. Let me mull it over for a while and talk with Geoffrey alone. Perhaps I can get him to talk. If I can do that I will convince him to come down here and talk to you. Peter Scott will be in a maximum security hospital for the next thirty days so we have some time."

Jesus, I thought. I have no idea what happened to Kenny. I didn't see him at all that weekend. They are wrong about this. It appeared as if the conversation was coming to a close so I backed up about ten feet and then walked by the semi-open door of Detective Marks' office on my way to the men's room. I pretended that I didn't even see them. I went into one of the stalls for a minute. I needed to think about what

I had just heard. They knew that we never made it down the Shore. No big deal. I will just tell them it was so long ago that I forgot. The primary thing that was bothering me was, why was Grand pop trying to link what happened to Kenny Masterson to me. After all, the two had nothing to do with each other.

A few minutes later I made my way back to the conference room where everybody was waiting for me. The questions were a rehash of what I had already answered what seemed like a million times. I continued to insist that the initial rape, as it was now being called, happened down at the Shore, not revealing that I had overheard Grand pop and Detective Mark's earlier conversation. Two hours later we were on our way home. No one had eaten anything since breakfast so everyone was starved. Aunt Vivian produced a bag of cookies from her huge purse.

"For emergencies, and this is an emergency," she giggled. The tension between her and Mom seemed to have abated a bit. Of that I was very glad. Between the five of us the bag was empty before we got home.

Kevin A. Carey

Once we were back home, Mom opened up her pocketbook and pulled out a small piece of paper. She handed it to me. It had Jay's grandparents' phone number on it. I thanked her and ran upstairs to the phone in Mom and Dad's room for privacy. I quickly dialed the number on the paper. Pop-pop answered.

"Hi, it's Geoffrey, is Jay there?"

"One minute, Geoffrey, let me see if he wants to talk to you," Jay's grandfather answered rather sourly.

Surprised by his tone of voice I said, "Of course he wants to talk to me. Why wouldn't he? He's my best friend."

Pop pop was so abrupt with me and I couldn't figure out why. After a few anxious minutes, Jay picked up the phone, "What do you want, Geoff?" he said, sounding just as sour as his grandfather.

Why was he so angry with me? "What do you mean, 'what do I want'?" I paused. "What is wrong with you?"

"Don't you know," he whispered in the phone. "You've ruined everything. I have to live with my grandparents. My father has to go to a hospital for

368

crazy people. And you can never visit our house ever again."

"So, you're telling me that it's my fault that we got caught?" I whispered quizzically.

"No," Jay replied. "It's your fault for not sticking to the story that we had agreed on before we went to the fucking hospital. You had to blow it; you had to tell them everything, even about you and me. What does that have to do with anything, anyway? That was private. No one was ever supposed to know about that. Now they think I'm a queer too."

I began to whimper. I tried to apologize and explain to him that I didn't mean to tell them anything, but they had tricked me.

"You are such a wimp," he yelled. "Maybe it is true what they say about you. Maybe you are a faggot."

His words struck me like a hundred newly sharpened daggers. "Jay, how can you say those things about me? You know they aren't true."

"Don't call me Jay anymore, it's Jason to you from now on!"

369

"What do you mean?" I cried.

"I have to go now." With that he hung up.

I sat on the side of the bed with the phone receiver still to my ear. I was in shock. My world had been turned upside down and now I had just lost my best friend. I wanted to crawl into a corner and die. I finally put the phone back down on the receiver, lay down on the bed and cried myself to sleep.

I never got a chance to say goodbye to my grandparents. They left to go back to Washington before I woke up. Mom said that I was sleeping so soundly that they thought it was best if I got some good sleep. Then she said something that really got me angry, but I was too tired to react much. She said, "I'm sorry that you and Jason had a fight. I think it's best this way, don't you?"

"How do you know we had a fight? Were you listening in on our conversation on the extension?" I asked.

"It was for your own good."

"How could you? Don't you trust me? Do you hate me that much?"

She reached out and tried to give me a hug. I pulled back and told her not to touch me. She said to me as her eyes glossed over yet again. "It's not you that I don't trust, it's Jason. Don't ever think that we hate you. You are our son. We will love you no matter what."

"Then stay out of my business!" I snapped.

She looked sympathetically into my eyes and said, "We have all been through a great deal these past couple of days. Why don't you go down to your room now and get some rest?"

"Yeah, like a little rest is going to bring my best friend back," I screamed, stomping off to my room down in the basement.

*****

The week passed by at a snail's pace. Except for the daily, totally unnecessary trips to Dr. Weinstein's office I hibernated in my room, worked on my German, French and Russian and retreated into my private world where I could travel to far off places and

371

nobody could bother me. It was so much more pleasant than reality.

I tried several times to call Jay but he refused to take any of my calls. I completely shut Sharon out of my life because I could not tell her what had really been going on with me. I made Mom field all of my phone calls. She didn't like it at all. She only did it so that she would not lose what little hold she had on me. She told Sharon that I was too sick and weak to talk to her right now but I would call her when I felt better. Sharon must have finally gotten the hint because she stopped calling.

After the first week of seeing Dr. Weinstein everyday, I only had to go every Monday, Wednesday and Thursday. I had no idea what the point to it all was. He would ask me how I was feeling, I would say fine. He would talk some nonsense; we would play with his dolls and sometimes even draw pictures. This was therapy for kids, not teenagers. I played along just to make everybody happy.

During the second session with him he gave me a blank notebook and a pen. He wanted me to start to keep a journal. He said I could write anything I wanted to in it, and that I didn't have to show it to anybody but him. What a waste of time, I thought. However, in time I found that writing helped me to release a lot of the frustration I was keeping inside of me, and it really did made me feel better.

My fourteenth birthday came and went without the fanfare of the year before. Boy, what a difference a year makes, I thought. The day after my birthday, Grand mom called and asked me if I wanted to come down and visit for a few weeks before school started again. Although I feared that I was going to have to answer some more tough questions while I was there I gladly accepted. It sure as hell beat seeing Dr. Weinstein every other day. Besides, Mom told me that Coach would be coming home from the hospital in a couple of days and my anxiety level was building. Despite all the assurances everybody was giving me, I did not trust the man one bit. I knew deep down that he would come after me the first chance he got.

Mom and Dad put me on a plane the following Monday morning. I must admit that the second the wheels left the runway of the Philadelphia International Airport I felt a huge weight lift off of my shoulders. Grand mom and Grand pop were waiting for me at the gate in Washington D.C. They were both all smiles. They each gave me a great big hug and we walked arm-in-arm all the way to the baggage claim area.

I spent the first few days getting settled in and reacquainting myself with my old room. I worked diligently on my language lessons. Grand mom and I went shopping everyday and we always ate lunch at one sidewalk café or another in Georgetown. I was having a great time and I was able to forget all about home and all of the shit that I had to deal with there. Not once did either of them bring up any of the craziness that was going on back at home. I was so thankful yet on my guard because there was no way I was going to get away without being interrogated yet again.

On Friday morning Grand mom had an appointment to get her hair permed and a manicure and pedicure. There was some big dinner party on Saturday evening, which we were all invited to. Grand pop and I also went and got our haircut. I managed to convince the barber and Grand pop to only style it and not to cut off any of the length, which was well below my shoulders.

After the haircut Grand pop and I drove into D.C. We parked on the street near the Lincoln Memorial. "Let's go for a little walk," he suggested. As we walked towards the monument Grand pop pointed out things that he had shown me several times before. I was polite and listened anyway.

When we reached the steps to the Memorial, we climbed about half way up and sat down. "It's beautiful, isn't it? A true symbol of our freedom."

"Yes," I mused with him, "it really is."

"Do you feel free, Geoffrey?"

"What do you mean by that?"

"Oh you know. Does it scare you that Mr. Scott is now free, after everything he has done to you?"

I hesitated a moment, but answered honestly, "Yes, I mean, I don't know. I just don't trust him. You know what I mean?"

"I think I do." Grand pop paused for a moment. "Geoffrey, I need to ask you a very important question."

Oh shit, I thought, and I was having such a great time. I internally braced myself for the worst, but outwardly I appeared as if everything was all right. I said, "Sure, what's up Grand pop?"

"Well, you've told us that when this whole thing with Coach Scott began you were down at the Shore at Mrs. Scott's parents' summer home."

So much for outward appearances. I began to sweat and turn pale.

He continued, "I happen to know that isn't quite true. It's only you and me now and I promise I would never do anything to hurt you or put your life in jeopardy. What really happened that weekend?"

I knew right then that it was finally time to tell the truth. I began to talk, "I remember it like it just happened yesterday," I said. "I was all ready to go down the Shore to celebrate Jay's Pop-pop's birthday. I even went up to the Ben Franklin up the street to get him a little present. I didn't have a lot of money, but I got him something small to show him that I was thinking of him. Mom had already bought him some golf balls, which I was to give him but I wanted to give him something personal, you know? I got to Jay's house and chain-locked my bike to the fence post in the backyard. I knocked on the backdoor. At first I got scared that they had left without me because nobody answered right away. Coach finally came to the door and invited me in. I figured he had just gotten out of the shower because he only had a towel wrapped around his waist. He was acting kind of weird and explained that Shelly and Jay were out running a few last minute errands and would be returning shortly. He gave me some milk and cookies and told me to go into the living room and wait and watch some television. I did as I was told and went into the living room, turned the TV on and sat down on the couch. A few minutes later Coach came in from the kitchen and sat down right next to me, and when he did his towel fell off. I turned my head in embarrassment, but he didn't seem to mind. Before I knew what was happening, he was making me touch him all over. Then he took my clothes off and carried me upstairs. He put me in the shower. At first he was really gentle, but suddenly I felt his thing up against my butt. I realized that he was trying to push that thing inside of me. I got scared and told him no, but it was too late. He gave this big push forward into me. The pain was unbelievable when it went inside of me. It hurt so bad."

I began to cry. I think Grand pop was getting a bit more information than he had bargained for. He put his arm around me as I continued my story. "I must have passed out shortly after that because I don't remember anything until I woke up on the Scotts' bed. My wrists and ankles were tied to the bedposts. I was in so much pain. Then the unthinkable happened."

Grand pop was visibly shaken by what I was telling him. "How much worse can it be?" he asked.

He knew in his heart that it had to be much worse than I had told anyone to this point. He told me that he had the doctor explain the rectal examination to him in a way that was not explained to Mom and Dad. He said that Mom and Dad had enough to deal with for the time being and they did not need to know all of the graphic details.

Grand pop again put his arm around my shoulder as I continued on with my story. "He had the sword in his hands that his father had given him from the war. You know the one, with the blue sapphires encrusted in the handle?"

"Oh Jesus Christ," Grand pop exclaimed in utter disbelief. "Yes, I am aware of it."

"Well, he threatened me with it. Then he turned the handle side towards me."

Grand pop cut me off in mid-sentence, by the expression on his face and the tears rolling from his eyes, he knew exactly where this was leading. "I think I've heard enough."

"I am so sorry, Grand pop."

"No son, it is I who am sorry. Sorry for not recognizing there was a problem much sooner."

"It's not your fault. I hid it from you on purpose. I had to."

"I'm sure you believed that, but trust me, you didn't have to. I would have understood."

Even though Grand pop didn't want to hear anymore I felt that I needed to tell him the rest. Perhaps by telling the whole truth for the first time I could make sense in my head of what happened. I gathered all of the courage I could muster and went on, "Everything after that kind of makes no sense to me."

Grand pop looked confused. "What do you mean by that?"

"After he shoved the sword up my butt, I must have passed out again. But when I woke up, Shelly and Jay were there. They kept insisting that it was Sunday. I knew that it could only be Saturday. In the end they convinced me that it was in fact Sunday when "The Wonderful World of Disney" came on T.V. I mean, I have no idea how I could have lost a day. He must have hurt me so bad that I slept through an entire day."

Grand pop was staring at me the same way Jay and Shelly did when I told them. "You're sure you don't remember anything else?"

"Positive," I said. "No matter how hard I try to remember anything else there is just nothing else in my brain to remember. But can I tell you something weird?"

"Sure," Grand pop said.

"Well, I have nightmares about what happened almost every single night since it happened."

The look on Grand pop's face was one of despair. He really was grieving with me. "I'm sorry, but I'm not surprised."

"Anyway, at the end of the dream, I see this other boy. He's pretty far away. I am always yelling at him to run."

Grand pop looked at me and asked the strangest question. "Could that other boy be your friend Kenny Masterson? Geoffrey, can you tell me what happened to him? Again I promise that nothing bad will happen to you if you tell me."

"I don't know," I said. "Why does everybody think I know what happened to him? How would I know that?"

Grand pop looked agonized. "You are absolutely certain that you have no memory whatsoever about whatever transpired that Saturday evening?"

381

"No. I told you and Shelly and Jay, and everyone else for that matter, over and over again. Why does everybody keep asking me that question? Don't they believe me? Don't you believe me?"

"Oh Geoffrey, what secrets are locked inside that brain of yours? I believe you when you tell me you don't remember what happened. Honestly I do. Don't worry about that anymore. Please always remember I care about you. I just wanted to understand the complete situation so that I can help you, and I think I do now." Grand pop turned his head for a moment to wipe the tears from his eyes. Then he said something else that really freaked me out. "Son, when that mind of yours is ready to release whatever secrets it is hiding I will be here to listen to you to help you, to protect you."

Did Grand pop know something about the supposedly missing time in my brain that he wasn't telling me, I wondered. He looked down at his watch and commented that we had better get going. We got up from our spot on the steps of the Lincoln Memorial and walked back to the car. I clicked a few more pictures along the way, finally putting my camera back in action.

"You and that camera," Grand pop said. And then almost so that I couldn't hear him he said into the dead air around him, "Where was that camera when you really needed it?"

Once we got in the car, Grand pop turned toward me and again said something really strange: "Geoffrey, you will never ever have to worry about that evil man ever again. I will personally see to it." With that the subject was dropped and never brought up again for the rest of the vacation.

I flew home about two weeks before school was to begin. In a way it was good to be home again. There was much to be done before the school year. Mom insisted that we go clothes shopping, to get a new wardrobe for the school year. I focused my attention on my future and I was looking forward to going back to school despite the fact that I was going to be so busy. But I was ready for it. I was ready to forget about this horrible summer.

I now closed yet another chapter on my life. I walked over to the fireplace and tossed the almost empty photo album into the fire. I had plenty of pictures of D.C. in happier times, and I could only hope that the flames would symbolically burn away some of those horrid mental images.

CHAPTER SIXTEEN

I grabbed the next album from the box. This one was by far the strangest collection of memorabilia. Not only were there photographs but also post cards and newspaper clippings. What I now consider to be one of the most significant events of my life, what I call the turning point, was now all laid out in before me. Although there were no photographs of my own to record this momentous event, there were several newspaper clippings and I had saved them all. Reading them now brought back so many emotions. I can still remember it like it was yesterday.

I had only been home from Grand mom and Grand pop's a couple of days and I was in a pretty good mood even though I had to go back to see Dr. Weinstein. I came down the stairs and went into the kitchen. Mom was intently listening to some news report that was being broadcast on the radio. The broadcaster announced, "Again, we have just received word that a private jet has crashed on its arrival into Toronto,

Canada's International Airport. The jet, belonging to a local accounting firm, left Philadelphia International Airport early this morning. First reports indicate that there are no survivors. A spokesman has told WIP News Radio that there were seven people from the local tri-state area on board. All names are being withheld pending verification and notification of next of kin. WIP News Radio will bring you further details on this breaking story as they become available."

Mom turned the radio off, poured me some orange juice and sat down in the chair next to mine. "Honey," she said, "your grandfather just called and told me to put on the news. He told me about the plane crash we just heard the reporter talking about. They believe that Mr. Scott was on board that plane. Now I know that Mr. Scott is not a very nice man, at least in your eyes, however, we would never wish him dead, would we?"

I could not believe what I was hearing. "Are you sure?" I said sounding much happier than I should have. I was jumping for joy inside at the possibility that the bastard could never hurt me again. I looked over at Mom who had noted my tone of voice and was not very approving. I tried to change my expression to look more serious, but I could not hide my obvious glee.

By noon it was confirmed that Peter Scott had indeed been on board the ill-fated plane. I had just finished making myself a peanut butter and jelly sandwich when the phone rang. I was closest to the phone so I picked it up. I couldn't believe who was on the other end. It was Jay. "Geoffrey, is that you?"

"Yes," I yelled, almost jumping for joy. Coach was dead and I got my best friend back. It truly was a glorious day.

"Meet me in the cave in fifteen minutes, and don't tell anyone where you are going or who you are meeting," Jay said in a monotone voice.

I was so elated! I quickly ran out of the house telling Mom I'd be back in time to go to the doctor. Jay needed me and nothing else in the world mattered at that moment. We both arrived at the cave at the same time. We got off of our bikes and stared at each other. My heart was exploding with joy at seeing my best friend again. I wanted to run to him, but I decided that it would be better if I waited to see what he was going to do. Finally, after a brief awkward pause we walked towards each other. He reached out to me, gave me a big hug and started to cry. Jay was never the type to be outwardly affectionate to anyone so I was pleasantly surprised.

Jay spoke first, "I am so sorry. I missed you so much."

"I'm sorry too," I said.

He quickly changed the subject, "I guess you've heard about my dad?"

"Yeah, it's been on the radio and television all morning. I'm sorry, Jason." I tried to sound convincing, but I was failing miserably.

He suddenly grabbed both of my arms and pulled me right up to his face, looked me square in the eyes, and whispered, "You're not sorry he's dead, and neither am I. I'm glad the sick bastard is gone. I hope it was a long and painful death. I hope at this very moment he is rotting in hell for the pain and suffering he caused us. He made our lives a living hell and I want him to suffer for it for eternity. And it's Jay to you, Asshole!" I smiled for the first time in a very long time. It was so good to have my best friend back.

"I brought something to celebrate this momentous occasion." Jay said gleefully. He cautiously surveyed the area for any people and then he pulled a bottle of vodka out of his pants.

"To the bat cave, Robin," he quipped.

I blindly followed him into the cave as he took a swig from the bottle.

"Where the hell did you get that from?" I asked.

"Where I always get it, from the mother fucker's bar. He keeps his bar well stocked and never misses anything I swipe. There are cases and cases of this stuff locked in the big closet in the recreation room, and I have an extra set of keys. Besides, what difference does it make now, the asshole is dead!"

Jay took another swig and passed the bottle to me. Except for a few rare sips of mixed drinks and beers at my parents' parties, I never had a chance to really try alcohol. I guess this was my big chance and I definitely didn't want to hurt Jay's feelings. I took the bottle, put it to my lips and chugged down two big gulps of what amounted to fire water. "Jesus Christ," I screamed trying to catch my breath. "This shit's enough to kill you!"

Jay could not stop laughing. "I thought you were an old pro at this."

"Me? What makes you think that?"

"You know, the way you are around girls, and all. Even though we've never talked about it you just seemed like the type."

"Fuck, no. But obviously you are!"

"Oh yeah. It really does dull the pain. I call it my medicine."

Jay continued taking big gulps from the bottle, not bothering to pass it back to me. I finally grabbed the now half empty bottle from him and took another mouthful. This time the alcohol didn't seem to burn as much. "Jay? How long have you been, you know, drinking to help the pain?"

"Oh, I don't really remember when it all started exactly. Maybe a year or so ago. One night Mom and Dad were out at some dinner party and the liquor cabinet was left open. I decided to try it out. It was great. Dad, being on one of his usual rampages, had just got done beating me before they left. The alcohol started to numb the pain. I knew that I had discovered my new best friend, besides you of course."

"Gosh," I said, "How did I miss it all this time? Why didn't you share this with me sooner?"

"Because I knew you probably would not approve," Jay said, staring down at the ground.

I decided to let it go for now. We finished the bottle and talked shit and laughed. It was so much fun. I looked down at my watch and saw that it was almost 3:00 already. I had to be at the shrink by 4:00 so I announced that I had to go and stood up. Bad idea, I thought. The cave began spinning and I fell backwards onto the dirt floor. I started to laugh. I could not get up. Jay tried to pull me up, but he just ended up on the ground next to me. We were a mess. We were both drunk as skunks. Somehow we stumbled out of the cave. I suddenly got this queasy feeling in my stomach. I leaned over one of the big boulders, which helped to shelter the cave's entrance, and threw up my guts. It was so gross, but I was in no condition to care. There were chunks of vomit all over my shirt and pants. It was even in my hair. Still, nothing mattered. I felt great. I thought how wonderful life was, and then I passed out cold.

When I was again coherent, I saw that we had somehow made our way to the entrance of the park. The world was still spinning out of control. Jay managed to somehow get us to my house. The only thing I remember is walking up the driveway, trying to act normal and pretend that nothing was wrong. I looked up and there was Mom standing at the front door and she was steaming. "It's after 5:00 young man. Where the hell have you been? You missed your doctor's appointment." She seemed to be completely ignoring Jay so I said, "Look Mom, look who's here. It's Jay."

"I see that," she said as her nose rumpled up. "Jesus Christ, what have you two been doing? You've been drinking. Haven't you? You disgust me." Without another word she grabbed both of us by our arms and took us over to the fence and sat us down. She then went over and got the garden hose and turned it on us.

Although it probably was not her desired effect, it felt great.

I looked down the driveway and made out Ben coming up on his bike. Mom called him over and handed him the hose. She told him to squirt us if we tried to get up and run away. She said, "I am going to call your mother, Jason. I cannot believe it. The first time you two get together and you cause trouble. You're nothing but trouble, young man." She finished her tirade and stomped off. I was too out of it to even move. Ben didn't have a thing to worry about. Jay and I just sat there on the pavement and smiled at each other.

Several minutes later a car pulled up in front of the house. It was Jay's mother and grandparents. Mom went down to the curb to meet them. The only thing I could see were the extended hugs and hand shakes which they exchanged. The four of them were upon us in nothing flat. Pop pop looked down at us and began shaking his head. "How pathetic," he said in disgust. He turned to Mom and asked her if she had any coffee to make a strong pot to sober the both of us up.

Kevin A. Carey

Mom protested, "Aren't they still too young for that?"

"Now, Jeannie, if they are old enough to drink, they are most certainly old enough for coffee."

Mom turned and went into the house to make the coffee. Shelly started to cry at the sight of us and walked into the backyard. Mom-mom and Pop-pop went to console her, completely ignoring us for the time being. Ben continued to guard us with the hose, squirting us occasionally just for the hell of it. Mom returned with a silver tray in hand. On it was a full pot of coffee, milk and sugar, a plate full of freshly made Rice Krispy Treats and several mugs and spoons. Jay's grandfather started shaking his head vehemently back and forth when he saw the spread. "Jeannie, why did you go to so much trouble? This is not a tea party!"

I could tell that Mom was quite insulted by the remark but she did not say a word as she placed the tray on the picnic table. Pop pop directed us over to the table and made us sit down at opposite ends from each other. Mom began pouring the coffee into the mugs. Pop pop stopped her after two cups were poured. He picked up a Rice Krispy Treat for himself and said, "We don't need the coffee, and they do. Don't add any milk or sugar. These boys need to drink it black. They can handle liquor, they can handle black coffee." Pop pop was sitting on the small bench at the head of the table. He looked at the both of us and sternly asked, "What makes you guys think that you are grown-up enough to drink?" We both held our heads in shame and didn't say anything.

"Jason, I'm shocked at you. You, of all people. You need to be strong. You are the man of the house now, and this is totally unacceptable behavior. What possessed you?"

I looked over at Jay and saw a smile pass across his face. He said, "We were celebrating."

"Celebrating what?" he asked in exasperation.

Before Jay had a chance to answer the question I said, "That's our little secret." With that the two of us started laughing uncontrollably. Both Shelly and Mom were crying. I'm sure they understood.

Pop pop grabbed Jay by the back of his shirt collar and told him that he had better straighten out and fast.

"I think it's time we took you home," he said. "I see you've already had a shower. Thanks, Jeannie, great job, and thank you for the coffee and Rice Krispy Treats."

Mom must have been really angry because she grabbed me by my ear and told me how humiliated she was. She dragged me along, as she walked everybody to their car.

Shelly turned to Mom and said, "Jeannie, I know it has been a very difficult couple of months for all of us. I really am sorry for everything that has happened. You must hate me. I don't want to lose your friendship. It means too much to me."

Mom finally let my ear go and went over and gave Shelly a big hug. "You are so right," she said, "I don't want to lose your friendship either. I am sorry about Peter. If there is anything you need please call me any time of the day or night. I mean that."

"Thank you. You are a doll. I do hope that you and Doug and Geoffrey can come to the funeral." Shelly looked over at me and said, "That is if he wants to come."

"It would be an honor. Wouldn't it?" she said to me as she pulled my ear again.

"Yes," I muttered.

Mom asked Shelly, "So have they found a cause for the crash yet?"

Shelly said with an occasional tear streaming down her face, "Of course details are very sketchy right now, and the FAA is doing an investigation which can take up to a full year to get results. The preliminary word is that a flock of Canadian Geese were passing by and got caught in the engines of the plane, clogged them up, and caused the plane to go down."

CHAPTER SEVENTEEN

Even now as I sit back on the couch in my apartment in Georgetown I have a great big smile on my face thinking back on that day. I felt absolutely no sense of loss for Coach Scott. He deserved what he got. The hangover I suffered the next morning, no matter how painful, was well worth it. Actually the feeling of euphoria far overshadowed the pain of the hangover.

Coach's funeral was another ordeal. It was almost two weeks before it could take place. It took that long to identify what was left of his body. Mom and Dad and I arrived at the funeral chapel right before services were set to begin. The place was packed with executives, civic leaders, friends, neighbors, family and the curious. The press was covering the event as if a head-of-state had died. We were immediately escorted to one of the front pews by one of Jay's cousins. Coach's bronze casket was resting on a rolling cart in the center of the aisle in front of the alter. It had an American flag draped over it signifying Coach's military service. There were sprays of flowers everywhere. I turned around in my seat. The Mastersons were sitting right behind me. Mrs. Masterson was clutching her newborn baby girl. I whispered hello. She introduced me to the new baby. Holly was her name. I looked down at the entrance of the chapel and saw Jay and Shelly preparing to enter with Mom-mom and Pop-pop. As they walked up the aisle a silence fell over the gathering and the service began.

It seemed to go on forever. People from various parts of Coach's life eulogized him and praised him for all of the wonderful and tireless deeds he had performed for his community, his job and his family. It really nauseated me. When it was finally over the family began filing out of the chapel. As Jay passed me he whispered, "I have a surprise for you. Meet me at the front of the chapel by the casket."

Several minutes later, after everyone had exited and headed for their respective automobiles for the procession to the cemetery Jay and I reentered the now empty chapel except for Coach's coffin and a couple of undertakers who were waiting to take it out to the hearse.

Jay slowly led me up the aisle. "I have to show you something," he said as he pushed the flag away. Before it hit the floor one of the undertakers ran over and grabbed it. Jay seemed not to be paying attention to any of that. He unlatched the clasps of the coffin.

I could not believe what he was doing. The last thing I needed to see was what was left of Coach. I nervously said, "I don't know if this is such a good idea Jay."

"Chill out and close your eyes," he said as he popped the final latch and flipped open coffin. When I again opened my eyes Jay was holding the sword in the palms of his hands. I shivered. I could not believe what I was seeing. Jay looked into my eyes, tears now streaming down. He said, "I want you to have the satisfaction of knowing that it is gone, buried, forever. You will never have to see it again. It can never threaten you or hurt you ever again."

We both stared at it for a long time, the tears coming easily to both of us. "Here, take it," Jay said.

I took the sword from him. I felt its power. My mind was racing replaying memory upon memory. I felt the room spinning out of control. I heard an incredible amount of screaming. I looked up and there was Kenny Masterson lying on Coach's bed with his arms and wrists tied down. Then I heard someone yelling from behind me. It was Coach. He was firmly pressing down on my shoulders. He shouted from behind me, "Do it Geoffrey, do it, and don't stop until it is finished." I lifted the sword over my head.

All of a sudden I was jolted back to reality. Jay and one of the undertakers were trying to take the sword away from me. Jay looked at me with tears in his eyes and said, "It's over, Geoff, it's finally over."

I could not believe the images that were now flooding into my mind. Every horrible, grotesque second of that weekend was now playing itself out in excruciating explicit detail.

"It's over. He can't hurt you anymore," Jay said.

All I could utter in my trance-like state was, "I just need to be alone."

401

"I understand," he responded and acquiesced to my wishes leaving me alone in the front pew. Shockwave after shockwave tore through my body as the memories returned. There was no longer a missing day. I now knew I had deliberately murdered one of my friends in cold blood. The guilt that gripped my heart took my breath away. I cried like I had never cried before. It was as if the floodgates had broken wide open and were finally releasing all the pain and hurt that I had stored inside of me for so long. I cried for what I had been forced to do to Kenny. I cried for what Coach had done to me. Most of all, I was crying for the innocent ten year old boy who died alongside Kenny that day.

As the tears continued to stream down my face I felt someone put their arm around me. I turned to find Mom sitting next to me. She too had tears in her eyes. She said, "I did not realize until now what a tortured little boy you are. I am so sorry for not being a good mom and being there for you no matter what. I promise to try and change that. Now, when you're ready, we'll go."

I asked for one more minute alone. She said okay, quietly got up and headed towards the entrance to the chapel. Of course Mom could never know the truth, no one could, that would be something I was going to have to take to my grave. I cried a little longer, and then the tears stopped. The incredible feeling of sadness that I had felt only moments ago was now replaced with an unbelievable sense of release. I got up and never looked back. I opened the doors to the chapel. I could not help but notice what a beautiful, bright, sunshiny day it was and how wonderful it was to be alive.

CHAPTER EIGHTEEN

They say when one door closes another one opens. That is exactly what happened on the day Coach was buried. When we arrived home, I went up to my room to change out of my suit. I undressed mechanically, the gruesome images of that horrid weekend still raging through my head. I neatly hung up my suit, put it away in the closet and changed into some shorts and a tee shirt. I picked out a book that I had read so often the glossy photos were beginning to fade and the pages were tattered. It was a pictorial of the French Riviera. I was hoping that it would distract me and clear my mind. I looked around the room, stopped and noticed my dresser. It was covered in plastic. Dad was getting ready to repair the ceiling from water damage that seeped through the roof from a recent rainstorm. Seeing the plastic instantaneously jolted me back to that horrifying scene two years earlier. I could vividly see Kenny wrapped in the same kind of plastic that was covering my dresser. As tears welled up in my eyes I knew I had to get out of that room and fast. I quickly made my way down the stairs, silently passing Mom and Dad who were sitting in the living room reading their respective sections of the newspaper. Mom looked at me for a brief moment and could sense I needed to be alone. She smiled tenderly and went back to her reading.

I went out the back door, unfolded one of the lounge chairs, placed it in the direction of the sun's rays and sat down. It felt so warm and wonderful against my face. I closed my eyes, taking in the warmth, and felt a profound sense of relaxation for the first time in a very long time. I tried to clear my mind of all the bullshit that was in it. I opened the book I brought with me and turned to the chapter about the Cannes Film Festival. It all sounded so glamorous to me. Someday, I thought, I'm going to go to Cannes. I stared down at the page, but could not concentrate on what I was reading. There were just too many questions going through my mind. Questions I knew I would eventually have to deal with. One thing very clear. I was the one who had killed Kenny. Coach had made it perfectly clear that no matter what had happened, I was the one who was responsible and I would be the one held accountable for Kenny's murder. I thanked God that the only other person who could implicate me was Coach and he was dead and buried and hopefully rotting in hell. The only other person I had to worry about was Grand pop. Did he know what really happened? Did he somehow find out? I knew he had the means to find out such things, and he had implied only weeks earlier that he knew something more than I did. I recalled his words exactly. He said, "Oh Geoffrey, what secrets are locked inside that brain of yours? Now don't worry about that anymore, you will never have to worry about that again. I will personally see to it." That statement led me to only one conclusion, that Grand pop was somehow responsible for the crash of the plane that Coach was on. It was no accident. The answer lay right in the newspaper account of what had happened. I had read it over and over again. The article said that when the plane was about fifteen minutes away from the airport, the pilot radioed the tower and said that he was going to need fuel when he landed.

That in itself was a strange statement given that refueling was a routine kind of thing. Then an eyewitness, himself a pilot, speculated that, "something must have gone wrong with at least one of the engines and the pilot (of the corporate jet) was trying, unsuccessfully, to glide the plane into the airport." The thought occurred to me that perhaps my own grandfather was trying to protect me, even if it meant the loss of innocent lives. Did he love me that much? Despite the moral dilemma going on inside my head, I was truly grateful to him. I worshiped the ground he walked on. I was more determined than ever to be just like him someday.

Of course, I could never be certain of any of these theories. How could he know what really happened? He was only trying to put pieces of a puzzle together, pieces that appeared to fit. Nevertheless, he had no solid proof, no evidence that I was aware of. My best course of action would be to do nothing and to keep all of this newfound knowledge securely locked inside of my head. My heart grew heavier and heavier as I laid there contemplating all of these things.

*****

I must have dozed off for a while because I didn't hear the truck pull up in the adjoining driveway. I was jolted awake by a loud bang. Through my blurry eyes I saw a moving van in the driveway. The loud bang was the sound of the doors swinging open against the sides of the truck. The house next door to us had been empty for several weeks already. I recalled the day Mom came in telling us, "Mrs. Larson is moving into a nursing home near her family in Florida." Not that I'd miss the old bat or anything. She always seemed so fussy. Every time I would walk across her lawn to get to my house, she'd shoot out of her front door hollering at me. "Get off my lawn, young man!" Needless to say, I did all I could to avoid her. At least now, I recall thinking and wishing, there was a chance that someone younger with kids would buy her house. As I peeked over the fence it appeared that my wish had come true. I counted at least six of them. One of them caught me looking, came up to the fence and introduced himself. "Hi, my name is David."

"Hi, I'm Geoffrey," I said.

"Looks like a good book," David said.

"Yeah," I said, "It's one of my favorites. It's about the French Riviera. I especially like the part about the Cannes Film Festival."

David appeared to show genuine interest. Perhaps he was just being polite. "That is so cool. Have you ever been there?" He asked.

"No," I replied, adding with some enthusiasm, "but mark my words, some day, some day."

David just said, "Wow!" and smiled. "We're moving in next door to you," he pointed toward Old Lady Larson's house. The moving men were unloading furniture from the back of the truck. There were three kids playing in the yard behind David. "Those are my brothers. I have no sisters. And that's my mother over there telling those men where to put everything." Then he pointed toward an older woman sitting on a lawn chair next to his mother. "That's my granny. She lives with us too. She may be old, but she's a lot of fun."

"So, where's your dad?" I asked him.

"Oh, my parents are divorced."

Just then Mom came out to water the lawn. I introduced her to David.

"It's nice to meet you David," she said.

"If you'd like to come over, I'll introduce you to my family," David offered.

"Yes, that would be very nice."

His mother, who insisted we call her Belle, sure seemed different. She reminded me a lot of Aunt Vivian.

"Can I offer you a beer, Jeannie?" Belle asked.

"At two in the afternoon?" Mom responded a bit taken aback.

"Yeah, well it's Saturday. Happy hour began at least two hours ago," Belle laughed.

"No, thank you," Mom declined politely.

Belle grabbed three more lawn chairs and set them up next to her mother's, Mrs. Gilda Holland, whom she introduced to Mom and me. Belle motioned for Mom and me to have a seat. "Listen Billy, stay in the yard with the ball," Belle hollered out to one of her kids playing in their new backyard.

"You do have your hands full," Mom said, a tad bit overwhelmed by all the activity. Mom then looked at Belle with this puzzled look on her face and asked, "How do the movers know where to put everything?"

"Oh, honey," Belle assured Mom, "my brother works for the moving company and he got me a swell deal. Besides, everything is marked so there are no mistakes. I'll introduce you to him when he comes back for another beer," Belle said as she pointed towards her well-stocked cooler.

"Oh," Mom said and then added, "Is there anything I can do to help?"

"You're a sweetie for asking, but really, I've got everything under control."

After some brief conversation Mom stood up and said, "It's very nice to meet you, Belle and Mrs. Holland. I do need to be running, though. Come along, Geoff."

"Geoff is welcome to stay if he wants to," Belle interjected.

411

"Only if he doesn't get in the way," Mom agreed, giving me one of her "and that's an order" looks. She then headed back to watering the lawn.

David took me on a tour of his new house. Although I had been inside of it many times before, it was like being in a different place. It even smelled different. We reached the top of the stairs, made a quick right and David proudly announced, "This is all mine. I have my very own room. I have always had to share a bedroom with my younger brother, Larry. Mother thought that since I will be a freshman in high school this fall, and am becoming an adult, I should have my own space."

I nodded my head and said, "Me too! I'll be a freshman too."

"Great," David said, "Maybe we will be in the same classes."

"Well," he said as he looked around the room, "the movers have unloaded all my stuff, so I guess I can put it away."

"I'll be glad to help you," I offered.

"That would be great," David said enthusiastically. "The quicker we get done the more time we will have to explore the neighborhood. That is if you don't have any plans this afternoon."

"Nope," I said. "I'm free all day. The world's at our feet. Or at least the neighborhood."

David smiled at me again and said, "Yeah it is, isn't it."

The first box we opened had a couple of posters in it. The first one we unrolled was of Marilyn Monroe in the famous scene with her dress swirling around her waist. "That's from the movie, The Seven Year Itch," David said, adding, "I just love that movie." The second poster David unrolled was of James Dean on a motorcycle. "Isn't that a great poster?" David asked with a big smile on his face.

"Yeah," I said. My mind flashed back to Kurt. We had met only briefly the summer before but the impact had been a lasting one. Now everything became clear. I was getting a second chance and this time, I promised myself, I was not going to blow it. Of course I was going to have to be absolutely certain before I jumped to any conclusions.

Our conversation turned to stuff like what the neighborhood was like and who my friends were. I looked around the room noting that mostly everything was unpacked so I suggested that we hop on our bikes and do the tour of the neighborhood and meet up with some of the guys.

Even though I had mentioned Jay in our conversation I hadn't told David about Jay's dad. I decided that I had better tell him that we had just buried his father earlier in the day, just in case it came up when we met some of the other guys. "You see," I said, "Jay's dad, we all called him Coach because he was the head of the park's little league, died in a plane crash a couple of weeks ago."

"Was that the one that's been splashed all over the news? The one where the small corporate jet crashed as it was landing somewhere in Canada?"

David seemed really interested in the details, but I wasn't in any mood to talk about it at that moment. There was no way I was going to reveal anything about the shit that asshole put me through to a complete stranger.

I said with exasperation, "Look, it's no big deal. He's dead. He's right where he belongs, six feet under. Now, please, let's change the subject."

"Hold on Geoffrey, don't take your anger out on me. I was only curious."

I suddenly felt ashamed and said, "I'm sorry David, I didn't mean to lose my temper like that. It's just that it's a long story and I'd prefer not to get into it right now."

"Okay, I won't pry anymore. I'm sorry," David said.

"Thank you," I sheepishly responded, hoping I had not offended my new friend too much.

"Hey," I smiled, "I have a great idea." I knew what I was about to suggest was probably a big mistake. But hell, I thought, Jay is spending the day with his family. He'll never know, and I'll make sure David doesn't say a word to anybody. I hesitated as I thought about what I was about to suggest.

David looked at me in anticipation and said, "So, what's this great idea of yours?"

I threw all caution to the wind because I needed to go to the cave. Perhaps it would help me clear my mind. I suggested, "Let's go for a bike ride down to the park. I have something really cool to show you. But you have to promise not to tell anyone, especially not Jay." I spit in the palm of my hand and then held it out to David. He gave me this horrified look. "Yuck, how gross. You do some strange things here. Go wash your hands."

"Sorry," I said, "it's just the way we solidify a promise."

"I think my word is good enough, don't you?" David said with a rather skeptical look on his face.

"Yeah, I guess so," I said feeling rather childish as I walked down the hall to the bathroom. I quickly washed my hands and turned to leave. To my surprise there was David standing at the bathroom door staring and smiling at me. "How long have you been standing there staring at me?" I asked.

Ignoring my inquiry David continued to smile at me. He said, "I'm sorry we don't do those kinds of things where I come from."

"It's okay," I said.

David reached out his hand to me. I reached for his and we shook hands. It was really weird, yet really great. At that moment something strange and wonderful happened inside of me. We both smiled at each other and lingered for a second still holding on to each other's hand. We finally unclasped our hands. My hand was shaking and soaked with sweat despite the fact that I had just dried them moments earlier. I glanced over at David. He was wiping his hand on his shorts. Yes, I thought to myself, he felt it too.

We headed outside without another word. Belle and her mother had moved their lawn chairs to the front now so they could instruct the moving men where to put the odd bits of stuff that weren't labeled. I took note of one of the moving men in particular. He was very tanned and muscular and had a shaved head. I quickly turned away from him when he caught me staring at him.

"Hi," He said. "I'm David's Uncle Drew."

I turned back around to him, still a bit embarrassed, hoping he wouldn't notice that I was turning red. "Hi," I answered back.

"It's great that David has made a friend already. It's pretty tough moving into a new neighborhood and not knowing anybody. Especially at his age."

"Yeah, I know what you mean. I remember when I first moved here. I thought it was the end of the world."

Drew laughed and asked, "How long ago was that?"

"It will be four years ago this very week as a matter of fact."

Drew laughed again saying, "So, you're an old timer."

"I guess so."

"Come on Geoff," David cut in, "we've got some exploring to do!"

"I guess I gotta go. Nice to meet you," I said.

"See you around," Drew said as David and I got on our bikes and rode down the driveway.

"So," David asked, "you know all about my love for old movies. What do you like?"

"Oh," I said, "I'm interested in learning languages and reading about different places around the world."

"Like Cannes?" David asked.

"Yeah, like Cannes," I said letting my mind wander.

"I'd love to go there too. Wouldn't it be neat if we could go there together someday?" David commented, smiling at me.

"Yeah, it would," I said smiling at the thought of it.

"Here it is," I said. "Black Rock Park. It is called that because all the quarries and rocks are jet black. They say it's the only park around with such black rocks. I don't know if it's true or not, but it makes a great story." We got off of our bikes and walked past the ball fields to the edge of the woods.

"Where are you taking me?" David asked. "Is it safe?"

"Well, most of the adults seem to think that it is overrun by druggies, but if you're careful there's nothing to worry about."

"Sounds intriguing and dangerous," David said.

"Nah, not with me as your guide," I reassured him.

"If you say so," David said sounding rather skeptical.

We walked along a dirt trail through the densely wooded area until we came upon a small clearing where the cave was hidden. I didn't see Jay's bike or any sign of him, but the rocks and bushes used to hide the entrance to the cave had been moved aside. Our secret cave was exposed to anyone who happened along. I put my finger to my lips and motioned David not to make a sound. I listened intently. I heard a faint rustling noise coming from inside the cave. There was no doubt that there was someone in there. I didn't know if I should run or be brave and confront this intruder. Before I had a chance to make that decision a figure appeared at the entrance. There stood Jay, looking in my direction and swaying with an almost empty bottle of vodka in his hand. I watched as he focused first on me and then on David. He said, "Hey, slowpoke, where the hell have you been? I tried calling your house but your mother told me that you were out. So I decided to come down here without you."

"Sorry," I said, not really meaning it.

"So, who's that?" he inquired, pointing toward David. "What is he doing here?"

I could hear the anger well up in his voice. "This is David," I said. "He just moved in next door."

As if David wasn't present, Jay said, "Yeah, and what the fuck are you doing bringing someone else here? This is our secret place."

David turned toward me and said, "I can see I'm not wanted here. I'll be leaving now."

"No, wait," I said. I didn't want him to go and I knew that Jay was drunk and shouldn't be left alone.

"David," I said, "I'm sorry. He's obviously drunk and doesn't know what he's saying."

"It's okay," David said. "You need to be with your friend right now, or rather he needs to be with you."

I wondered to myself whether he meant what I think he meant, and then quickly replied without much thought, "No, David, it's not like that at all. Jay likes girls." I could not believe what I had just blurted out.

421

David cut in, "Geoff, Geoff, it's okay. I understand. I really do, and I'm really glad, because I wasn't sure."

Jay looked at both of us with this dumbfounded expression on his face.

David continued, "Now go back to your friend and get him home safely. I think he needs you more than I do right now. Don't worry, I'm cool."

Boy was I relieved. "I'll show you the way back home."

"It's okay. I'll just follow the path back to the playing fields."

"Yeah, then go to the entrance of the park and go all the way up the hill until the street ends, then make a left. Your house is a couple of blocks down."

"Don't worry, I'm really good with directions. Call me when you get home."

"Sounds great," I replied. David turned around and headed down the dirt path. I now focused my attention back to Jay. "What the fuck is your problem?" I shouted at him.

"Me?" Jay shot back. "What do you think you're doing bringing a total stranger here, to our secret place?"

"David is not a stranger," I retorted.

"Oh, bullshit, you just met him, didn't you? He's a stranger, Geoff."

Jay had it the other way around. He was acting more like the stranger now.

"You had no right bringing him here, no matter how well you think you know him," Jay shouted.

"Give me a break. I was just showing him around the neighborhood."

"I think it's more than that. I heard that shit you were talking right before he left and the way you two were gawking at each other. It makes me down right sick to my stomach. It's true, you are a big queer," Jay snapped.

"You're drunk!" I yelled at him.

"I'm just getting started," Jay said, slurring his words and producing yet another bottle of vodka seemingly from out of nowhere.

I grabbed the bottle from his hands and smashed it against some nearby rocks. Glass and vodka went flying in all directions. Luckily, none of the glass ricocheted back at us. I was furious with Jay. I screamed, "No, you're not just getting started. As a matter of fact you are finished."

He was still clutching the first bottle of vodka, which was almost empty. I grabbed it from him with little resistance. This time I threw it further away. It too shattered into a million pieces. Jay fell to his knees and began crying shamelessly.

"Now look what you've done asshole!" he screamed at me. "You've ruined everything."

I felt so sorry for him. I reached out to put my arm around him but he jerked away from me yelling, "My father is dead. You cannot and will not ever touch me like that again. I'm not a faggot like you. Do you understand me?"

"Yeah, I hear you," I said very offended and hurt, not knowing what to say.

Jay continued. "And one more thing, if you ever tell anyone outside of your family about the horrible things my father did, I will deny it all and call you a liar. The hell my father put you through will be nothing in comparison to what I will do to you. When my father died so did the secrets. We cannot ever talk about him and what he did to us, ever again. Do you hear me?"

"Jesus Christ," I exclaimed. "Why would I want to tell anyone else about your fucking asshole of a father? Get a grip. He's dead, rotting in hell, paying for what he did to us and God knows who else."

"Good," Jay said, "but don't ever forget what I just told you. I mean it. You open your fucking mouth to anyone else and I will hunt you down and you will wish it were you who were dead."

I heard what he was saying loud and clear and I believed every single word that spewed from his lips. "Let's get out of here," I said. "I'll help you get home."

Jay didn't say a word, but silently followed me all the way to his house. It was evident by all the cars parked out in front that there were still a lot of people there. I snuck him in the back door and took him down

425

to the recreation room. I sat him down and told him not to move. A noise came from the top of the stairs. Someone was coming down the steps. Thank God it was only Shelly. She was surprised to see us.

"Jason, honey, where have you been? We've been worried about you."

I answered for him, "Hi Shelly. He's okay. I found him down at the park. He had a little bit too much to drink, so I brought him home."

She stared at me for a moment, not sure what to say. "What do you mean, you found him?"

"I was riding my bike through the park and…"

Jay interjected, "Tell her all of it, Geoffrey." He turned to his mother, "He's got a new boyfriend, already. Dad's not even in the ground one day and Geoffrey's making new friends, forgetting about his real friends."

Before I had a chance to open my mouth in protest, Shelly said to Jay, "Well, what do you expect? Why, with the behavior you have been displaying lately, I am surprised you have any friends at all. Besides, it's obvious to me that Geoffrey still is your best friend. He cared enough to bring you home. He could have left you there, then God knows what might have happened to you, perhaps the same fate as your friend Kenny." She then turned to me and added, "Thank you, Geoffrey. You've been a great friend to Jason. You're invited here anytime."

"Thank you," I said to Shelly. I turned to Jay and told him that I was still his best friend and that I was here for him.

"Yeah, yeah," Jay said incoherently, "now get outta here."

I nodded to Shelly and excused myself. I left out the back door so I wouldn't have to confront any of the guests and made my way home.

That night as I lay in bed it was not Jay and his shenanigans that I was thinking about. It was David. He looked so good today, especially in the pair of short shorts he was wearing. He had curly blonde hair and blue eyes. He was much taller than me and his long legs were so muscular. God, it was so crazy, but I was certain that I was falling in love with him. The more I thought about him the stronger the longing I felt towards him. My imagination was filled with images of us being together. It felt as if I had grown wings and taken flight. I felt like I was soaring through the sky like an eagle.

Wow, I thought to myself as I now stared down at the first pictures I had taken of David. I continued to smile as I leafed through the next couple of pages of the photo album, again drifting back through time...

Mom popped her head in the bedroom door and told me to get up and get ready for church. I rolled over and looked at the time. It was already nine o'clock.

As we left the house at a quarter to ten, David and the rest of his family were coming out of their front door. My heart leapt at the mere sight of David from across the driveway. Belle announced that they were on their way to church, although she wasn't exactly sure as to how to get there. Dad, finding it a bit odd that anyone would venture out without a clue, chuckled and suggested she follow us. I went over and said good morning to David and apologized to him for Jay's behavior the previous day. He smiled at me, bid me a good morning and said to forget about it. Apparently Natalie and Ben had made friends with David's brothers, for in no time they were all running around playing with each other. Mom started to yell at the kids, "Come on now, stop playing. You're going to get your nice clothes dirty." Everybody piled into their respective station wagons and off we went to church.

After mass Mom introduced Belle and her mother to some of the other women. David and his brothers all stood in a neat line while Belle proudly introduced each one. I grabbed David away and told him I wanted him to meet some of the guys. As we walked towards a small group of guys, Mark, an acquaintance from school, called out to me and asked, "Do you think they will make you captain of the junior varsity wrestling team this year?"

"I don't know," I answered blushing.

"Oh, come on," Danny, another friend, continued, "they have to. You're the only guy on the team with an undefeated record."

David whispered into my ear, "I didn't know you were a wrestler, and undefeated. Wow, I'm impressed."

I turned red with embarrassment as another kid, Barry, chimed in and said, "Yeah, he's really good. He's got a great take down technique and you should see his Half Nelson move."

Barry, finally noticing David, turned to me and said, "So, Geoffrey, who is your friend?"

"If you guys let me get a word in edgewise!" I quipped. Everyone laughed. "This is David," I said, "he just moved into the neighborhood yesterday. He is my new next-door neighbor. He's going to be a freshman too."

"Cool," one of the guys said as I introduced David to each of them.

"They are all also on the wrestling team," I said.

Just then Ben came running over to us and said, "Come on, Dad's taking all of us to Denny's for breakfast."

"Who's all of us?" I asked him.

"Us and our new neighbors, come on!"

"Okay," I said. "Sorry guys, we gotta go now. See you all on Wednesday."

"Nice to meet you," David said.

As we walked away, David turned to me and said, "I have to admit I'm not much into sports, but I'd love to see your Half Nelson move sometime, whatever that is."

I laughed and told him it was no big deal. "But seriously," I said, "I'm not much into sports either, though my grandfather says it makes you a well rounded person, and to get anywhere in life you have to be well rounded."

"I suppose that makes sense," David said. "I see life as an adventure. It isn't just getting there; it is enjoying the journey as you go and being yourself. That is one thing my father did teach me."

"What do you mean by that?" I asked.

"It's a long story. I promise to tell you when we have more time."

With that we piled into our respective cars and drove off to Denny's. On the way mom commented to us how proud she was of all of us. She said, "It sure is nice that we are making friends with our new neighbors and making them feel welcome."

Once at the restaurant we had to sit at two separate tables. David's grandmother graciously offered to sit at the table with the younger kids. David and I, being the eldest in both our families, sat at the table with Mom, Dad and Belle. Boy, Belle sure could talk up a storm. She gave us her family's history in less than two hours. They had moved all the way from Wichita, Kansas, although her roots were originally from this area. She told us that she had worked at the main headquarters for Pizza Hut as a Quality Control Manager.

"My favorite pizza place," I said.

"Well now it is going to be even better," Belle proudly announced. "You see, when I decided to leave Kansas, Pizza Hut offered me management position. I will be the District Manager for the eight Pizza Huts in this area."

She continued to talk incessantly about each of her children; their different personality traits, characteristics, likes, dislikes and stuff like that. She was really proud of her kids. I was especially fascinated to listen to her dote over David, who blushed the whole time. I think she liked David the best. "He loves old movies," she said smiling at David. "Why, he knows all of the old time actors and actresses. He can even recite dialogue from many of the movies. He is so amazing. Who knows, maybe he'll be a big shot movie director someday."

"Oh, Mom," David said, red as a beet now. "Stop it, you're embarrassing me."

I looked over at David and smiled and said, "Wow, a movie director. How cool is that!"

"That's Mom's dream," David said.

"So what's your dream?" I asked.

David perked up and said, "I want to be an actor on Broadway."

"Wow," I said in awe.

Belle continued to smile at David and said, "That's nice dear. You've never told me about that. It does sound like a good idea though, because they say acting makes you a better director."

Belle turned to me and asked, "So Geoffrey, what do you want to be when you grow up?"

"That's an easy one," I said as my mother shot a nervous glance at me. "I am going to work for the United States government and the President of the United States, just like my grandfather."

Now it was David's turn to be in awe. "Your grandfather works for the President of the United States?"

"Yes," I smiled proudly.

"Wow! Have you ever met the President?" David asked.

"Oh yeah," I beamed. It was now my turn to shine. I hadn't gotten to talk about Jay's and my visit with President and Mrs. Nixon last summer in such a long time. It was a story I would never tire of telling. Mom and Dad smiled politely as I talked, although I knew they were tired of the story. Belle and David listened intently, throwing out a couple of questions now and then.

When I finished, Belle asked, "So what exactly does your grandfather do for the President?"

I could see Mom tense up again. I carefully considered my answer, then said, "You know I honestly don't know what he does. He's never really told me."

David looked at me funny and started to laugh and asked, "So, how do you know you want to be just like your grandfather if you have no idea what it is he does?"

"I know it sounds weird," I said, "but I've always known that's what I've wanted. I am learning many different languages and my grandfather is helping me with my studies by picking out all of the right classes to take."

By the expression on Mom's face, it was clear that she was quite uncomfortable with what I was saying. "Geoffrey, dear, I don't think Belle and David want to hear about this. Don't you remember what your grandfather told you?"

"Yes," I answered as I went back to my breakfast, finishing the last of what was on my plate.

David's curiosity peaked. "So, Geoffrey, what did your grandfather tell you?"

"Nothing," I lied. "Nothing at all."

Belle apparently could sense the tension in Mom's voice and my sudden change in mood. She looked over at David and said, "I think it's time to change the subject."

The waiter was now coming over to our table with check in hand. Dad promptly paid the bill, and we were out of there and on our way home. I couldn't see David for the rest of the afternoon because he and his family were spending the afternoon with their Uncle Drew. When we got home I went straight to my room, changed my clothes, and pulled out two notebooks from two different hiding places. One hiding place was more secure than the other. In fact, to get to that notebook it took not one but two strategically placed combination locks. I figured that if someone found the hiding place they would have one hell of a time getting to the notebook. One notebook was for the doctor and the other one was only for me. That notebook was where I recorded my real thoughts and feelings.

I took both notebooks and a pen and went outside to the smaller of the two picnic tables in our backyard. Everyone knew that when I had my notebook out that it was very important that I be left alone. This was to be my quiet time to do my homework for my special doctor. The first thing I did was scribble some nonsense into the notebook that Dr. Weinstein would see, so that he could try to analyze me in our weekly sessions. I felt that these sessions were a complete waste of time. But it made everybody else happy and kept them off of my back so I did it. With that finished, I quickly went to work in the second notebook.

> 1. *Kenny. Besides Coach, could anyone else who knows exactly what happened that horrible night? Grand pop seemed to know something, but what? Yeah, he knew the truth about not going down to the Shore. He knew that I had spent the entire weekend at Coach's house. He also knew that Kenny had come to the house looking for Jay, but nobody was home. Did he put two and two together? Did he have a chance to question Coach before Coach died? Would Coach have*

told him anything? I suppose I could ask Grand pop straight out if he talked to Coach. But then, would he get suspicious? Would it completely ruin my chances for a government job if Grand pop knew that I had murdered someone? I needed to come up with a way to ask Grand pop if there was anything Coach may have told him without giving myself away. Then there was Jay and Shelly. They also knew where I was that entire weekend. Did one or both of them surmise what happened that Saturday? Did Coach tell Shelly what happened that Saturday? Did Coach finally give in to Shelly's insistent probing and confess to her? I suppose I could start by questioning Jay, however, he's been so out of it lately, with his drinking and all. Jay and I however, were so close that we told each other anything and everything. Though now I wasn't so sure. He just seemed so distant and troubled. He should be the happiest person alive now that his asshole of a father was dead. I know I certainly was. How was I going to get him to stop drinking?

2. *The Plane Crash. It's pretty obvious, at least to me, that it wasn't an accident. Why did Grand pop do it? I know he is involved. There's no other explanation. He told me that I would never have to worry about Coach again, and then not too long after that, Coach ends up dead. Coincidence? I really don't think so. If I asked Grand pop, would he be honest with me? Even if he had something to do with it do I dare mention it to him? I mean, he did me a favor. He did us all a favor. But still, to satisfy my curiosity, I needed to know.*

3.   *David. David is a whole other story.
        He's not really a problem at all. He has
        all but admitted to me that he also likes
        guys. Of course, I am going to have to
        continue to hide it and not let anyone
        else know, especially Jay. If Dr.
        Weinstein ever discovers that I like guys,
        he will tell Mom. Well, if being a
        homosexual is a disease, then I don't
        want to be cured of it. Besides, I don't
        believe it is a disease. I don't feel sick
        inside. It all seems so natural. What
        makes me feel sick is to have to keep it
        all bottled up inside of me. I know that
        love between two men is not an
        acceptable thing in society, but my gut
        tells me it is not wrong no matter what
        people say. How am I going to tell
        David? He has got to know.*

4.   *Sharon. David has got to know that I am
        only using Sharon as a shield to hide*

behind. He has to know that no matter what everyone says about us, Sharon and I aren't having sex. I messed up last summer with that guy at the pool, Kurt. Given everything that has happened it's probably better that way. But not this time. This time I know better who I am and what I want, even if it means having to hide it. The sooner David knows how I feel and what is going on inside of my head, the better my chances with him will be. Of course there is always the question of what if I am completely wrong about him. What if he isn't gay? If I come right out and tell him, I risk losing another friend.

The backdoor slammed and out came Mom and Dad. I quickly closed both notebooks and put them in my book bag.

"You've been out here a long time, son," Dad said.

"I just have a lot on my mind," I said.

"It's okay," Mom said, "this summer has been very difficult for you. One we all would rather just as soon forget."

"You can say that again!" I exclaimed.

"Geoff," Dad said, "your mother and I need to talk to you. We've given you most of the summer to think about what happened and to work with Dr. Weinstein without any interference from us, but we feel it's time as your parents to know what is going on with you. We really don't know nor do we quite frankly understand. It seems as if you have shut us out of your life and your mother and I are not very happy about it."

"What do you mean?" I asked, feeling my defenses quickly go up.

"I think you know what we mean," Dad answered. "You are fourteen years old. You are old enough to know the difference between right and wrong. In fact your grandfather thinks you should be treated like an adult, although sometimes I'm not so sure about that given your recent behavior."

"What's that supposed to mean?" I asked, defensively.

Mom continued to keep silent while Dad controlled the conversation. "You have never discussed with us what was going on between you, Jay and Mr. Scott."

"Do we need to go into that again?" I asked, now annoyed.

"Yes, as a matter of fact, we do. You have never told *us* all about it. *Only* Dr. Weinstein."

"Wait," I said, now visibly upset, "do you think that I wanted Coach to do those awful things to me?"

"Did you?" Dad asked.

"No way!" I hollered. "This is a stupid conversation."

"Calm down, Geoffrey," Mom said, "your father is only trying to help you."

As difficult as it was, I sat there quietly while Dad continued on. "Didn't you tell the doctor that you looked forward to your little meetings with Jason and Mr. Scott?"

I hesitated a second to think about my answer. "Well, yeah, I guess so. But I was under a lot of stress. I was afraid that if I said that I didn't like it, that Coach would come after me. Jesus, the man threatened to kill me if I ever told anyone. I was scared to death. I really was."

Mom was starting to cry. "So, you're not a homosexual?" she asked.

"Of course not!" I exclaimed.

"Is Jason a homosexual?" Dad asked.

"Absolutely not," I answered.

"You don't know how good it is to hear you say that Geoffrey," Dad said, obviously relieved.

"Do I still have to go and see Dr. Weinstein?" I asked.

Mom answered that one. "Yes, I am afraid so. Unfortunately, it will take a long time to work through those unnatural things that happened to you. You may not understand it now, but someday you will."

"It just seems so dumb," I said. "I mean I'm tired of drawing pictures and playing with his stupid dolls. If Dr. Weinstein hasn't figured it out yet, he never will."

Apparently Dad was not listening to a word I was saying. He had an agenda and he intended to make his point no matter what. "Geoffrey," he continued, "Is the pain of what happened so bad that you have to turn to alcohol?"

That question took me totally by surprise. "What?" I asked, truly bewildered.

"We've let go of the incident that occurred a few weeks ago, but yesterday when you came home, your mother smelled alcohol all over your clothes. Be honest, Geoffrey, how long has this been going on? We need to know so that we can get you some help."

I turned my head and looked away for a moment. I didn't know if I should tell them about Jay and jeopardize our friendship even more. If anyone was going to help him, it was going to be me. I was so confused; I didn't know what to say.

"It's okay, son," Dad said. "Your mother and I are here for you. We want to help you. You've made a lot of bad decisions in your young life. We want to help you change that."

That was the last straw. I sat straight up on the bench and shouted, "No matter what I tell you, you're not going to believe me, so why should I waste my breath?"

"Oh God, Geoffrey, it is true, isn't it?" Mom cried.

"Is what true?" I yelled.

"Geoffrey!" Dad shouted as he slammed his fist down on the wooden table. "If you don't stop shouting, I'll use my belt on you. You're not too old for that!"

I quickly came to my senses, although I was still very angry. The vision of Jay's bloody black and blue butt passed through my mind.

"You're an alcoholic!" Mom stated with tears in her eyes. "Where did we go wrong? We've been good parents. We've done the best we could."

"You're fucking crazy," I shouted. "I am not an alcoholic."

"You apologize to your mother for that language, young man!" Dad shouted.

"Why?" I growled. "Mom makes all these accusations before she even hears all of the facts."

"That's enough out of you!" Dad yelled.

"Now who's shouting?" I yelled back.

Dad continued, seeming a little bit calmer, "We are not leaving this table until you tell us about your drinking problem."

"First of all," I said, "I don't have a drinking problem."

"Then what do you call it?" He asked doing his best to keep his cool.

"I've been drunk one time, and believe me, I have no intention of doing it again."

Dad ploughed on, "Well, then how do you explain yesterday?"

"You smelled it on my clothes, not on my breath," I argued.

"What were you doing with it on your clothes? Bathing in it?" Dad asked sarcastically.

"I was helping a friend, if you must know," I said.

"Keep talking," Dad snorted.

I looked Dad straight in the eye and said, "Look, this is something I have to deal with on my own. You are just going to have to trust me."

"How are we supposed to trust you after everything that has happened?"

As soon as I heard that statement I knew that I was all alone in this world, probably never to be believed again. But I had to keep my cool and play their game if

I was going to get anywhere. I learned that lesson all too well, thanks to Coach. I chose my words carefully, "I am not an alcoholic and I am not a homosexual. I'm sorry that you don't believe either of those things." I then lowered my voice and said something that took everybody by surprise, even myself. "I'm working too hard to live up to my grandfather's wishes. If you, or anybody, comes between me and the goals that I have set for myself, I will never forgive you and you will never see me again."

Mom and Dad sat there in total disbelief. Dad finally said, "That's quite a big threat for such a young boy."

"Young man," I corrected him. "Yes, it is."

I knew that the one person my father feared was Grand pop. I also knew that Dad was not very happy with his father-in-law's participation in my academic and extracurricular life. However, it was evident that he had absolutely no control or say in the matter. I continued, "I will go to him and tell him that I want to live with him and Grand mom, and tell him how horrible it is living here."

Mom was crying and Dad was so upset he was shaking. He stood up, not very steadily on his feet. "I don't know who you think you are, mister, or where you learned to act like this, but don't think you are going to get away with this."

With that, he took Mom by the arm and guided her back into the house. I was finally alone to comprehend what I had just done. I had declared war on my own parents and our home-life would never be the same. I thought about something Grand pop told me the last time I saw him. He said, "You, Geoffrey S. Brooks, are the master of your own destiny." I realized now what he meant. I had just taken control of my destiny.

CHAPTER NINETEEN

I was now staring down at more blank pages. The last half of the photo album was completely empty again. I did that intentionally. It was probably my morbid mind at work. I just could not get into taking pictures anymore that summer. As quickly as the bug had returned to me, it just as quickly left me. While the pages of the album were blank, my memory certainly was not.

I had two days before the start of the new school year to talk to David and try to explain to him how I felt about him in a way that wouldn't offend him if he weren't interested. First, however, I had to try to talk some sense into Jay. I woke up early the next Monday morning. Instead of calling Jay I decided to show up unannounced. I told Mom I was going out for a bike ride to clear my head a bit. She just shrugged and said something like "okay," but she didn't look at me. She was avoiding my gaze ever since yesterday's confrontation.

I got on my bicycle and rode straight over to Jay's house. As I was getting off my bike, the front door opened and out came Chief Baxter. He walked past me not even seeing me. "Hello, Chief Baxter," I called out.

"Oh hello, Geoff. Sorry. I am still in shock over Mr. Scott's death."

"Yeah." I said half-heartedly, "It is terrible."

"Yeah it is," he said as he waved goodbye, casting his head down and walking away.

Shelly was at the door holding it open for me. She was drying tears from her face. I thought, even though I felt nothing for Coach, it must be really difficult to lose your husband. I tried to console her, but she seemed not to hear me. She suddenly pulled me close to her, started crying and told me that she missed him so much. Feeling a bit embarrassed, she let me go and tried to straighten up and stop crying. She looked me square in the eye and said, "May I ask you something Geoffrey?"

"Of course," I replied.

"In spite all of Mr. Scott's problems, don't you think he was still a great guy?"

Jesus, the man was an asshole! Why couldn't she see that, I thought. However, I knew that I had to lie. I said, "Yeah, he was."

By the look in my eyes she knew I really didn't mean what I said, but she did not try to challenge me. "So what brings you here so early. Jay is still in bed."

"That's okay," I said. "Can I ask you something?"

"Of course, Geoffrey. You know you can always ask me anything. That will never change, honey," Shelly said.

"Do you know that Jay has a problem with, you know, alcohol?" I said having trouble getting the words out of my mouth.

Shelly's eyes began welling up with tears. "To be honest, no I didn't realize it until you brought him home on Saturday. I guess I was caught up in my own things. But don't you worry about a thing. Jason and I had a long talk yesterday and he promised me that it would never happen again."

"And you believed him?" I asked.

"Yes, of course I did. He has never lied to me," she said, not really believing her own words.

I thought for a minute, and then I diplomatically stated, "I'm sure Jay means what he says, but sometimes it's hard to keep promises."

"What are you saying? Do you really think he has a big problem?" Shelly asked as if it were a new concept.

"Yes I do," I answered sadly.

"Why are you so sure?"

I thought about it for a second and then decided that it was time to break a sacred trust. "The first time we got drunk together, the day that Coach died, Jay showed me the keys to the liquor cabinet in the dining room and the walk-in closet in the recreation room where boxes of booze are stored."

"Oh, you know how boys tell tall tales with each other. How would he get the keys to those places?" she said.

"Apparently it wasn't too difficult, and I know he has a couple of sets just in case he loses a set," I said.

"So," Shelly said, still not comprehending what I was telling her, "if he has such a big problem how do you suppose we can help him?"

I could tell that she was trying to appease me, but I was not going to let this one go. "First, throw away all the booze in this house."

"But it's under lock and key in the liquor cabinet in the dining room."

"And in the walk-in closet in the recreation room," I added.

"Yes. You're right. How did you know that?"

"I just told you, Jay has keys to both places," I said, sounding rather frustrated.

Shelly looked at me in complete disbelief. "Are you sure?"

"Absolutely. They are on his keychain."

"You wait here a minute." With that, Shelly tiptoed upstairs and quickly returned. She showed me the key chain and said, "This one?"

"Yup."

"There are so many keys here. I have no idea what they all do. I don't even know which one belongs to the liquor cabinet," she said.

"It shouldn't be too hard to figure out," I said.

It didn't take us long to find the right key. At first glance the many bottles appeared to all be there untouched. But then Shelly looked again and noticed that many of the bottles were half to three quarters empty. "Hmm," she said. "That's strange. We don't have that many parties. Why would so many bottles be open and almost empty?"

"Jay has a flask," I said.

"So you're telling me that he sneaks into this cabinet and fills up his flask and then takes it somewhere and gets drunk?" She said in complete disbelief.

"Yes," I said without a single note of doubt in my voice.

"Do you know where he goes?" she asked.

That was one question I was going to have to avoid answering. "Oh, you know," I said, "anywhere he doesn't think he will get caught."

"Okay. It couldn't have been going on too long," Shelly mused.

"You haven't checked out the walk-in closet yet."

I could tell that she still didn't completely believe any of this yet. She locked the cabinet and took the key off the keychain.

"There are others," I said.

"Others?" She asked quizzically.

"Keys," I replied.

Shelly said nothing as I followed her down to the recreation room and the locked room that held, from what Jay boasted, all of the liquor you could ever want. After several attempts with various different keys, one key slid comfortably into the lock. She turned the key and the door swung open. When it did I was horrified at what I saw. Not only were there lots and lots of cases of booze, but also in one corner were several rolls of plastic, long chords of rope and six big cinderblocks. I did my best to maintain my composure. All the while images of Coach throwing Kenny's body in his plastic coffin, weighted down by cinder blocks into the swamp were whizzing through my head. Shelly didn't seem to notice those items. She went straight for the boxes of booze. Many of them were empty except for a stray bottle of wine or two. Shelly was finally genuinely concerned, perhaps even convinced that she had a major problem to deal with.

"Now do you believe me?"

"Yes, Geoffrey," she said, finally defeated, as she wept. "I guess I am going to have to talk to Jason again and get rid of all of these bottles. I'll call my father right away."

There was suddenly a loud crash of shattering glass behind us. Shelly and I whirled around to see Jay standing there holding the end of a now broken bottle. He looked so evil. At the moment he looked just like his father. "You asshole!" he growled. The comment was obviously directed at me. Before I had a chance to defend myself Shelly knocked the broken bottle from Jay's hand and slapped him hard across his right cheek. "You go to your room right now, Mister."

Jay stood there defiantly, not moving. He looked straight into my eyes and said, "I don't ever want to see or hear your name ever again. Get out of my life you fucking faggot!"

Shelly went to slap him again but Jay had already backed up expecting the blow this time. I was in such shock that I didn't know what to say or do. Shelly looked over at me and said, "Thank you Geoffrey. You have been a great friend and Jason will realize that some day. Now you'd better go. I can handle it from here."

But Jay wasn't finished yet. He wanted to pick a fight in the worst way. I tried to pass him but he put his fist up to my face. It was my turn to act tough. I grabbed his arm, twisted it and held it behind his back. "Don't even think about it," I yelled at him. "You know you wouldn't have a chance."

Jay glared directly into my eyes. He was not merely looking at me; he was piercing my inner soul. The expression on his face conveyed the intense disgust and hatred he was feeling toward me. Worse than the anger was the look of betrayal. I didn't really feel that I was betraying him. I felt that by helping him I was being his friend. I cared too much for him to stand by and let him ruin his life. But the Jay that I had come to love had turned into a mean, frightening person. It hit me like a ton of bricks: Jay was becoming his father. I realized then more than ever that he needed to get help. I could not stand by and watch him turn into the monster his father had been. I said goodbye to Shelly and let go of Jay's arm and calmly walked up the stairs and out the front door, never turning back. I had hoped when Coach died that the reign of terror was over. I was wrong. Coach's meanness had manifested itself in Jay, but not in me, I thought as I made my way back home, not in me. I refused to let the self-loathing and self-hatred take a hold of my life as it had Jay's, despite the degrading messages that Coach tried to plant in my brain. I was angrier than ever. Even with Coach dead, it was not over. For Jay, alcohol numbed the effects. For me, it was language studies and geography books. I dropped my bike on the front lawn and ran straight up to my bedroom and lay there and cried because I knew that Coach would haunt both of us for the rest of our lives.

CHAPTER TWENTY

I gazed up from the photo album open in front of me. A pall of sorrow came over me. I never did get the chance to help Jay because that was the last time I would ever see my best friend. I expected to see him at school, but that never happened. Shelly called Mom a couple of days later to tell her that she had to get Jason away from the memories. What Shelly would never understand was that those memories would never go away.

A couple of months later, right before Christmas, I was reading the newspaper looking for a story for my weekly current events assignment. I opened the paper, turned the first page and there, right in the center of the page, was a picture of Jay and his Mom and Dad. Ironically it was one that I had taken in happier times. They were all smiling. By all outward appearances they were the happiest of families. Anyone who saw this particular photo would envy their closeness. My heart quickly sank as I read the small article under the picture, "Distraught son of local fallen hero shoots his mother before turning the gun on himself..." The rest of the article focused on Coach. What a crock of shit, I angrily thought. In the end Coach had won; he had destroyed two more lives, even from beyond the grave. I sat there in complete shock, unable to cry. Jay had died and a piece of me went with him. He had been the first love of my life. The only consolation was that Jay was finally at peace, and would never suffer physically or emotionally again. My final wish for Jay was that he wouldn't encounter his brutish father on the other side. I grabbed a pair of scissors from my desk and neatly cut out the article and picture and pasted in the last page of the photo album. After that, I quietly left the house and went back to the cave, our cave, and said my final farewell to Jay.

As I was leaving, I noticed a single wild rose growing out of the side of the rocks. I went over and gently picked it, brought it home, and pressed it into the photo album. I found several other pictures of Jay that had not made any of the previous albums and made a collage on that last page with the pressed rose and news article.

No, I decided, as I returned to the here and now, this book was not going into the fireplace. I closed it and put it back in the box.

CHAPTER TWENTY-ONE

There was only one more photo album left in the box. Actually it was more like a scrapbook than a photo album. After I had read about Jay's death, I had pretty much lost interest in photography. On the front of it was a picture of David and me posing in front of the Schubert Theater in New York City. Yes, David had done it. He had made it to Broadway. This picture was taken the night of his Broadway debut. He had taken over the role of Bobby in the musical that had won nine Tony Awards and the Pulitzer Prize, "A Chorus Line." God, I was so proud of him. It was such an incredible night, complete with a surprise party attended by the entire cast, even Marvin Hamlish, the musical's composer. More importantly, his whole family and many of his friends were there to cheer him on. Even my mother and father made the trip. David was great. He had come such a long way in a short period of time, from a "talking tree," as he once described it to me, in his first grade play to a Broadway Star!

To me David had always been a star. My fondest memory was of our first kiss. It was the first time I was kissed by another guy out of love instead of some sick game, and it was wonderful. Thinking back, it was really pretty funny and, no matter how awkward the moment, it was sheer magic. Right before it happened, I was feeling really low. I just wanted to sit in a corner and cry. Mom had taken Ben and Natalie shopping, leaving me alone in the house. As usual, before she left she barked all kinds of ridiculous orders. "Don't answer the telephone. Don't answer the door. Don't let anybody in the house, no matter who it is. Don't make a mess. Don't go anywhere without leaving me a note telling me where you're going and when you'll be back."

After they finally left I sat on the couch in the living room and just stared into space. I was suddenly jolted out of my little trance when I heard loud knocking at the front door. Not heeding Mom's orders I went and opened it. There stood David with this funny grin on his face. He said, "Hey, I noticed your

Mom leaving with the kids so I thought I'd come over and see what was up."

"Not much," I replied half-heartedly. "Come on in."

I let him in and closed and locked the front door behind him; something Mom had taught us to do when she wasn't home.

"What are you so glum about? You look like you've just lost your best friend."

I couldn't hold back the tears any longer. "I kinda just did, someone who was once my best friend," I said showing him the newspaper article. He quickly read the article and came over to me and gave me a big hug and promised me that everything was going to be all right. David's strong arms felt so good around my shoulders and waist. I eventually stopped crying, but I could not let go of David. Then, without warning, he pulled back from me just a little bit, stared into my eyes and gently pushed back a long strand of hair that was covering my eyes. And then it happened. His lips touched mine. Shocked, knees buckled and we both tumbled to the floor, just missing the edge of the coffee table. David seemed embarrassed. He was lying on top of me now. He tried to get up. He said, "I'm so sorry. I don't know what came over me. I've never done anything like that before."

I grabbed his arm before he had a chance to move too far. I looked right into his beautiful baby blue eyes and said, "Don't be sorry. I'm not." Then I pulled his face to mine and started to passionately kiss him. It was a bit awkward as it took David a little bit of time to figure out exactly where his lips should be. After a few seconds, he lifted his head away from my face and said, "Wow. That was great. Where did you learn to kiss like that?"

Now was not the time for confessions. "From my, aah, girlfriend," I said. "But it's not what you think."

With a puzzled look on his face, almost ready to cry, he said, "I don't understand. I must have made a big mistake. Please tell me it's not true."

I started to stammer, praying that I could make him understand. "It's not like that. Sharon is a wonderful girl. She talks too much, but she's a really nice person. Oh God. I'm really messing this up. David, I know how I feel inside. The problem is nobody else understands it. So, to make it, you know, look good, I go out with Sharon. I know this may sound kinda strange, but she knows how I feel about guys, and she helps me keep up the charade. I swear, if I didn't know any better I'd think she'd prefer to date women rather than men."

David, who had now rolled off me and on to his side just stared at me intently and didn't say a word.

"You do understand, don't you?" I just wanted to scream at that moment.

"Yes," he finally said. "Now, tell me again how you feel inside." He was smiling that devilish smile of his again.

"I have a better idea," I said. "Let me show you." With that I grabbed him and kissed him and would not let him go. I have no idea how long it lasted. We both jumped to our feet when we heard keys jiggling in the front door lock. Mom walked in the door first. She smiled at David and said hello, and then she looked at me and with a stern voice said, "What is one of the rules while I am out of the house?"

"Not to invite anybody in. But," I added, "this is different. It's David."

"Maybe so, but a rule is a rule."

David turned to me. "Maybe I had better be going. I'll talk to you later, Geoff."

I sat back and sipped my beer trying to hold on to that and the many wonderful memories of David that followed our first kiss. We experimented with our newfound love for each other whenever we got a chance.

Sharon continued to be a big part of my life: In fact, the three of us would become inseparable. Sharon and I were accepted as a "couple" by the whole school and Sharon came to understand how David and I felt about each other. I was not surprised — but was grateful — when she told me one day that she was cool with everything and that I remained her special friend. I urged her to date other guys but she wouldn't. She said that it was me she loved regardless of the consequences. Sharon and I went to our junior and senior proms together, and enjoyed ourselves immensely. Everything else we did together was always with David in tow.

I did envy David, who was more confident about who he was and his sexuality. He was often harassed because he was so open, but he didn't seem to let it bother him — at least he never tried to hide behind a girlfriend. David grew to really like Sharon, and while he didn't understand why I couldn't be more open, he went along with our little subterfuge and our happy threesome made the best of our time in high school.

CHAPTER TWENTY-TWO

I lost some of my passion for photography but Ben, taking after his older brother, had become an avid photographer. He enthusiastically documented my seventeenth birthday party, including several shots of the three musketeers — David, Sharon and me — looking like we were having the time of our life. The party was actually a bit of a distraction, because I was focused on the birthday present I'd received earlier in the day. What made matters worse, I couldn't even talk about it. I was about to realize my dream of following in my grandfather's footsteps.

The morning had begun with a cryptic phone call from the man himself. Grand pop asked me to meet him in the back parking lot of the Players Club, a small community theater about ten blocks from where I lived. He said it was a big secret that should not be disclosed to anyone and that I'd understand afterward. All kinds of bells and whistles went off inside my head. I was a little frightened, but also intrigued, by the cloak and dagger routine. I suppressed my doubts and wondered what my grandfather's mysterious summons meant.

An hour later, I was in the back parking lot of The Players Club. Grand pop pulled up. He was alone. I jumped into the passenger's side of the car and we drove away. I asked him where we were going, but he said, "Not so fast, you'll find out in good time." He made lots of small talk asking how my summer was going and how things were going with my girlfriend. We even talked about David. He told me that he knew that David was gay, but that as long as I stayed on the straight and narrow, everything would be okay. I wasn't real sure what he meant by that, so I decided to let it go without comment. He then told me how proud he was that I was doing well with my language studies and that the events of a few years earlier seemed to have strengthened my resolve for perfection.

We drove into downtown Philadelphia and pulled into a parking garage off Broad Street. I recognized the building immediately: It was where Grand pop had worked before he retired. After working in Washington D.C. most of his life, he had been transferred here in early 1973. After only eight months of working in Philadelphia he decided to retire. For the past two years he had been enjoying his retirement, playing golf almost everyday and taking Grand mom on frequent trips to places he used to visit alone.

"What are we doing here?" I asked.

"Patience, son, patience," he said.

We got out of the car and walked over to an elevator where we were met by a marine in his dress blues. He saluted Grand pop, whose importance still amazed me. The young marine silently led us into the elevator clearly marked "Private" and escorted us up to the local offices of the National Security Agency. We walked into a huge open office filled with dozens of people diligently working at their desks. Nobody appeared to notice us.

We were ushered into a corner office at the far end of the floor. A tall, lanky man of approximately 55 years of age was standing behind the desk. Bottle cap-thick lenses in black plastic frames sat on the bridge of his nose, making him look geeky as well as intense. Grand pop introduced me to Mr. Stanley Lokowski,

Director of the Eastern Special Operations Unit of the National Security Agency, then excused himself and abruptly left the room.

I was left alone, seated uncomfortably in front of Mr. Lokowski's desk. I was actually beginning to shake and had an urge to bolt from the room but I managed to keep my cool. Mr. Lokowski asked me to call him "Stan" and began our conversation by impressing upon me the importance and absolute need for keeping our conversation completely confidential. Now I was really scared but kept my composure, not wanting this stranger to see my fear.

As he spoke, Mr. Lokowski seemed to know everything about me, except my hidden homosexuality. Thank God for that. He complimented me on my foreign language abilities, adding that such skills are only developed over time and with a lot of hard work. He finally got to the point of our meeting, telling me that the NSA was always looking for individuals with the special talents that I possessed.

"Learning foreign languages comes easily to me," I said.

"Which ones are you studying?" He asked.

"German is my favorite. But I also know French, Russian and a little bit of Spanish. Russian is harder because I've had to learn on my own since it's not offered at my high school."

"Excellent. We will get you a Russian tutor. But I also understand that you have tremendous discipline," Stan casually threw out.

"What do you mean by that?" I asked skeptically, focusing more on the discipline part of the comment rather than the Russian tutor part.

"I understand that you are a tough guy. By that, I mean you have had a really difficult past to deal with and you've managed to do that quite well and keep your sanity. I also am pretty sure that you know how to keep a secret, probably better than most adults."

My defenses up, I retorted. "What the hell is that supposed to mean?"

"Now, Mr. Brooks. There is no need to get worked up. I only meant that you have a resilience second to none," he calmly said.

I was absolutely livid now. "What do you think you know about me?" I almost shouted.

While waiting for an answer, a knock came at the door and Grand pop entered the room. "Geoffrey, Geoffrey, calm down, everything is alright," he said. "I've been listening to what's been going on in here and perhaps I can be of some help."

My mind was racing so fast that all of my thoughts were blurring together into one big angry knot and I was losing control, something I swore I would never do again after Coach died. "Somebody had better explain to me what is going on here," I said.

"You are a very special person," Grand pop continued. "You have had to put up with much adversity in your young life, none of it deserved. Yet you have managed to grow into a happy, healthy young man."

But," I interjected, "Stan — Mr. Lokowski — is insinuating some strange things about me."

Laboring to salvage the situation, Grand pop said softly, "He is only saying that you are an amazing guy."

"Well then, what does he mean when he says I know how to keep secrets?"

"I've hated to bring up past events because I know you've been plagued by terrible nightmares. Unspeakable things happened on that weekend six years ago that should never have happened to you, or anyone else for that matter."

"Yeah. But why is that relevant now?" I shrieked.

"I know you once told me that you did not remember what happened after Mr. Scott raped you. I believed you then. However, I am pretty certain that you have regained your full memory, that you remember the entire weekend, with all of its gory details."

I sat there in complete shock as all of the memories of that weekend replayed themselves in my head, as they had done at least once a day since my memory had returned. I was shaking so badly that I couldn't even hold the glass of water that Stan had just handed to me. It suddenly occurred to me what this was all about. I had finally been found out. I was about to go to jail. I was going to be put away for a very long time for the murder of Kenny Masterson. The tears began to flow uncontrollably. I shouted out, "But you don't understand. He made me do it."

Grand pop was up to me in a flash. He gave me a big bear hug and said, "It's okay son. It's over. You don't have to keep those terrible things locked up inside of you anymore."

I continued to cry saying stuff like, "Will I have to go to jail? I don't want to go to jail. I'm so scared."

Grand pop looked at me and said sympathetically, "No. No. No. That is not what this is all about. Please relax." Then he turned to Stan and said, "Today is my grandson's seventeenth birthday. Would you do me a favor and bring him a small glass of scotch. I think he could use it right about now."

It burned all the way down my throat, but I was grateful for the scotch. I finally asked, "How did you find out?"

"Oh, I've known for a long time. Remember when we learned what Mr. Scott had done and you had to talk to the police?"

"Yes," I nodded.

"Well I did some serious digging and questioned Mr. Scott relentlessly while he was locked away in that mental hospital. He finally broke and told me what had happened. I am so sorry. Maybe I should have exposed him then. However, I had your best interest in mind, and as long as you couldn't remember what had happened I thought it best to remain quiet, so I devised a plan. I knew that as long as Mr. Scott walked this earth he was a threat to you. Therefore, I decided to take matters into my own hands. We here at the National Security Agency have resources far beyond anyone's wildest imagination. Rigging Mr. Scott's plane, quite honestly, was a fairly simple procedure. The only thing we had to find out was when Mr. Scott was planning to fly using his firm's corporate jet. The other thing we had to consider was where the plane was going. Although he often flew to Houston, Texas, we also knew that he flew pretty regularly to Toronto, Canada. Canada was the ideal destination because once the plane was outside of the United States; the crash investigation would be handled in a different manner, giving us time to tie up any loose ends. It was a simple matter to have one of our "inside people" at the firm check Mr. Scott's itineraries on a daily basis. When we were absolutely certain that he was going to be on that plane, with no chance of changing his plans then we would make our move. It didn't take too long before word came into us that Mr. Scott had a meeting to attend in Toronto that he absolutely had to attend. Like I told you, our job was a simple one. We brought in our own ground crew during the night and had them recalibrate the instruments that affected fuel levels. The plan was for the plane to go down over water, making the investigation all the more difficult. That unfortunately did not happen. The ace pilot on board, a former air force fighter pilot, managed to get within seven miles of the airport before he couldn't hold it anymore. Thankfully he crashed into a field next to a cemetery, killing no one on the ground. Of course, as you know, all five of the passengers and the two crewmembers were killed on impact. The crash investigation went better than we could have ever hoped for. We got a lucky break when the FAA focused on several Canadian geese found in both jet engines. Those geese, which had severely clogged both engines were determined to be the cause of the accident. Somehow they overlooked the fact that the plane was totally empty of fuel. We were in the clear, as we had expected to be and here you are today, a happy, healthy, brilliant young man."

I sat there in complete awe of what I was hearing. I didn't know what to say. My grandfather must have truly loved me to go to such great lengths to protect me. When I finally was able to catch my breath again I apologized for my earlier outburst. I asked, still not believing it all, "You did all of this for me?"

"Yes, after the years of cruelty and punishment inflicted on you at the hands of this monster I decided that this was the very least I could do for you."

It was now Stan's turn to speak. He took a deep breath and paused for a brief moment to formulate his thoughts and to give me a chance to calm down. Once he had my complete, undivided attention he said, "Okay Geoffrey, I won't torment you any longer. This organization, The National Security Agency, is willing to groom you to become a Language Specialist and a

Special Operations Agent. If you accept this offer you will become one of an elite few, who are responsible for protecting the United States from its many enemies, just like your grandfather did." He continued on, "If you accept our offer, your grandfather will continue to be your guide and mentor. He will personally see to your personal and spiritual growth and make certain that you get the education we require until you are ready to officially join the agency."

I sat there in stunned silence. It didn't take an Einstein to realize that such opportunities don't come along everyday. I really didn't know what being a Special Operations Agent meant, but since it was very important I felt scared and vulnerable, but it all sounded so wonderful and the opportunities sounded endless. At only seventeen years of age, I was being given a chance to make my mark. Plus, I would continue to develop my language skills. It was everything I had dreamed of. I finally blurted out, "Yes, of course, yes!"

Grand pop smiled broadly and proudly and said, "Congratulations, Geoff. You have a great future ahead of you."

CHAPTER TWENTY-THREE

I flipped the page of the scrapbook. There were several photos of my high school graduation, including a great shot of David, Sharon and me in our caps and gowns. It was a bittersweet day. It brought to an end a chapter in our lives none of us would ever forget. We continued to spend much of the summer together. Our parents let us all go down to the Shore for senior week. We were wild. Although we each had our own room, David and I slept in one room enjoying a week of complete freedom.

The summer came to an end way too fast. The three of us spent our last day together crying up a storm. The next day, Sharon and David, leaving separately, went to New York City. Sharon was attending NYU with aspirations of becoming the first woman to run her own Fortune 500 Company and David was planning to study Performing Arts at Columbia University. I left for UCLA to continue my language studies and my grooming for the National Security Agency.

As our college years flew by the three musketeers had less and less contact with each other. In March of my senior year Mom sent me an engraved invitation. It was announcing that in August David would be taking over the role of Bobby in the Broadway hit "A Chorus Line." A surprise party would be following at the world famous Sardi's Restaurant. In the letter that came with the invitation Mom said the entire family would be making the trip to New York City with Belle and the rest of David's family. I was so excited. I had not seen David in over two years and had exchanged only a few letters. I had only been back in the United States three months after spending a year and a half in Europe honing and sharpening my language skills.

I quickly made reservations to fly to New York City for David's Broadway debut. God, I hoped he still cared, if only a little. I made Mom promise not to tell anyone except Belle, who was getting the tickets for the show, that I was coming. I wanted it to be a complete surprise.

I planned the excursion for months and couldn't wait much longer. Not only would I get to see David but also I'd have a few days of much needed rest and relaxation.

The plane seemed to take forever getting to the gate when we landed at JFK, and traffic into Manhattan from the airport was even slower. I finally checked into my hotel room in Chelsea at about 2:00pm, freshened up and headed down to Greenwich Village for a bite to eat. I loved the shops, restaurants and the easygoing atmosphere of the Village. This gave me the opportunity to be myself, to be gay in a gay environment, without fear of what people would think or say. Furthermore, since New York City was so big nobody would recognize me if I happened to hook up with another guy. Mom and Dad were staying somewhere near the theater in midtown some forty blocks away. I didn't have to catch up with them until about 7:30pm.

There were so many restaurants to choose from. I randomly picked one that looked good and ventured in. The place was abuzz with activity. As the hostess led me to a small table I couldn't help but notice that there was a woman intently staring at me. Boy, these New

Yorkers can be so rude. I thought. She kept staring and staring. I stared back at her. The bizarre thing was that she kind of reminded me of Sharon whom I hadn't seen since the day we all parted for college. This woman however could not be her. She appeared so animated, humorous, so easygoing despite the fact that she couldn't take her eyes off of me. The Sharon I knew, on the other hand, wasn't easy going about anything. She had always been way too serious about everything. Yeah, I was pretty sure Sharon would have achieved her goal of becoming a high- powered business woman, probably with a couple of kids, a well tanned lawyer for a husband and a house in the suburbs.

I browsed through the menu. Everything looked good, especially after the airplane food I had eaten flying in from Los Angeles. Narrowing down the possibilities was going to be a problem. "I'd recommend the grilled salmon," came a voice from behind that could only be Sharon's.

"My God," I shrieked, "It is you!" We stood in the middle of the restaurant hugging each other and jumping up and down, making complete fools of ourselves. One of the women Sharon had been sitting with came over and joined us, affectionately putting her arm around Sharon's waist.

"Geoffrey," Sharon said, "this is Susan.

"I've heard so much about you," Susan said shaking my hand.

Sharon told Susan that she'd be over in a minute and then sat down across from me.

"It is so good to see you, Sharon. Is this the business ladies who lunch that I hear so much about back in LA?" I quipped, stopping to take a good look. Sharon seemed to be beaming. "Wow, you look great. I guess this New York life style really does agree with you."

Sharon looked over at Susan then back to me. "I guess no one told you?" she asked, sounding coy, and a little mischievous.

"No," I replied, "I haven't spoken to anyone from home except Mom and Dad in like eons. I just got back from Europe less than three months ago. I was living there, studying for the past year and a half or so, and now I am trying to complete my degree."

"Oh Geoffrey, I am so proud of you," Sharon beamed. "You achieved exactly what you set out to do."

"Well, yes, you could say that, I guess. I am on my way to completing a very long journey," I blushed.

"No Geoffrey, the journey is just beginning. Our life is one very long journey, although sometimes the route takes us in a direction we least expect. Why, look at me. These are not business acquaintances, these are my friends. I dropped out of college my junior year. After all, whom was I trying to kid? Running a company is not my idea of fun. I am currently working as a legal secretary to support myself. Not quite what mommy and daddy had planned for their little girl," Sharon said with a great big smirk on her face.

I didn't know what to say. After thinking about it a second I asked, "Are you happy with your decision and the person you have become?"

"I. have never been happier than I am at this moment, and it is only getting better."

"You really are, aren't you? I can see it in your face, in your eyes. There is sparkle like I have only seen one other time," I smiled.

"And when was that?" she asked.

"I still remember it. Don't you? It was the day I first kissed you at the pool."

Sharon blushed and said, "That was a very long time ago, we were just kids. I was a little girl. A lot has happened since then. We both grew up. You discovered that you preferred boys; I assume that hasn't changed?"

"Absolutely not!" I whispered.

We both laughed and Sharon continued, "Once I let go of that fierce determination and relentless drive, I discovered that there was a whole other life out there waiting to be lived. A life of enjoyment, fun and now with Susan in my life, it is a life filled with love."

I was in shock. "Susan is your…"

"Lover? Yes. I discovered, albeit later than you, that I was gay. I guess I've always known and that's why it was so easy to hide behind you." Sharon paused a moment, "That hasn't changed has it? You're still not open about yourself, are you?"

"No, I am still more closeted than I would like to be, and, of course, I'm still single."

We both broke out in laughter. It wasn't as if we were laughing at something funny. It was more like an emotional release. There was such a profound sense of joy that we could now be together as ourselves. No more facades, no more games. We were just two people who had shared so much and now could reveal our true selves to each other.

I joined Sharon and Susan and another lesbian couple at their table. We spent the next hour talking and laughing, reminiscing about some of our torrid moments and teen adventures.

Sharon was not aware that David was still living in New York City or that he was getting ready to make his Broadway debut. It didn't take much to convince her and Susan to come to the show. I quickly got hold of Belle at the hotel where she was staying and she assured me that she could get two more tickets, especially if one was for Sharon. Boy, was David in for a surprise!

We all arrived at the theater at 7:30 sharp. As I suspected, everyone was surprised to see Sharon and me. Everybody thought that we were still an item until Sharon made it perfectly clear that she was a proud lesbian. "Closets are for clothes," she proclaimed, glaring at me while she said it.

The show was fabulous. David received thunderous applause. Afterwards we all waited for him at the stage door. David came out to a crowd of supporters. There were so many people around him that he didn't see me at first. He went over and gave his mother a big hug. When he lifted his head from her shoulder our eyes met. He let go of his mother. We both just stood there and stared at each other. Finally he reached out and also gave me a big hug. He started to cry and whispered into my ear so that only I could hear him, "God, I've missed you so much. I thought you fell off the face of the earth, and then your mother said that there was no way you could make it out here. I was so disappointed. You jerk. You made me crazy on purpose. So do you have a boyfriend, or are you still trying to be the good ole American boy next door?"

"David, David," I said, now crying too, "You haven't changed one bit. You still talk too much and too fast. I have missed you so much and no I don't have a boyfriend, and yes I am preparing for the job I have been preparing for all of my life and I will be moving to D.C. next month to pursue my career, so to answer you question, yes, I am still closeted, although I think most people have figured it out. How about you? Do you have a boyfriend?"

Although I was secretly hoping to hear that he was available, my heart sank when he introduced me to his boyfriend who was patiently standing behind him. David turned to him and gave him a big hug and a kiss. I don't know what I was expecting. I guess I just wanted things to be the way they were before we went to college. But things change. People change. I tried to smile. I'm sure David saw the disappointment in my face despite my attempt to hide it. Oh God, what a fool I am, I thought.

Thankfully Sharon had made her way over to us and another celebration ensued giving me a chance to compose myself after my obvious disappointment. The partying went on until the wee hours of the morning. David was full of surprises that night. During dinner he announced to everyone that after his six month contract with "A Chorus Line" ran out, he was signing a five-year contract with The National Theater in Washington, D.C.

I glanced up from my dessert at the announcement. Of course I was happy for him, but how was I going to live in the same town with the man I obviously still loved and couldn't have? I had to get it through my thick skull that David had moved on with his life and that from now on I was just another friend to him, nothing more. At least if we were in the same town I'd get to see him once in a while.

At the last minute, at both David and Sharon's insistence, I decided to stay in New York for a couple of extra days. Sharon, David and I spent three wonderful, fun-filled days together. It was like old times, except that Sharon had her girl and David had his guy, and I had no one. At the end of the visit David saw me to the airport. I did my best to be upbeat. God, it was so hard to just be David's friend. The emptiness I was feeling inside was all-consuming, but I knew I could not let David know what I was going through, although I think he knew. As we parted he gave me a hug and whispered, "Don't worry. He'll never leave New York. He's too attached to it."

As I sat back on the couch, holding on to the last book of memories, I thought to myself how much of a long haul it had been to get here, but here I was. I had made it and I was happy. In spite of all the difficulties, I was now very happy.

I was jolted out of my trance-like state by the sound of a key unlocking the front door.

"Honey, I'm home," he said as the door swung open. He was carrying a bottle of champagne and a dozen beautiful red roses.

"You shouldn't have," I said.

"This is a special occasion. Isn't it?" he asked as he looked over at the couch.

"Well, yeah, I guess so."

"What have you been doing all day? This place is a mess."

"Reminiscing," I said.

He put down the flowers and champagne and came over to me. "Kiss me, Geoff," he said.

I grabbed him and pulled him to me. I was almost light headed at seeing the man that I had grown to love so much. I pushed him down to the floor where we rolled and kissed and laughed. An envelope fell out of the breast pocket of his suit jacket. I picked it up. "What's this?" I inquired.

"Just my way of saying Congratulations and I love you!"

I opened the envelope. Inside were two tickets to Cannes. "I love you too, David."

Kevin A. Carey

About the Author

Kevin Carey was born in suburban Philadelphia. He graduated from Millersville State University in Lancaster, Pennsylvania with a degree in Foreign Languages. He has extensively traveled the world and experienced life from a perspective not afforded many. This, his first book, a thriller, is about how a young man named Geoffrey Brooks became a Special Operations Agent for the world's most prestigious spy organization while coming to terms with his homosexuality. Geoffrey Brooks has been touted as the gay Jack Ryan made famous by award-winning author Tom Clancy. Already working on his second novel, insiders are raving about Geoffrey's latest mission: Fighting for a country he loves while fighting for the man he loves. Kevin is proud to share these stories with you, drawn from his insider knowledge of the international spy community.

Printed in the United States
828200001B